VALLEY
of FIRE

Center Point
Large Print

**This Large Print Book carries the
Seal of Approval of N.A.V.H.**

VALLEY of FIRE

JOHNNY D. BOGGS

CENTER POINT LARGE PRINT
THORNDIKE, MAINE

This Center Point Large Print edition is published
in the year 2014 by arrangement with
Kensington Publishing Corp.

The text of this Large Print edition is unabridged.
In other aspects, this book may vary
from the original edition.
Printed in the United States of America
on permanent paper.
Set in 16-point Times New Roman type.

ISBN: 978-1-62899-087-4

Library of Congress Cataloging-in-Publication Data

Boggs, Johnny D.
Valley of fire / Johnny D. Boggs. — Center point large print edition.
pages ; cm
ISBN 978-1-62899-087-4 (library binding : alk. paper)
1. Nuns—Fiction. 2. Outlaws—Fiction. 3. Treasure troves—Fiction.
    4. Large type books. I. Title.
PS3552.O4375V35 2014
813´.54—dc23
                                                    2014005555

For Deborah Kerr and Robert Mitchum

Prologue

The Lord works in mysterious ways.

Yeah, you've read that before. So have I, and I ain't much when it comes to picking up books. Well, ain't nobody ever accused me of being a writer. Rapscallion. Gambler. Liar. Whoremonger. Drunkard. Cardsharp. Horse thief. Two-bit assassin. Son of a bitch. Been called them things, and worser. Yet I have come to believe that, indeed, the Lord does work in mysterious ways.

How else could you explain why I sit, one more time, in this damp, stinking dungeon in Las Vegas, New Mexico Territory, legs shackled, sentenced to hang? Fitting, I guess. The padre who frequented that old orphanage always said I was bound for the gallows, so I've accepted his prophesy as gospel. In eight hours, it will all come true.

But how I, Micah Bishop, wound up here . . . well, that is one thing I'm still trying to figure out. And I ain't got much time to reach some satisfactory conclusion.

These words I write for the undertaker and the ink-slinger reporting on my execution for the *Las Vegas Daily Optic*. These is the facts, or best guesses, as I know them.

My name is Micah Bishop. Maybe. I'm an orphan, but that's the name the Sisters of Charity

7

told me that my ma or pa had given me. I am thirty years old, or thereabouts. I have been accused of killing a gambler in this burg a few months ago, which, if you must know, is true. It wasn't, though, exactly murder. I called it self-defense, but nobody believed it. Nobody on the jury, or in the entire courtroom, or anywhere in the territory believed it.

Except two people. Maybe. Sister Rocío and Sister Geneviève, would believe me, but they wasn't around to testify on my behalf. It don't matter. Besides, they wasn't in that bucket of blood when I dealt this b'hoy named Gomez out of the game, permanent-like. The county solicitor would likely have objected to anything them two nuns had to say under oath regarding the untimely passing of Manuel Gomez, since those two nuns didn't witness the shooting.

But if not for Rocío and Geneviève, I wouldn't be here. If I'd never heard of the Valley of Fire, if Geneviève had not busted me out of jail, if Sean Fenn hadn't been such a greedy bastard, if priests and Spaniards hadn't done such a dirty, rotten thing more than two centuries ago, if Sister Rocío hadn't been so damned honorable and good, if and if and if and if . . . well . . . it's like I said. The Lord works in mysterious ways.

So here I sit. Alone. Just me, a candle, a couple writing tablets and a few pencils. There's a Bible over in the corner, next to the slop bucket, but I haven't cracked its spine yet. Too busy writing.

Is this my confession? I don't know. Maybe. I'm trying to figure that out, too.

Just like I was always trying to figure out Sister Geneviève Tremblay. And even old Sister Rocío.

Maybe it'll all make sense to me when I'm finished writing. Or more than likely, I won't know the truth till some trusty hangman springs that trapdoor open and I get dropped into eternity.

For me, it all started here in Las Vegas after I'd sent Gomez to meet his maker, after I was first sentenced to hang. It began like this. . . .

Chapter One

Continental Arms Company calls its little pepper-box pistol "Ladies Companion," and, honestly, it ain't much of a gun. But when that five-shot .22 is an inch from your eyeballs, it might as well be a cannon.

Even when it's held by a nun.

"I didn't bust you out of that hellhole ten minutes ago," Sister Geneviève said, her hand not wavering a bit, "to have you quit on me now. So sit down, Mister Bishop, or I scream, and that mob hauls you back to jail, or, more than likely, straight to the gallows tree"—her finger tightened ever so slightly on the trigger—"providing I don't wallpaper this pigsty with your miserable brains."

We was in a hotel room, and it was a pigsty, but not as bad as the one I'd been in just minutes earlier. I was in that pigsty on account of a sawed-off little runt called Gomez, who caught me dealing off the bottom over at Hernandez's Gambling Parlor on La Plazuela, then had the stupidity not only to pull a pistol out of his waistband, but to send a ball through my hat, part my hair, and scar my scalp. He would have done a lot more damage had he gotten off his second shot. He didn't, but only because I put a bullet in his gut. After which, the good citizens of Las Vegas bruised me considerable, hauled me off to jail, and sentenced me to hang in less time than it has taken me to write this all down. There wasn't no grand jury or coroner's inquest. They hadn't even given me a trial. How was I supposed to know that the late Gomez was Felipe Hernandez's brother-in-law? Felipe Hernandez owned not only Hernandez's Gambling Parlor on La Plazuela, but a big freight line than ran from Raton Pass to Santa Fe, and an even bigger rancho just north of town. And by now you've likely figured out that he also owned the mayor, marshal, and some mercantile in New Town, where the hangman had bought his rope.

Well, they could have strung me up right then and there. But they give me a day or so to rot in the jail. Torture, I call it. Making a body think about that hemp scratching your throat, wondering what it'll be like, if your neck will break or if you'll just kick and choke and strangle. Sons of bitches.

Guess there ain't no point in trying to explain that I was innocent. Sure, I had killed Hernandez's brother-in-law, but I had warned Gomez not to pull that pistol, had told him he was making a bad mistake, and he had gotten off the first shot and come a couple inches from killing me. That made it self-defense, even if I had been cheating, which nobody could prove unless I confessed, and that certainly wasn't in the cards. I had been protecting my person. Same as I'd been forced to do with that drover in Missouri, and that outlaw down in the Indian Nations. I hadn't killed nobody in Texas, but them Texans seemed to suspicion just how come other men's horses kept following me home.

That was my story. And Sister Geneviève's? That was what I was trying to figure out.

Staring at that pepperbox, her gloved hand so delicate on those rosewood grips, her finger tighter than I'd like against that trigger, I began to suspicion that Sister Geneviève wasn't no Sister at all. Granted, I had spent some years trying to forget what those nuns had tried to beat into me back at that orphanage, but my memory told me that nuns usually didn't have such cold brown eyes, and seldom looked so beautiful, not to mention deadly. Maybe they'd cuss a little when

11

riled, but I doubted if nuns carried pepperbox pistols. And, sure as hell, I'd never heard of a nun busting a fellow out of jail a few hours before he was scheduled to die. Even the Pope, I figured, would frown upon a Sister going that far to save a gent's soul.

I didn't have to figure how Felipe Hernandez would take my escape. Sounds from the street drifting through the open window told me that, plain enough.

Criminy, just a few minutes earlier I had been confined in the worst jail I'd ever struck, picking over the hog and hominy I expected was my last meal, washing it down with cold coffee—and no sugar, mind you—wondering if I'd wet my britches when they come to string me up. About that time the jailer, a toothless old coot named Evers, had ducked his head into the hallway and said, "A nun's here to see you."

I had rolled my eyes.

"Boy," Evers said, "iffen I was you, I'd see her."

"You worried about my eternal damnation?" I asked.

He snorted and spat. "I don't give a hoot 'bout you, mister. But that sister, she looks finer than frog hair cut eight ways. Was I younger and condemned to die, I'd be of mind to pray with a gal like that."

"Hell, Evers, send her in."

Old Evers was right. This nun walked in,

clutching a Bible in her right hand, and pressing the silver crucifix she held in her left to right pretty, full, rosy lips. Dark as that pit was, I couldn't see her too well, and considering how she was all decked out in a loose dress of black serge with white coif and black veil covering most of her head, about all I could make out about her was her face.

A beautiful face. Perfect nose, not a blemish about her, with such soulful brown eyes. When she got closer, over the stink of the dungeon, I could even smell lilac on her person. She looked younger than me. Lowering the crucifix, she told me, "I am Sister Geneviève of the Sisters of Charity."

Sisters of Charity? That sent a chill up my spine, recalling to mind them years just down the trail in Santa Fe where I had spent most of my childhood getting walloped by nuns who had looked nothing like her.

She turned to ask Evers, "May I enter the cell to pray with him?"

Sounded perfectly French. Not that I knowed what perfect French sounded like.

Evers, miserable reprobate that he was, shook his head. "Nobody's allowed inside, Sister. Marshal's orders."

Marshal's orders? I thought. *You mean Felipe Hernandez's!*

"Very well," she said, and bowed in the filth and muck that covered the flagstone floor. Once she taken to praying in Latin or some foreign tongue, Evers left and locked the big oaken door behind him.

Soon as Evers turned that key, she looked up with eyes not so much soulful but rather harder than a beer bottle. "I need you to take me to the Valley of Fire."

"Ma'am?" *Valley of Fire?* At first, I figured it was some Catholic talk, about me telling her the wickedest things I'd done—which would have taken considerable time—and feeling the fires of Hades before getting absolution and avoid going to the bad place.

"You heard me." She sure wasn't speaking Latin. Or French. She sounded like the hard-rock madam at that hog ranch a few miles north of Trinidad, Colorado. She asked again, her voice far from forgiving. "Can you take me there?"

That inquiry was the last thing I expected, and I spilled most of my cold coffee over my duck trousers and almost sat down in the slop bucket. "Ma'am?"

"Take me and others to the Valley of Fire."

This was summer. The Valley of Fire, or Fires, as some folks called it—as if it wasn't hot enough already down there with just one fire—lay east of the *Jornado del Muerto*, the "Journey of the Dead" along the old Camino Real, maybe a day or so from Lincoln . . . but more than a hundred and seventy-five miles from these gallows. Brutal as that country was, it did seem more inviting than what Las Vegas offered me. But there was one little thing. . . .

"Sister," I said, "much as I'd like to help you out, I don't think Felipe Hernandez is gonna let me guide you nowhere."

She was standing. "Let me worry about that. If I get you out of here, will you help me?"

"Hell, yes!" I felt no pressing need to meet up with Saint Peter.

"Deputy!" she called. Had to call twice more before Evers unlocked the door and headed down the hallway.

"That was quick. You—" He almost choked on the quid of tobacco he was gumming when she stuck that pepperbox in his face.

"Let him out," she said, spoken like the word of God.

She didn't give him time to stall. When he just stood there drooling brown juice into his beard, she cracked him upside the head with that little pistol, and brought her knee up savagely into his groin. Old Evers went down, and her knee went up again smashing the poor fool's face, then she pounded the back of his head with her Bible and the pepperbox. He fell hard against the flagstone, and I feared she had killed the reprobate. That .22 disappeared in the folds of her habit while she grabbed the ring of keys he had dropped.

Faster than David could sing a psalm, we was

out of that jail, skedaddling in the shadows. Seemed to me like we was making a beeline for the livery stable, when all of a sudden we both heard old Evers screaming and cussing from the door to the jail. Made me wish she had hit that loudmouthed jailer harder, maybe even killed him. As luck would have it, Felipe Hernandez happened to be riding right past the jail with a bunch of his gunmen. So much for sneaking to get us some horses. Shots was fired, and every drunk in town came flying out the saloons along the plazuela. Instead of running to the livery, we cut down an alley and hurried up the back stairs of El Hotel Gallinas, making it to the second floor. The good Sister had a key, and after she unlocked the door to room 22, we quickly found ourselves panting and listening to the ruction being raised outside.

Wasn't much of a room, illuminated only by a couple candles, but El Hotel Gallinas ain't much of a place to hang your hat. Once I had caught my breath, I thanked her for her trouble and told her I'd see about fetching a horse and be on my way. That's when I was suddenly looking down the same pistol barrel that old Evers had seen before she'd knocked his lights out.

That's when she told me, "I didn't bust you out of that hellhole ten minutes ago to have you quit on me now. So sit down, Mister Bishop, or I scream, and that mob hauls you back to jail, or, more than likely, straight to the gallows tree, providing I don't wallpaper this pigsty with your miserable brains."

I didn't sit. "How you plan on getting me out of here?" I jutted my jaw toward the window. Since she sure wasn't deaf, she could hear those shouts from the darkened streets. Men was cussing a whole lot more than she'd just cussed me, and I could savvy that Felipe Hernandez wanted me brung back dead, and he didn't care what they did to the gal who had sprung me loose, either.

"I got you this far." She jerked her head toward the cot. "Sit down!"

The bed squeaked.

"You said you'll guide us to the Valley of Fire."

Who was *us?* I wondered. Being honest for a change, I said, "A man about to hang's likely to agree to just about anything." I smiled.

She didn't.

The pepperbox came closer to my eyeballs. I'd expected what she had just done—a nun, helping a convicted murderer bust out of jail—to weigh heavily upon her shoulders, to cause her to tremble, and cry, and maybe fall into my arms. Instead, I got another good look down the barrel of that little cannon.

"Are you really a nun?" I asked.

But she must've not heard me because she was saying, "Sister Rocío insisted that you were the only one. . . ."

"Rocío?" Instinctively, my right hand felt the back of my head.

Her eyes hardened. "You know Sister Rocío?"

I rubbed my noggin. "An old one-armed crone?"

Sister Geneviève's head bobbed just slightly.

"She cracked my skull and knuckles a million times back at the orphanage."

My rescuer didn't trust me. Not yet. "Where was this orphanage?"

"Santa Fe." For effect, I emphasized. *Sisters of Charity.* Next to St. Vincent's." That was the hospital the nuns had started right after the War of the Rebellion. Later, them nuns had formed the orphanage, and then what they called an industrial school for girls. Those sisters wandered all across the Rocky Mountains begging for money, for help.

"She was older than dirt back then, and I left, what, sixteen years ago. She couldn't be alive after all this time. She looked liked she was about to bite the dust when I knowed her. She must be dead. You must have another Sister Rocío."

"Left arm amputated at the elbow. Blind. She just turned seventy-three."

"Seventy-three? I thought she was a hundred when I knowed her." Still, I couldn't stop smiling. "Good for Sister Rocío!" I meant what I said, but I was also thinking, *That old hag's mind has gone. She's mistook me for some other wayward lad she tried to beat sense into.*

"She insisted that you're the only one who could take her there." Geneviève Tremblay was whispering to herself, but I heard.

When I stood, she pointed that pepperbox right at my stomach, but my fingers slowly reached inside my vest pockets, though I knowed they was empty. Then I checked the mule-ear pockets on my britches, but they was the same.

"Thieves," I said.

"What are you talking about? What are you looking for?"

"Just a rock. An old black piece of lava. Watch fob. Rocío gave it to me right before I run off—before I left." I smiled. "That and a heavy silver Cross of Lorraine."

"Lava?" she asked.

"That's how the valley got its name," I explained.

It must have convinced her that I was honest, sometimes, because she lowered that gun, and said, "I'll take you to Rocío."

Outside, among all the shouting from the streets, came words like *muerto*, *guero*, and *puta*. The population of Las Vegas, New Mexico Territory, sounded mightily riled.

"I don't mean to sound skeptical, Sister, but the way I figure it, old Evers has told everyone that it was you who busted me out of the calaboose. They'll likely search your room." In a pig's eye. Criminy, there wasn't no *likely* to it. At that moment, I heard floorboards groaning and spurs chiming just outside the door to our room.

Footsteps stopped, and the doorknob squeaked. I grimaced. The door opened, but Sister Geneviève didn't even look away from me. I was about to risk getting my eyes shot out, or my head blowed off—those "Ladies Companions" are known to misfire and shoot all five rounds at once—but stopped myself as a man entered the room, and quickly shut the door behind him.

"It's not my room," she said. "It's his."

The long-legged gent swept off his wide-brimmed black hat and stepped into the candle-light. He wore a black robe, and a silver cross hung from his neck. I was only beginning to suspicion that Sister Geneviève wasn't a nun, but I damned sure knowed this guy wasn't no priest, and not because of the Texas-sized spurs he had strapped to his boots.

"Hello, Bishop," Sean Fenn said.

Me? I faced the hangman's noose here in New Mexico, but only on account of some misunderstanding and having killed a relative of a powerful hombre. Unjust decision, if you ask me. But Sean Fenn? That son of a bitch deserved to die.

Chapter Two

"You're a lucky man, Bishop." Sean Fenn moved to the dresser, opened a drawer, fetched out a bottle of Jameson and two tumblers.

I hadn't felt too lucky when I recognized Fenn, but sight of that Irish whiskey—providing it was Irish and not forty-rod poured into a Jameson bottle—made me feel a mite better . . . till Fenn poured two fingers in one of the glasses, and handed it to the nun. The second, he filled with four fingers, and took that one for his ownself.

"I don't feel lucky," I said.

Outside, it sounded like the entire population of Las Vegas was running around. I could hear Felipe Hernandez barking orders in Spanish, then English. I could still hear a lot of cussing.

"You should." Fenn sipped his drink. "First, Hernandez wanted to bring in a lot of his relatives to see you swing, including his sister and cousins in Santa Fe. That's how we found out you were in jail. Hadn't been for Felipe's sense of honor, of justice, you'd be dead by now, and we wouldn't know what to do."

I ran my hand over the beard stubble on my face. "The Valley of Fire."

"That's right." Fenn downed the rest of his Irish.

"Even you could find it, Sean. It's pretty hard to miss. It's a big valley."

Sister Geneviève hadn't touched her whiskey, so Fenn, smiling, took the tumbler from her hand and passed it over to me. I barely tasted the peat as I shot down that Irish.

"Big valley," Fenn said, "but what's buried there isn't big." He moved to the window, pulled back a curtain, peered outside. "The train will be arriving directly. We should be at the depot."

Shaking my head, I almost laughed. "We? I think Señor Hernandez might object to that." I was getting tired of making that point and nodded at his getup. "Even that outfit won't help you, Sean, not after you got a nun to bust me out of jail. They won't trust nobody."

Fenn was moving, kneeling by the bed, reaching underneath. With a grunt, he began dragging something across the plank floor.

I got off the bed.

Kneeling beside him, the nun helped pull a long pine box from underneath.

I frowned. "A coffin?"

Geneviève pulled off the lid, leaning it against the dresser.

"Get inside," Fenn told me.

Now, I don't never try drawing to inside straights. I don't put my hat on a bed, don't bet on a horse with four white feet, and such things like that, but it ain't on account that I'm of a superstitious nature. But lie down in a coffin?

"I'll do no such thing!" I said, all indignant-like.

About that time, we heard the hotel's front door open, and a bunch of boots downstairs, more shouts, and the proprietor saying something that nobody could make out on account of the cussing and commotion.

"Alive now," Fenn said, "or dead after they hang or shoot you. Your choice, pard."

I pulled off my hat, grumbling, but a moment later found myself lying inside that box.

"You too, Sister Gen," Fenn said.

She protested worser than I'd done.

"They know you busted him out of jail," Fenn said. "They'll be looking for you, or any nun."

"How about a priest?" I said, but Fenn was already shunning his robe and crucifix.

"Get in," Fenn snapped at the nun. "We don't have much time."

He was right about that. Boot steps sounded on the stairs.

Geneviève climbed in on top of me. She was small. I wasn't that big, but it got to be a tight fit . . . yet, rather pleasurable. I mean, I could smell that lilac real good. She squirmed, trying to get comfortable. I moved my arms, put them around her back. Our faces were close, but she turned hers, pressed it against my shoulder, and sighed.

"Y'all look might cozy," Fenn said, and I

watched him head to the door. The fool hadn't put the lid on yet.

The door opened, closed almost immediately, and I caught the scent of something that didn't smell nothing like lilac. Fenn appeared over me and the nun again. Geneviève? She couldn't see on account that she was lying facedown, but I'd clumb into the pine box like a dead man. Fenn held up a flour sack. He was smiling at first, till he opened the sack.

His face turned into a mask, and he started to lower the sack, then just plain dropped it. It landed on the nun's back, then slid down to my right.

"God!" I sucked in my breath, tried to hold it.

Sister Geneviève gagged, almost threw up.

Even Sean Fenn had trouble speaking. "Be . . . quiet." His eyes was watering, before I squeezed mine shut, trying not to breathe, trying not to smell, trying not to gag or lose my breakfast. He moved away, came back with a shell belt and a Winchester rifle, put those in the coffin, too. The barrel leaned toward me, making it harder for me to fetch, especially once the lid was on. And soon it covered us, trapping us inside darkness with the smell of dead, putrefying rats.

A drawer opened, and moments later, Fenn began working a screwdriver quickly. Boots and cusses came down the hall, doors opening and shutting all along the second floor. I had to breathe again. The nun sucked in a lung-full, and gagged.

"You"—I tried to whisper, tried not to send Jameson and coffee and the slop they served me in jail all over the sister's habit—"should have . . . just run for . . . the livery. Could've stole some horses . . ." I couldn't smell her lilac anymore.

"That"—she spit, gagged—"was never . . . our plan."

"And this was?"

"Quiet, damn it. Quiet or we're all dead." Sean Fenn spit. Spit again. Tried to spit out the taste of dead rats that filled the air. It sure filled the coffin.

Might be, I thought briefly, *this is Hell.* In close confines with a beautiful, young woman, her lying on top of me, and us both trying to keep from retching, the stink of dead rats strangling us.

The door busted open. To keep the bile down, I bit into the coarse wool of the sister's outfit. I don't know what Geneviève bit into.

"Good, you've finally arrived," Fenn was saying. "This is my brother's coffin. Take it down to the depot."

"¿*Qué?*"

"¿*Señor?*"

"Gawd-a'mighty! What's that—"

"My dead brother," Fenn said. "Killed. Butchered by Comancheros on the Texas Panhandle."

Idiot. Comancheros hadn't acted up since the

Comanches pretty much quit fighting years ago. Sean Fenn talked like he wanted them boys to find me.

"I am taking his remains home to our dear mother in San Diego, California."

"Good," came a voice, followed by a spit. "Get him out of here."

"But"—Fenn poured it on too thick—"aren't you here to assist me in my hour of need?"

One fellow gagged, and I heard boot steps staggering down the hallway. Didn't hear him vomiting, which was a good thing, because that sound would likely have been too much for the nun and me.

"We're looking for an escaped killer."

Boots shuffled.

"But," Fenn begged, "for the love of God, I need—"

Them boys was gone.

"You can vomit now," Fenn said. "But not too loud. Be back in a few minutes."

And the bastard left us there.

Well, we didn't lose our supper. Didn't speak. Scarcely breathed. Summer nights still get cool in this part of New Mexico, but that coffin became a furnace. Made them dead rats smell even worser.

A few minutes later—that felt like a week—the door opened again, and I heard Fenn directing a couple boys to take the coffin to the depot. One of the gents muttered a prayer in Spanish, then the coffin came up—and after a loud "*¡Maldita sea!*" from one of the hired men—our head end came crashing down. It's a miracle the lid didn't pop off, what with only four screws in place. Even a bigger miracle that the hired pallbearers didn't hear my grunt and Geneviève's gasp, then us choking at the stench, sucking in air, holding our breath, praying. Sean was cussing them boys for their stupidity.

"*Señor*," came a pleading voice. "Heavy. *Es muy pesado.*"

"Yes, brother Gus was a large man. Pick it up. Gently."

Our heads were lifted. The men spit, gagged, sucked in breaths, started inching, grunting their way out of the room.

"The back stairs," Fenn directed them.

And so we went. Bumping. Cussing. Slipping. A couple times they lowered the casket, spit, prayed, grunted, and hoisted us back up. We could hear the commotion caused by everyone searching for me and the nun, but nobody bothered to stop us. Oh, I guess a couple fellows come by to see what was going on, but the sight of the coffin and the smell coming from what was inside doused their curiosity.

Finally, we got lowered gently onto the depot, and I heard Fenn thanking the fellows, the jingle of coins as he paid them off, and then, the most glorious sound.

A train whistle.

"Brother Gus," Fenn said, "we'll have you on your way home soon." Fenn's footsteps moved away from the platform, and there was nothing for me and Sister Geneviève to do but shift our bodies a bit (my arms having gone to sleep and my left thigh cramping), suck in more of that foul air, spit on each other to try to get the taste of dead varmints out of our mouths, then fall silent as the Atchison, Topeka, and Santa Fe train pulled into the station.

Well, all sorts of folks come to the platform. Most of them, I warrant, was under the direction and employment of Felipe Hernandez. Nobody would be getting aboard that train without some inspection.

"I am Sean McMurtry," I heard Fenn telling somebody, "bound for San Diego with the body of my dear brother, Gus. Murdered in Texas a week back." At least he had dropped the bit about Comancheros.

"I see, señor."

That voice caused me grave concern. It was Felipe Hernandez.

"I know what it is like to lose a loved one. To have a loved one murdered."

"Yes, indeed," Fenn said. "I heard about that. Your brother-in-law, correct?"

"*Es verdad.*"

"Shot down in cold blood by that cowardly murderer Micah Bishop."

28

"Have you seen a nun during your time here, señor?"

"No. I have spent much of my time in my hotel room, awaiting the train. Spent this evening telling my brother all the things I should have told him while he lived."

That was another thing I disliked about Sean Fenn. He fancied himself an actor, but, for my money, he wasn't no Lawrence Barnett. John Wilkes Booth, maybe.

"And you have seen no strangers?"

"Señor Hernandez. I am a stranger in this town."

"*Sí*. Forgive me."

"*¡Patrón! ¡Patrón!*"

Merciful God, somebody was calling Felipe Hernandez. He must have left while the locomotive coughed and belched, because the next voice I heard was not that of Hernandez. It had a German accent.

"You ship your dead relation home?"

"That's right, Conductor." Fenn was talking. "To California. Here is my bill of lading."

"It is in order. Load"—he got a whiff of the rats—"it in the last boxcar."

We got hoisted again, began tilting one way, then the other. I just prayed those dead rats wouldn't fall out of the flour sack.

"I will ride with my brother."

"*Nein*. Against the railroad's policy."

"I was very close to Gus."

29

I couldn't hear, but am certain Fenn slipped the conductor a greenback or two because I heard the door open to the boxcar, felt us being slid in among sawdust or straw or hay or something. Another sound came from inside the car. It sounded like . . . but I couldn't make that one out. Then came a man's grunt, followed by Fenn thanking the boys who had loaded the coffin into the car.

The train jerked back, then I heard the conductor yelling, "All aboard!"

Sean Fenn said, "Leave the door open, if you please, gentlemen." He laughed. "So I can breathe fresh air."

Moments later, two long blasts of the horn, then hissing, squeaking, and we were moving. Heading south. Away from Felipe Hernandez and this bloodthirsty town.

Almost.

"Señor!"

"Yes, Señor Hernandez?" Fenn didn't sound too friendly. That wasn't acting.

"Perhaps you could answer this question for me. . . ."

I didn't hear the question—too much noise from the train, bells ringing, the locomotive grunting, and a pounding within the boxcar.

Couldn't make out Fenn's reply, either.

The train was moving mighty slow.

"I didn't quite catch that, Hernandez."

Heard that plain. Fenn had dropped the *señor*.

Some other shouts were lost in all the commotion, then I heard something I did recognize.

The report of a pistol.

Chapter Three

Pretty soon, it sounded like Gettysburg out there. I tried to push open the lid to the coffin, but didn't have much room, especially with the nun lying on top of me.

"What are you doing?" Geneviève Tremblay raised her head off my shoulder, bumped it against the lid. Groaned. A bullet tore a hunk through the coffin, buzzed my ear, thudded into the lid.

"Mother of God!" The nun dropped back onto me, heavy, almost knocking the breath out of me. Or would have, if I hadn't expelled all the air in my lungs when that bullet practically made my presence in a coffin fitting.

A horse whinnied. Another answered.

Horses?

Bullets sang out. The train seemed to be picking up speed.

"Push up!" I yelled at the nun.

"What?"

"Put your back against this lid." Just talking filled my mouth with the stench of dead rats.

She understood. She worked her hands between

31

my arms and pressed against the bottom of the coffin. I lifted my arms on either side of her body, pushing the lid.

I pushed harder. Her body strained. She drooled on my chin. The rats smelled deader. Harder we pushed. Straining. Hell, there was only four screws in that thing.

The lid came flying off. The nun rose, and toppled over the side, crying out in pain. I sucked in air that didn't stink of rats, sat up, reached for where I knew that Winchester should have been.

It disappeared.

The train lurched. So did I. The flour sack emptied its contents. I forgot all about the shell belt and the Winchester that was gone. I grabbed my hat, and flung myself out of the coffin, landing on straw, and something else.

I cussed.

"That's what it is," Fenn called out in the darkness.

I began peeling the fresh horse droppings off the palm of my hands.

It occurred to me that no guns was shooting. I looked toward the sound of Sean Fenn's voice, waiting for my eyes to grow accustomed to the new darkness.

A match flared, and I caught Fenn's face, then followed the light. It grew brighter. Then, glorious light.

Fenn had fired up a lantern.

By that time, the train was moving at a lively clip.

I glanced around. Sister Geneviève was on her knees, shaking her head, then locating Fenn. She came to her feet in an instant, but didn't cross herself, didn't pray, didn't do one thing but make a beeline for Sean Fenn and slam a fist into his jaw.

'Twas a sight that made a pagan like me proud.

Sean Fenn had four inches and thirty pounds on me. He was a big gent, tougher than a cob, but the nun's fist had sent him backward. Unfortunately, he didn't fall out of the boxcar.

"Rats!" Sister Geneviève sounded more like a fire-and-brimstone Baptist than a nun from the order of the Sisters of Charity. "Rats were not part of the plan!" She lowered her hand and began massaging the scraped knuckles.

Fenn laughed and touched his jaw, turned to me and shrugged.

The nun went about straightening her habit, her hood, then reaching inside the coffin. For a moment, I thought she was after the dead rats, but she pulled out the shell belt, and tossed it to Fenn, who was lighting a cigar from the lantern's globe.

Behind me, I heard hoofs scraping the floor, and turned, finding two bay geldings. Off to the other side, I spied a burro, two goats, and a crate full of chickens.

A rooster crowed.

Figuring my palm was as clean as I'd get it, I picked up a handful of hay, rubbed my hands in it, then brought the straws up to my nose . . . just to breathe something other than dead rats. I turned my head and spit, then dropped the hay, and faced Fenn.

He held the Winchester. He was a fast one.

A grunt caught my attention. Turning, I seen Sister Geneviève on her knees, hands pressed against the foot of the coffin. Stupid, I know, but my first thought was *Is she really praying over those rats?*

Then the coffin moved. She was pushing it.

I stepped out of the way.

She give me a cold look. "Would you mind helping me?"

"Helping you do what?"

She didn't answer, just stared into the coffin, and pushed again. At which time, it struck me. I walked to the front, grabbed the box, pulled it to the open door where the wind blew hard and the air smelled of piñon. I stepped to the side, grabbed the pine again, and me and the nun pushed that box full of dead rats out of the car, and into the night.

Sean Fenn never lifted a hand to help. He did withdraw his cigar, blow smoke, and say, "Thanks."

I stared out at the rolling darkness, breathing deeply, letting the cool air wash me clean.

Finally, facing Fenn again, I asked, "What happened back there?"

"Yes, Mister Fenn. Explain that gunfight, if you please." The nun had taken my lead, and stepped to the open door. The wind whipped off her hood, and I got an even better look at her face, though it was dark despite the lantern. Her dark hair blew. Her chest heaved in breath after breath.

Fenn stared at her.

"The depot?" I had to remind him.

"Oh." He shifted the rifle under his armpit, puffed on the cigar a mite, then withdrew the smoke, and wet his lips. "I bought that coffin in Vegas. Had it brought up to the room."

"And?"

"Turns out, Felipe Hernandez owns the funeral parlor."

That figured. The man owned everything else.

"Guess one of his kin told him," Fenn said. "Made him wonder why, if my brother had been killed in Texas, I waited till Vegas to put him in a coffin." He grinned. "Then one of his men mentioned that I'd said poor Gus was killed by Comancheros."

"I knowed it!" I couldn't help myself. "I knowed that lie would trip you up, get us all in a heap of trouble."

"Well, we got away." Fenn flicked his cigar into the night, backed up a few steps, and drew his revolver. He punched out the empties and began reloading the chambers from the shell belt the nun had tossed him. Facing the Sister, he added, "And the dead rats helped us get away." He stared at me.

"Not yet." It was Geneviève who spoke.

"How's that?" Fenn didn't look back at her. Didn't even look at the Colt he was reloading. He kept his eyes on me, the untrusting cad.

"We haven't gotten away." She was kneeling—not in prayer—by the horses, which did smell a lot better than what we'd been smelling.

"Oh, Hernandez will come after us," Fenn said. "But he can't outrun a train." Fenn pulled back the hammer, lowered it gently, and dropped it into the holster he wore. He had filled every chamber with a .44-40 shell. Most folks kept the one under the hammer empty so they wouldn't blow off a toe or entire foot, accidentally.

"He can send a telegraph." That came from me.

Geneviève and Fenn looked my way, their expression seeming to say, *He's not the idiot we thought he was.*

Fenn stepped toward the door, holding his hat on his head as he peered into the night.

"Even you can't shoot a telegraph wire," I said. "From a moving train. In the middle of the night. Without a moon."

"Besides," Geneviève added, "they might have already sent that wire."

I will admit that I felt pleasure in that distraught

look on Fenn's face, despite the fact that if I got caught, I'd be dead real soon.

Fenn started with, "There's a chance—" but quit before he made a complete fool out of himself. There was no chance. No chance at all.

Sister Geneviève stood and moved closer to the two horses. She spoke to them softly, reached one, and began rubbing her hand over its neck. The second horse tilted its head and gave her a nuzzle. She hadn't put her hood back up. The nun, I mean.

She peered over the nearest animal's back. "I don't see any saddles."

I got her meaning. "Likely in a baggage car, or with the folks who own these mounts." But I was looking, too, causing the hens to cluck, the rooster to scratch, and the goats to start peeing.

The laugh from Sean Fenn sounded full of contempt. "You can't jump horses out of a moving train."

He was right, of course.

Heading south out of Vegas, we was moving at a right fast clip. But before long, the train would turn west, bound for Santa Fe. Pulling any load through Glorieta Pass wasn't easy. Around there, the train would slow to a crawl. We'd ease the horses off then, hoping they didn't break their legs, or we didn't break our necks, and ride on to . . .

Valley of Fire? Bareback? Three people on two horses?

Horses wasn't the problem. What if Felipe Hernandez telegraphed ahead to some stop like the station by Starvation Peak? Or Bernal? Fulton or Rowe? Nah, that wasn't likely. Most of them places had only telegraph repeaters to send the message down the line and water tanks. The train didn't even stop between Vegas and Santa Fe, except to take on water.

"Come to think on it," I said, being struck with genius, "best thing would be to get off at Romero."

On cue, the horn tooted, and the train began to slow.

"We wait till they get water, and when the train begins to move out, we get the horses out."

"And the brakeman?" the nun asked.

"It's still dark," I said. "Got to take the chance he won't see us."

"Two horses. No saddles." Fenn was annoying me.

"You know me, Sean. Horses tend to follow me around." I grabbed a hold on one of the wall slats as the train jerked to a stop. "There are a few homes around there. Might could find us some saddles and blankets and such. It's an easy trail. South from Romero to Anton Chico, Puerto de Luna, Fort Sumner, and down toward Lincoln. Easiest way to get to the Valley of Fire."

Actually, the easiest way was to take the train south, get off at Socorro, ride east to that lava flow. But that was also the easiest way for us to land back in the Las Vegas pit.

Fenn motioned us to hide behind the mound of hay them two geldings was eating, then he turned down the lantern. Above the hissing, I heard footsteps outside, and spotted the glow of a lantern as the brakeman made his way toward the locomotive and tinder.

Geneviève and I knelt in the darkness.

"I guess I shouldn't have pushed that coffin out of the car," she whispered.

"I'm glad you did." I did not add *providing that brakeman don't notice that it ain't in here.*

"Evenin'." The brakeman had stopped to chat with Fenn.

"Hello. I told the conductor I was riding in here with my dearly departed brother." Fenn motioned toward the coffin that wasn't there.

"I heard. Sorry about your loss."

"Thank you."

"You need anything? Got coffee in the caboose."

"Not now, but thank you. Maybe the next stop. When is that?"

"Bernal. We stop every seven, ten, twelve miles or so."

"Coffee would be fine then. At Bernal."

I heard more footsteps.

"Ah," the brakeman said, "here comes the conductor."

When Fenn turned to look up the tracks, the brakeman pulled a pistol. I didn't see it. Didn't see the brakeman at all, but that metallic sound of a hammer being cocked I heard just fine.

"I must ask you, sir, to step out of the car." That brakeman was a cool one, and smart. He'd struck up a right friendly conversation, easing Sean Fenn into a false sense of security, and when Fenn had turned his attention toward the conductor, the brakeman had drawed his pistol, and pointed it at Sean's belly.

The nun turned to me. "Telegraph?" she asked, her voice barely audible.

My head shook. "Fenn's set-to back at the depot."

Fenn jumped out of the boxcar, and the conductor began demanding, his accent harsh. The chickens started squawking, and the goats bleating, but I got most of what riled and suspicioned the conductor and other railroad folks. What had been the meaning of that gunplay back at Las Vegas? Innocent passengers and AT&SF employees could have been wounded, or killed.

More folks was out there than just the conductor and brakeman. If one of them happened to take a look-see inside this car, my neck was good as stretched, and the nun was good as excommunicated, burned at the stake, put on the rack, or whatever they done these days.

Don't know if Geneviève was praying, but I sure was.

"Take his gun," the conductor said.

The boxcar door slid shut.

More shouts, but the only thing I caught was, "We have a schedule to keep."

The horn sounded.

"We will deliver him to the sheriff in Santa Fe," someone said. "Till we learn what was the cause of the shots in Las Vegas."

Moments later, we was moving again.

Either my luck held, or God had answered my prayer. Sean Fenn was out of the picture, and I was alone with a beautiful nun.

A goat peed on my boot. I cussed.

All right, we wasn't exactly alone. I hurried to the side, turned up the lantern just a bit, found the Winchester and shell belt. Thankfully, nobody had stuck his head inside the car, they'd been too much in a hurry to get Sean Fenn tied up—I assumed they had tied him up, or maybe put a ball and chain on his leg, and manacles on his wrists.

"We can stop in Bernal," I told the nun. "Get off there with these two horses. Can you ride bareback?"

She didn't answer. She stood at the door.

"Don't matter," I said. "I think I can borrow a couple saddles and bridles at this farm I know about. No sidesaddle, though. Not likely anyway. Sorry, Sister."

"I don't think we'll be getting off at the next water stop, Mister Bishop," she said.

I got her meaning. Leaning the Winchester against the wall, slinging the shell belt over my shoulder, I pulled hard on the door.

They'd locked the damned thing.

Chapter Four

Lordy, I slammed the stock of Fenn's Winchester as hard as I could against them wooden planks in that door. The Sister backed away from me like I had lost my mind, and, looking back on it, maybe I had. After all, I had been locked in a pen in Las Vegas that wasn't fit for a man. Now I was in a car full of bleating goats and cackling chickens and . . .

"Horses." I whispered the word, lowered the rifle, finally letting it drop on the hay and dirt. I rubbed my hands, sore from all the pounding I'd done.

"Horses," I said again, louder and made a beeline for the stoutest of them two bays.

Taking halter and rope, I led a gelding away from the hay. Sister Geneviève said nothing, just stood in the shadows, watching. I moved the horse close to the door, turned him around, and swept off my hat, tossing it toward the nun.

"Sister, take my hat. Walk over to the door.

Stand on one side of this hoss, and start waving the hat over his tail."

"What?"

I repeated those instructions, and she done what I asked, though I could tell she didn't care much for my genius. When she started waving the hat, I tugged down on the lead rope, clucked a bit, and finally the bay kicked.

You should have heard the string of cusses the nun dished out. She was lying on the floor to the left of the horse, scrambling away from the gelding. The cusses, of course, was directed at me. Never occurred to me that nuns didn't know that horses kick at things that are behind them.

"Reckon I should have warned you," I said. Would have been laughing, if I hadn't been so worried about getting hung.

She found her feet, brushed off the strands of hay and dust, and it's probably a good thing I couldn't see her face all that good, because I warrant she was giving me the evil eye.

"Again," I said.

"What?"

"Again. Wave the hat. Watch his legs."

"I'm not getting my head stoved in, Mister Bishop."

"We don't get that door open," I reminded her, "there's a mighty good chance we'll both be heading back to Las Vegas . . . where Felipe Hernandez won't be happy with you at all."

She bent over, picked up my hat, and slammed the dust off it against the rocking side of the car.

The whistle blew.

A moment later, the horse kicked again, the hooves slamming angrily against the door. Sister Geneviève dropped the hat.

"Again."

Three more times, I got that gelding to kick. The last time, the nun had almost gotten her hand smashed. Figuring she needed a rest spell, I dropped the halter rope, eased the horse away from the door, and walked to check on any damage. I was mindful not to get behind that big bay.

"Always give a horse a wide berth walking behind it." I decided I should give the nun a lesson in horses. I'd known folks to get their brains knocked out being careless around a horse, even a gentle one. "Or keep your hand on the horse when you walk around it. That's what I do when I'm saddling one."

"Enlightening." She didn't mean it.

One of the planks was busted, and I managed to pry it off, bending back the nails. I tossed the chunk to the rear and reached through. The air was cool. I couldn't see, so I turned up the lantern, then tried again.

"Can't . . . reach . . . that . . . bar." I pulled my hand inside, found the nun, and told her, "Couple more kicks should be all we need. Grab my hat, and we'll do her again."

"No."

"Sister . . ."

"You hold your own hat, Mister Bishop. Let her kick at your head."

"Ain't a *her,*" I corrected. "It's a boy horse. An unfortunate boy horse." I had to laugh at that.

I brung back the horse, handed the rope to the nun, picked up my hat, and got on the gelding's side. It taken awhile before the legs came up. I stepped quickly to the side, keeping my battered old hat from getting battered some more. The hooves against the wood sounded like a cannon shot. The bay snorted and shook his head in anger, jerking Geneviève around a bit.

I inched closer to the gelding again, started waving that old hat. He didn't take long before he kicked again, and finally, wood splintered.

"Once more," I said.

After the third kick, I told the sister to pull the horse toward them goats, and I yanked off another bit of broken wood. I found the bar in the lock, pulled it out, and dropped it along the rails.

A moment later, the door was open, the air was blasting, and the horn was tooting.

"Damnation!" I said. "Are we already that close to Bernal?"

'Course, it was still pitch black. Couldn't see

nothing outside. I turned down the lantern, picked up the rifle and cartridge belt. "Quick, Sister. We're going on top."

"What?"

"I'll climb to the roof then I'll pull you up behind me."

"Are you loco?"

With a sigh, I done some explaining. Nuns knowed all about goodness, about God and commandments and Heaven and Hell. But they didn't know much outside of missions and churches and monasteries.

Chances are, Sean Fenn had said there was a notorious outlaw in the livestock car. Knowing Fenn, he said that bad man-killer, Micah Bishop, was holding a nun hostage. When the train stopped for water at Bernal, the conductor, brakeman, and anybody else they could horn-swoggle would be standing outside, demanding my surrender. Or, maybe, Fenn had kept his trap shut, but those railroad boys would get suspicious. Or they'd want to check on the goats and chickens and horses. Any other similar notion might lead somebody to open that door.

I said, "Bernal or Rowe or Lamy. Eventually, somebody's gonna open that door. And I don't want to be inside here when they do. They get us trapped inside this car, there ain't no way out. On the roof, we got a chance."

"What chance?"

"I don't fancy being locked up inside. In a jail. Or in a boxcar. You coming?"

"Why don't we just jump off? Walk back to Romero?"

"Because I don't fancy getting my neck broke, neither."

"Nor do I, Mister Bishop."

"I won't drop you."

She didn't move.

"Do you want to get to the Valley of Fire or not?"

Not that I really wanted to go down south, but I couldn't very well leave this nun in the boxcar. I'd played my hand. The door was busted and open. Certain-sure, them railroad boys would be looking inside. And if they found a nun . . . well, then the nun would start talking and pointing, and I'd be hogtied and headed back to Felipe Hernandez and the gallows tree.

That persuaded her. She moved past the gelding, and soon stood, holding onto the wall, the air blowing the hood down and making the hairs on her head fly every which way.

"I'll go up first," I said. "You hand me the Winchester and shell belt then I'll help you up."

Even in the dark, I could tell how pale she was getting.

"I've done this a thousand times," I said. "There's nothing to it."

I'd done it, maybe, twenty times. Never in the dead of night. And never . . . "Son of a bitch."

It had started raining.

Lots of folks think it never rains in New Mexico Territory, but it does. Summer months bring in the monsoons, and them thunderheads can dump a river of water on a body in just a short time. But monsoons usually strike in late afternoon, not around midnight. This was one of those rare nighttime showers, slow, steady, cold, and making an Atchison, Topeka and Santa Fe boxcar dangersome and slippery.

Well, I'd started the ball. After jamming my hat on my head, I got a good hold on the wood, and swung myself into the night, into the rain. Wind and rain blasted me considerable, but I didn't mind. Fact is, it felt kinda cleansing, washing off the stink of dead rats, the stink of that Las Vegas cell, the stink of goat pee. Wasn't no trouble for me to climb right up those slats like I was on a ladder. I found a hold on the roof and just pulled myself up. Easy as pie.

I slid around, leaned over the top, yelled down at the nun that it was her turn.

Her head—the hood was back up—appeared like a timid mouse.

Then a notion struck me. "Sister, you need to turn down that lantern."

"But then I won't be able to see a thing."

That took some studying. The brakeman and the conductor knowed there was a lantern in here, but it had been turned down when they hauled away Sean Fenn. Now it was turned up. Maybe they wouldn't recollect. On the other hand, that could suspicion them some.

Hell's fire, the door had been locked, and I didn't reckon they'd be dumb enough to think the horse had gotten loose, wandered over, kicked open the door, which somehow managed to slide open. Oh, yeah, and knock the coffin out, too. Nah, they'd figure some friends of Sean Fenn was in here and them boys had gotten the door open and leaped out when the train had slowed.

Or . . . they might think them friends of Sean Fenn planned on helping him escape—which would mean they'd search every inch of the train, roofs and all.

Or . . .

"The hell with it," I decided. A body could think hisself to death. "Give me your hand."

Immediately, my mind figured something else out.

"No, hand me the Winchester first."

She disappeared just for a second, then pointed the rifle's barrel at my direction.

"Get your finger out of the trigger guard," I told her.

"What?"

I had to shout, for the wind had turned into a gale. Smoke stung my eyes, and the rain didn't do much to dampen the cinders blowing in my general direction.

"Take your finger off the trigger! I don't fancy getting my head blowed off. Accidental-like or on purpose."

"Oh." Funny. That nun had acted like she had plenty of experience holding that little .22 pepperbox, but the rifle seemed foreign to her.

She took her hand out of the lever, grabbed the stock, and hoisted it up. As I reached for the barrel, the train rounded a curve, the boxcar tilted, the wheels screeched, and the Winchester disappeared.

I would have cussed my miserable luck. Didn't hear the rifle bouncing along the tracks, but I did hear Sister Geneviève scream for God's mercy. That's what stopped me from cussing.

I almost slid off the roof, but I managed to grab the nun's hand before she went falling into the night. My right hand gripped her wrist, the other held tightly onto my hold on the roof, which was getting wetter and slipperier. The train finished rounding the curve, the car straightened, and the nun slammed against the car.

Her free hand locked on my wrist like a vise.

Unfortunately, the shell belt had been draped over that shoulder, and when she reached up to grab my wrist, the belt dropped alongside the tracks. Well, those were .44-40 cartridges, and since the rifle was long gone, and since I had no weapon, and the nun only had that little pepperbox, it wasn't like that was a major catastrophe.

She swung back and forth like the pendulum on a clock, into space and banging against the door. One of the horses snorted. The goats sang out. Oddly, enough, them hens stayed quiet.

Finally, the train began to slow down. I turned my head toward my hold on the roof, grunted, groaned, strained, and somehow managed to pull the nun up alongside me. When I had caught my breath, I turned to her and said, "Like I told you, Sister, there's nothing—"

"One more word from you, Mister Bishop," she warned.

I couldn't see her face. Didn't have to. I inched away from her, then noticed something.

The train was slowing, the horn was blasting, and we was stopping.

"Lay flat," I told her. "Don't talk. Don't move. Don't breathe."

Chapter Five

We had reached the water stop at Bernal.

I could make out the glow of the brakeman's lantern as he made his way from the caboose. I could hear the commotion as they filled up with water ahead of us. Naturally, the brakeman stopped by the boxcar on which we was riding.

"That's odd."

I recognized the brakeman's voice.

"What's that?"

He wasn't alone, but it wasn't the German conductor talking.

"You locked this door, didn't you? Back when we hauled that slippery gent off at Romero?"

"Yeah." He must have seen the open door. *"Yeah."*

After they climbed inside, I heard them moving around noisily right below us, leading the gelding to the other end, tethering her to the picket rope.

A minute or so later, they was back outside in the rain.

"Must have gotten loose." The fellow who wasn't the brakeman had to shout because the wind wailed like singing coyotes and the rain fell harder. Cold. Downright icy. Miserable weather to be in.

"Yeah," agreed the brakeman, who had shown such savvy and coolness when he had captured Sean Fenn. "And got angry, kicked the door, knocked out the bolt."

"Horses is a wonder."

"Let's get out of this rain."

A moment later, they was gone. They hadn't noticed the coffin was missing. They hadn't asked how the horse managed to slide open that door. They hadn't even questioned the lantern that was lit. Nor had they turned down the light.

I had expected them to figure out everything,

shout out a warning, but they acted practically stupid. Must have been the rain.

The train started moving, slowly at first, then picking up speed.

Sister Geneviève was speaking to me again. "Are we getting off here?"

I had done some more figuring. "No. We'll ride a spell."

"Outside. In the rain." She wasn't happy.

"Rowe is two stops down. After Fulton. They'll stop for water. We'll get off a little before we reach Rowe."

"And break our necks."

My head shook, not just to disagree with her lack of a positive attitude, but to get the rain off the brim of my hat and out of my eyes. "The train will be climbing by then. We'll slow to a crawl."

"And then? Backtrack to Romero? Follow that road you said down to—"

My head was shaking, but she couldn't see me. "No. Sean Fenn would suspect that."

"But we don't have to worry about Fenn anymore."

"I always worry about Sean Fenn. He ain't one to stay caught. Besides, Felipe Hernandez and the law will be after me, and that'll be one of the roads they'll be studying hard."

"Then why did you suggest it to begin with?"

"In case you haven't figured me out yet, I

ain't one for planning. I make things up as I go."

Sister Geneviève shocked me then. She laughed.

So, we rode in the rain. In the cold. In the night.

I studied on how to get the nun to the Valley of Fire. I also tried to figure out a plan to be shut of her, and go my own way, out of the territory and as far away from Sean Fenn and Felipe Hernandez as possible. Also, I tried to come up with something that made sense about why Sister Rocío would tell folks that I could lead them to the Valley of Fire. And why people wanted to go to that burnt-over patch of black rocks in some of the most miserable country you'd find in New Mexico.

I only got wetter.

Then, after a couple miles or more, I got smarter.

I sat up and faced Sister Geneviève. "What the hell are we laying out in the rain for?"

"You said—"

"I know what I said. But I misjudged them fellows running this train. Thought they was smarter."

"That is something to which I can relate."

Smoke blew in my eyes. Coughing, I shook my head and told the nun, "We'll just crawl back down, get inside the car, dry ourselves off. Then leap off the train when we're near the water tower at Rowe."

Rowe was a little more than a water stop. Back when they was laying tracks, a bunch of folks from the settlement of Las Ruedas had built a pipeline from the Pecos River to the railroad, and Rowe was born. It was a railroad town, although it wasn't much of a town. Nothing like Las Vegas or even Lamy, but most folks had stayed in Rowe after the rails were finished, and few had gone back to Las Ruedas. Rowe was all right. A person could find a little whiskey and something to eat. I could borrow a good horse and light a shuck for Arizona Territory. Rowe was practically civilized, and most of the folks living there were Catholic. They'd know what to do with a nun. Better than I knowed.

"What if they check on the livestock when we stop for water at"—she had to remember the name—"Fulton?"

"We can climb back up before then. Same as we just done. We're getting handy at that kind of thing."

I mean, we was up here. We'd lost a rifle and a shell belt, but I hadn't dropped the nun.

"They shut the door, Mister Bishop," the Sister said.

"But they didn't lock it," I said, arrogance in my tone. "They couldn't have locked it. We'll climb down between cars. Then I'll crawl out, push the door open, and help you get inside."

"Like you helped me get up here."

"I didn't drop you." Nuns was supposed to be forgiving, especially them from the Sisters of Charity.

Her shadow stayed nailed to the roof.

"Suit yourself," I told her, "but it's a shorter drop from the inside of a car to the ground, than it is from up here."

I stepped around her, with the wind and rain to my back, and realized there was only one car beyond the boxcar, and that was the caboose. Too close. I turned around, walking into the rain, into the wind, toward the next boxcar. Kept my arms out for balance.

The whistle blowed. The train rocked some more. She was huffing, heaving, groaning—the engine—beginning the climb into the mountains. She'd be climbing a lot harder in a few miles. I could make out the glow from the lantern the fools hadn't bothered to turn down inside the livestock car. It looked warm. Couldn't wait to get inside, providing I didn't break my neck trying to open that door.

Behind me, Sister Geneviève called out, "Wait, Mister Bishop!"

I waited. Even turned around. I could make out her figure as she rose, taking tentative steps toward me. I held out my hand to help her.

A second later, the train rocked, and the nun slipped. Her shape disappeared. She screamed.

I let out an oath. Called out for her.

"I'm all right!" she cried out.

I walked toward her voice. My boots slipped, and this time it was me screaming.

And sliding.

Right off the damned boxcar.

Somehow, my right hand grabbed hold of something, kept me from going straight into the pits of hell, slowed my fall, and gave me a chance to get a better hold. Oh, I went over the side, but somehow caught the top slats. My knees banged into the side of the boxcar. The goats started yelling again. My fingers gripped them slats tight. That left me still a passenger on the train, but I didn't know for how long.

"Mister Bishop!"

I looked up, could just make out the Sister's face from the glow of the lantern inside.

"I'm still with you, ma'am."

Her hand slammed into my face, prompting a few more offensive words.

"I'm sorry."

"It's all right." I spit out rainwater.

"Grab my hand."

"Sister, you stay put. For now."

"Grab my hand."

"If I grab your hand, I'll pull you off the roof."

Realizing the logic in that, she withdrew her hand. I moved down the side of the car. Still gripping the slats with my hands, I found the door and pushed with my leg. Get that door open, just a bit, just a little hole, and I could swing inside the car to my friends the goats and chickens and rooster and two geldings. Inside, I could open the door again and figure out a way to get the nun inside without killing her.

My left foot found a hold between the slats. My right leg stretched out and pushed at the door.

"What are you doing?" the nun called down to me.

"Trying to get this door open."

I pushed harder with my leg.

She said something, but the whistle and the wind and the rain and the clicking and the goats made it impossible for me to comprehend what she said. I ignored her, just pushed. Tightened my grip. Pressed harder with my foot stuck between two slats.

That was something I shouldn't have done.

I guess the gelding had also cracked the slat my foot was on. Loosened it, anyhow. Because it snapped. All my weight was on that piece of wood, so when it broke, I was falling.

The nun, bless her, screamed out my name—that, I heard—and grabbed my flailing hand, but she should have done what I had told her to do. Stay put.

She would have had a long, wet, but safe, ride into Rowe, and maybe on to Lamy . . . instead of falling into the darkness, into what seemed like eternity, with me.

The AT&SF rumbled on by. The lantern from the boxcar quickly disappeared, and we fell, our screams mingling together. We should have hit the ground by then, but, no, we kept on dropping.

It was like one of those dreams, where you're falling and falling. What's that I'd been told? If you hit the ground in your dream, you was dead.

I felt dead. Knowed I was dead.

We must have fallen off a bridge. That's what struck me first. What struck me next knocked the breath out of me, then everything disappeared, and I was freezing. And swallowing water. Cold, icy water. Then I understood. We'd fallen off a bridge, only not one over hard-rock earth. One over the Pecos River.

Chapter Six

The Río Pecos usually ain't that deep, but winter had been hard and the snowmelt was still running off the mountains, so she was running higher than normal. The Pecos ain't that wide, neither, so the Lord must have been watching over us. Or over Sister Geneviève, anyway.

I come up, breaking the surface, spitting out water. Yep, the river was up, and flowing good, and I heard the nun screaming. She was being carried downstream, toward them rocks. I had to save her. I had—

Hell's fire. I said I'd set the record straight in this here account. Tell the truth.

All right, if you must know, I didn't come up, spit out water, swim over to save the nun from getting drowned. Truth is, after hitting the water, I didn't remember a thing till I was coughing out water on the banks. On top of me, Geneviève Tremblay dug her knees into my back and pushed down hard with her small hands, forcing water from my lungs. Don't ask me how she'd done it, but she'd grabbed my arms and dragged me out of the Pecos.

It was her who'd saved my life, which was damned embarrassing, but that's the gospel truth.

Once she was sure I wasn't dead, she toppled off me, crawled a few rods, then sighed.

"Any other brilliant plans, Mister Bishop?" she asked after the longest while.

Couldn't answer. Couldn't move. My body was numb from cold, my head was splitting, and it's a miracle I hadn't broke no bones. After I started breathing normal, I rolled over, groaning, the rain still pelting my face.

"Well," I said after an eternity. "Sean Fenn, them railroad boys, Felipe Hernandez . . . they'll never find us here."

Then I fell asleep.

Dawn came, and still we slept. When I finally woke up, the sun was warm, drying, merciful, and so was the wind. Figured it must be nine or ten in the morning, which was early for me, but way late to be getting up when you're dodging the law. My muscles was stiff, but slowly I managed to sit up. It taken a good long while before I recollected everything that had happened, and realized why I was laying on the riverbank watching a nun wash her feet and legs in the Pecos.

Sister Geneviève pulled down that black wool, reached over for a stick, and pushed herself off a rock. She limped toward me, using a chunk of juniper as a crutch.

"You all right, Sister?" I called out.

"I'll be fine, Mister Bishop." She hobbled toward me.

Staring at the trestle over the river, she shuddered. When I looked at the bridge, I almost threw up. That had been a long drop. At least, it looked way up there from where we was. A wonder we hadn't gotten killed.

"Are we near Rowe?" she asked.

"No, ma'am. Not even near Fulton. The Santa Fe crosses the Pecos at San Miguel, but there ain't much to it."

She sat on a fallen tree and started massaging her right calf.

"You sure you're all right?"

"Pulled a muscle," she said. "What's in San Miguel?"

"Just a telegraph repeater, some railroad equipment. A few farms."

"You know a lot about the railroad." She pulled off her hood, and looked into the sky, letting the sun bathe her face with warmth. Her matted hair needed ten minutes with a curry comb, and her hand holding the makeshift crutch was cut and bruised.

"Helped build it," I said. "Grading." About the only honest job I'd ever really had. I didn't bother telling her about the time Sean Fenn and me planned on robbing the train between Springer and Raton. We hadn't gone through with it, though we had come up with a mighty good plan. Fenn had chased after a petticoat bound for E-Town high in the mountains, and I'd gotten drunk and passed out in the livery. By the time he come back, he couldn't find me, and the train had gone on to Raton and into Colorado. Them railroad boys never knowed how close they'd come to being victims of a holdup that would have made Jesse James and Sam Bass envious.

Even with her hair tangled so, Sister Geneviève looked mighty fetching.

I still couldn't come to terms with the fact that she was a nun. Maybe she wasn't one. "You sure you're a nun?"

"I pulled you out of the river last night, Mister Bishop."

Good answer. Most women I'd knowed never would have done that. I reckon she was with the Sisters of Charity. She'd even saved my hat, which was drying on a rock beside me. We just sat there in silence, getting warmer, drier, me sneaking a peek at her every once in a while.

Finally, she pushed herself up, leaning on that stick. "What now, Mister Bishop?"

I made myself stand, took a few tentative steps toward her, turned around, picked up my hat, studied the railroad tracks and the river, upstream, downstream, then wet my lips with my tongue. They was cracked considerable.

"Which way to the Valley of Fire?" she reminded me.

I nodded in the general direction. "From here, it's almost direct south. As the crow flies, I'd say maybe a hundred and twenty miles." I give her a hard stare, just so she wouldn't get some fool notion. "But we ain't crows."

She got some fool notion, anyway. "But neither the railroad detectives nor the law nor Sean Fenn would look for us if we took this most direct route."

I sniggered. "Oh, it's a direct route, all right, Sister. Straight to Hell." I motioned toward the river. "The Pecos goes another way. It's nice and cool here with plenty of shade. But after a few days, it turns hot and miserable and deadly. You won't find no water till Piños Wells, if there's any water there. Farther south you get, you're around what the Mexicans and Spanish used to call *Jornado del Muerto*, which means—"

"I know what it means, Mister Bishop."

"Well, you sure ain't walking there. Not with a bum leg."

She give me a direct look into my eyes.

God, they was beautiful, dark eyes.

"I thought you have a certain way with horses, Mister Bishop."

I choked back some fine cuss words. She was tempting me to steal horses, which I was mighty good at.

"Why?" I demanded. "What in tarnation has you so jo-fired to walk or ride better than a hundred miles through the worst country in the territory to dig up something in a valley of black rocks?"

"Don't you know?"

"No."

"Sister Rocío never told you?"

"She never told me nothing, excepting who Jesus's disciples was, how many Hail Marys I needed to say, and that I'd better eat all the posole in my bowl, or else."

"Maybe it'll all come back to you when you see the Valley of Fire."

Silence. Then, "It's worth your while, Mister Bishop."

That got me to figuring some more. It was also worth Sean Fenn's while. I mean, it's one thing for a nun to rescue a condemned man from the gallows. There was a story in the territory that one of them Sisters of Charity, Blandina had been her name, had helped out Billy the Kid in Trinidad. Not that it did the Kid any good seeing how Pat Garrett shot him down some years later. But Sean Fenn wouldn't have lifted his little finger—the one on his left hand that this fellow in Denver had cut off at the second knuckle, clean as you please, with a Bowie knife four years back—to save my hide. So maybe whatever was in them lava flows was worth my while.

But getting there . . . ?

I gave up. I couldn't win no argument with a nun. "Come on, Sister." I started walking downstream.

Two or three miles later, we come upon a little farm. Corral. Lean-to. Couple shacks. And a jacal. Didn't see no smoke from the chimney, but there was two mules in the corral, and a burro and a bunch of stinking goats. The problem, naturally, was that this outfit was on the other side of the river.

"We'll have to cross here, Sister," I told her.

She looked around for a bridge. 'Course, there wasn't one. She turned to me. "You're stealing . . . those animals? We'll drown for those?"

"We won't drown, and those animals can get us to Anton Chico. Pickings should be better down there. Then we can take off south, through the desert, toward your Valley of Fire and our graves."

She didn't move.

"I'll hold your hand."

She limped to the bank and stepped into the water. Sighing, I followed her. Stubborn. Her head was harder than mine. Frigid water took our breath away. It had been deeper up by the trestle, but it was wider here.

The nun slipped once, but caught herself before I could. She kept moving, making a beeline for the bank. The stones on the bed got slippery, but the water didn't get no deeper than my boot tops, at first. About midstream, Sister Geneviève stepped into a hole. That dropped her only to her waist, but she turned, and the color drained from her face. Next thing I knowed, her juniper crutch was flowing downstream without her, and her eyes rolled back into her head.

I lunged for her, but she splashed into the water before I could save her. Me? I went down and under, came up holding onto my hat, moving for her as she floated after her crutch. Like I said, it wasn't deep, but bitterly cold. I caught a handful of black wool, pulled her close to me, then heaved her up over my shoulder. Even sopping wet, she was light as a deck of cards.

Moving through the water, I carried her, climbed out of the river, and left a trail of water to the lean-to. There, I laid her on straw, then pulled off my boots, added to the water trail, and knelt beside her. She was breathing, but out cold. One of the mules brayed. I rubbed the stubble on my cheeks, trying to figure out what to do.

Finally, I spotted the blood, and gently lifted the black cloth of her dress.

I swore. Quickly, I removed my bandanna, wrung it out, whipped and rolled it as thin as I could make it, and wrapped it just under her knee. Spying a little branding iron in the corner, I grabbed it, tied the bandanna into a knot, then put the branding iron's stem atop the bandanna, tied the iron to it, started twisting until the bleeding had stopped.

Ain't no doctor, but I have had plenty of experience treating things like knife cuts and gunshots, dislocated shoulders, busted knuckles, and hangovers—things like that.

Way I figured things, she must have cut her leg on a rock when we fell off that bridge. She'd fashioned a bandage of sorts, but hadn't done nothing else. I reckon whatever rag she had for a bandage had washed off when she'd stepped into the river, the cold water just shocked her, and she'd passed out.

Good thing, too. Likely, she would have bled to death before she'd have asked me for help, and I hadn't been looking for some blood trail.

"Hey!" I called out to the jacal. "I got a nun here who needs help!"

Nothing.

I shouted out, "Help me!" My echo was the only reply.

Her crucifix reflected sunlight. I reached down

for the silver cross. It was actually a pin, fastened on a rawhide thong. Plain and simple. I unfastened it from the rawhide, pushed up the pin.

One of the mules brayed, and I got me this idea.

Leaving the nun, I left the lean-to, ducked inside the corral, and eased myself to the nearest mule, whispering to it like I'd known him all my life. I put my hand on his neck, rubbing in circles, moving down to his rear end. I snatched me a hair from the tail and hurried back to the lean-to.

Beside the unconscious nun, I worked on that stickpin, bending it back and forth till it broke off from the underside of the crucifix. I hurriedly tied one end of the hair to the big side. Wetting my lips, I pushed the skin on the sister's calf together with thumb and forefinger, then pushed the pin through.

First time, it didn't work. The hair slid off.

Did the same the second time. I started to think that I might have to find a knife, heat it up somehow, and cauterize the cut. But the fifth time, the horsehair went through like it was suture thread and the stickpin was a surgical needle.

Taken me twelve stitches, but I made them tight so she wouldn't have no ugly scar. I tied it off, bit off the hair-thread, and looked down at my handiwork.

Actually, I stared at the nun's leg. It was a work of God. Pure. Slim. Beautiful, even with the blood and bruises. I pulled down the black wool.

She moaned a bit, turned her head. I felt her forehead, but she wasn't feverish. Still, I fetched a saddle blanket off the corral post, and covered her with it. Then I ran to the jacal.

Someone lived here, that was a fact. A man. I could tell.

The bed in the corner was unmade, and the place stank of dirt, man-sweat, and tobacco. The skillet by the fireplace was full of bacon grease, and the coffee left in the cup looked thicker than blackstrap molasses. Finding a trunk next to the bed, I opened it. One of the shirts looked passably clean, so I ripped off the sleeve and tore it into strips. I smudged one in the bacon grease, then found a twist of tobacco on the table, bit off a chunk, and started chewing. On my way out the door, I spied something else, so I picked up the jug, and ran in my bare feet back to the lean-to.

Geneviève still slept. I lifted up her dress, saw she was still bleeding a mite between them stitches. I spit tobacco juice on it. Spit three or four more times to get that cut good and juicy because I knowed that the best thing you could do for a gunshot wound was to spit tobacco juice into the hole. It would fight off any blood poisoning. Big Tim Pruett had told me that, right before he died, and Big Tim had been one to ride the river with. Next, I slapped the bacon-greased rag over those stitches, and used the rest of the strips to fashion a bandage. I tied them good and tight, but not too tight, as I didn't want to cut off all the circulation.

I loosened the tourniquet. Color flowed back into her pale leg. Blood didn't soak the bandage.

Satisfied, I hooked the tobacco out of my mouth with a finger, pulled the cork out of the jug, and taken a swallow. I coughed, gagged, wiping the tears from my eyes and the snot dripping from my nose. I had me another pull, laid the jug beside the sister, and went to the corral.

Well, I had one of them mules saddled, reined to the corral, and was working on the big Jack when I heard the shotgun. Knowed it was a shotgun on account I heard the first hammer clicking, then the second. The second hammer taken some time to get set, which troubled me, because I feared it might accidentally go off. I turned around slowly, raising my hands, but not stepping away from the mule. I figured the man with the shotgun, iffen this was his mule, wouldn't be inclined to send two barrels from a shotgun and risk wounding or killing one of his mules.

He was one big Mexican. Looked to be the size of Goliath, with a beard like Moses. He sounded like I'd always figured Moses would have sounded. Strong. Deep. Demanding.

"Step away from Juanito, señor, so I can kill you without harming my mule."

Chapter Seven

Luckily, he spoke and savvied English.

My head tilted toward the lean-to. "There's a nun lying yonder. She cut her leg real bad. I need to get her to the doctor in Anton Chico."

"There is no doctor in Anton Chico."

"Well, there's a church. And a priest. And a midwife, I reckon."

"There is no nun, señor. You are a thief. *Por favor*, step away. That is a good mule. I do not wish to hurt him when I kill you."

Bless that nun, she picked that moment to moan.

The Mexican didn't lower the shotgun, didn't look away from me, but he'd heard. His eyes turned skeptical, but when the Sister groaned again, I could see the hesitation, the doubt underneath that massive beard.

He stood on the riverside of his farm, so he couldn't see inside the lean-to, and I wasn't sure that he wouldn't just kill me, and his mule, then do his investigating. So I spoke some more. "Her name is Geneviève. She's with the Sisters of Charity in Santa Fe."

He give a quick glance toward the lean-to, but I didn't move a hair. His eyes was back on me in an instant.

"Mister," I said, "I ain't got no gun. Not even a knife. And I ain't wearing boots. They's in the lean-to, so I ain't going nowhere. Look inside that lean-to. You don't want to kill me and find out you made a bad mistake. That nun, and God, sure wouldn't forgive you for murdering me, who's trying to save Sister Gen's life."

He had already started inching hisself around the corral, keeping that shotgun aimed in my general direction. He backed up till he had a clear look inside the lean-to, but I didn't resume breathing again till he had eased down them barrels of that shotgun. Crossing hisself, he seemed to forget all about me, and hurried into the lean-to.

I joined him, once my legs got to working again, leaving the second mule half-saddled standing in the corral. He had lifted the Sister's dress, and studied the leg. When he looked up at me, contempt masked his face.

"Did you do this?"

"No, I didn't cut her leg. She fell. Uh, she—"

"No." His head shook violently and muttered something in rapid Spanish that I couldn't catch. In a tone of disgust, he spoke to me in English. "Is this what you call doctoring?"

"Well . . . yeah . . . I mean . . ." For a moment, I thought he might fetch that shotgun off the straw and blow a hole in my belly.

Instead, he untied my bandage, tossed away the

cloth, and pulled a handkerchief from his mule-ear pockets. To my surprise, the handkerchief looked clean. His chin jutted toward the whiskey. "Hand me the jug."

I'd been demoted from surgeon to nurse. I done as I was told, kneeling beside him on the other side of Sister Geneviève, watching as he splashed that rotgut onto the white cotton, soaking it good, then began scrubbing around my stitches, wiping off the tobacco stains, the bacon grease, all the good doctoring I'd done.

That whiskey must have burned consider-able—it had certainly burned a wicked path down my throat—because, even unconscious, Sister Geneviève's eyelids tightened. She moaned, turning her head one way and the other. Beads of sweat soon appeared on her forehead.

The Mexican mumbled an apology in Spanish, wiping her brow with the whiskey-soaked rag, leaving it there, then running them massive fingers of his over my mule-hair suturing. Them stitches still held. She wasn't bleeding much.

"You should be a seamstress, señor," he said.

I told him, "I am, well, sort of prone to accidents."

The Mexican smiled, which surprised me, and rose. "Bring the Sister into my home. We will tend to her there. It is better than here. Cleaner, at least."

He must have forgotten that I'd been inside his

jacal, and didn't find it much cleaner than this lean-to. But he was walking away, shotgun in his arms, so I picked up Sister Geneviève and followed. Once I laid her down on the cot in the corner that served as the farmer's bed, I let my hand slip inside the pockets of her habit. I felt a couple pouches and a purse, but those wasn't what I wanted. I'd hoped to find that little five-shot pistol.

The Mexican told me to move, so I stepped away.

He was on his knees again, putting a bedroll at the foot of the cot, gently lifting the nun's bum leg, elevating it. "Señor, if you can get a fire going, we shall boil water. And heat up coffee and soup. When was the last time you have eaten?"

Criminy, now that he mentioned coffee and soup, my stomach started growling.

That Mexican farmer, he sure was thorough. While the coffee and soup warmed, he boiled the white shirt I'd ripped, then cut that into more strips and fashioned a real good bandage. I reckoned that he had suffered even more accidents than me. He seemed that good at doctoring.

Folks can fool you. I'd figured that farmer for some uncouth bum, but them big hands of his had a woman's touch. He was gentle as he refixed the Sister's leg, though I am proud to say he didn't find no fault with them stitches. He cleaned her leg some more, wrapped the bandage on good and tight, and covered Geneviève with a pretty blanket. He also removed the purse and pouches from her pockets, and left them beside the nun's side.

"Are you alone here?" I asked over his shoulder.

"*Sí*. Unless you count the mules, burro, and goats." He kept focused on Sister Geneviève. "*Me llamo Jorge de la Cruz.*" Grunting, he pushed himself to his feet, turned, and them Old Testament eyes of his blazed through me. He had just told me his name. Now, it ain't polite to ask a fellow his name, and he wasn't asking, but I could tell he wanted to know. Wanted to know my name, and a lot of other things.

"I am Big Tim Pruett." Hell, it was the only handle I could think of.

"You are not very big, señor."

I shrugged. "That's what they call me."

It satisfied him. "The Sister sleeps. That is good. Come, Señor Pruett. We shall eat."

While Sister Geneviève rested, we sat at the table, me on my second helping of tortilla soup, and Jorge de la Cruz slowly sipping coffee, glancing at the nun every now and then. At last, he asked me, "How did you get here?"

I wiped my mouth with my left hand, then wiped my hand on my trousers. He filled my empty tin cup with more coffee, and I sipped it.

I knowed that question would come along, so

I'd been thinking on an answer. "We was traveling on the westbound train." That much was true. "We left the train last night." So was that. "She is on her way to Anton Chico, and asked me to guide her."

"To the parish of San José?"

That must have been the Catholic church there, so I nodded.

He set his cup of coffee in front of him. "Why did you not follow the road from Romero to Anton Chico?"

"She's a nun. Wants to visit all the farms along the river."

Glory to God, he believed it. His head bobbed. "And how did she come to cut her leg so badly?"

"It was nighttime," I said. "She slipped, must have bashed her leg against a sharp rock. We was making camp just by the trestle. I didn't know she'd cut herself. And she didn't tell me. Stubborn, she is. Stubborn as a witch."

He didn't like that, but kept on listening, just listening and sipping and staring. Trying to catch me in a lie, but if there's one thing I was good at, it was lying.

I kept on talking. "Must have wrapped it herself. Never let on. I don't think she would have told me nothing, but when we crossed the Pecos to get to your farm, the cold water must have shocked her. She passed out."

That's something else Big Tim Pruett had taught

me. Adding a dash of truth to your lies makes any falsehood more believable. It sure was working for me.

"It's a miracle that I reached her before the current took her under and she drowned," I continued. "I got her to the lean-to, found the cut, made a tourniquet, and stitched her up."

"With a hair from Juanito." The Mexican smiled. Well, I thought he grinned. It was hard to tell underneath that thick beard.

"Actually, I think it was the jenny."

He nodded. "Ah, Lucía. *Bueno*. Lucía will like having helped save the life of a holy woman."

He wasn't done with his interrogation. "But where is your valise?"

I give him the dumb look.

"Clothes? Food? Bedrolls?"

"Oh. Well. She's a Sister of Charity. They take the pledge. You know, live in poverty. Them kinds of things. She figured on relying on the Christian charity of homesteaders such as yourself for food and lodging."

He chewed on that. And before he could ask another question, I slowly rose, saying, "If you don't mind, Señor de la Cruz, I'll go out and put on my boots. They should be dry by now."

After his nod of approval, I walked back to the lean-to. Got the boots on, and looked all over where the Sister had been lying down. No pepperbox. Nothing but the crucifix I'd broken to save her hide. That I picked up, slipping it inside my vest pocket as I walked to the river. Didn't find the Continental nowhere on that path.

I looked downstream and upstream and into the piñon and juniper woods along the river. Upstream came the faint sound of an AT&SF train's horn. The eastbound train was making its way toward Las Vegas, and that got me to fretting. A posse might be aboard that train. It also got me to thinking something else, because about that time the notion struck me that Sister Geneviève had lost her hideaway pistol. Made plenty of sense, what with her dangling from the side of a moving locomotive, falling off a trestle into a river, then getting practically swept downstream after she'd passed out. Yeah. That was it.

Satisfied, I returned to the jacal.

That's where I found the .22. It was in Geneviève Tremblay's right hand. She was awake, and had that "Ladies Companion" cocked and pointed an inch from the farmer's face.

Chapter Eight

"That had better be you, Mister Bishop." Once again, she sounded like that madam I'd knowed up around Trinidad. Didn't look at me, didn't lower the pepperbox, didn't take her eyes off the burly farmer.

"It's me," I said, once my voice box recovered from the shock. "That's, um, that's Jorge de la Cruz, Sister. We're at his farm. He fixed you up. No need thanking him with a .22 through his eyeballs."

Her finger relaxed on the trigger just a tad.

"Not for him, ma'am, you would have bled to death."

She lowered the pistol, and I stepped inside while she asked in Spanish for the farmer's forgiveness.

"*Es nada.*"

"Well," I let the good Sister know. "I mean, I done some good doctoring to yourself. Even fished you out of the river like you done me."

The big farmer nodded toward me. "It is Señor Bishop you should thank, Sister."

I decided he was a one standup guy for a farmer.

"He stitched your cut, stopped the bleeding." Then he was giving me a mean look, but not so Sister Geneviève could see, and I knowed why. He had stressed the name *Bishop*. I'd told him my name was Big Tim Pruett.

Well, a body never can get all his lies past scrutiny.

I give the farmer a polite grin and sat on the cot beside the nun. "I knowed I should never have given you that little pepperbox." Turning to the farmer, I explained. "For her protection, señor.

You know, not everybody in these parts is honorable, even to a woman of faith."

Jorge de la Cruz was by the hearth, filling a mug with hot soup. He picked my spoon up from the table, didn't bother washing or wiping it, just dropped it in the cup, and brung it over to me and the nun. "Here." He thrust the soup toward her. "You should eat."

"*Gracias.*" I helped her up, and she ate the soup like a wild dog fighting for supper. Famished.

While she ate, I did some fast talking. "I told Señor de la Cruz about you asking me to guide you to Anton Chico. How you fell on a rock, cut yourself, and didn't tell me. And I guess I shouldn't have give you that little popgun." I turned toward de la Cruz, smiling. "Thought it would be good, for her protection, and all."

He scowled.

I looked back to the Sister. The pepperbox was gone.

She handed me the empty cup, the spoon rattling inside. "May I have some more?"

Well, I just went back to the fireplace, ladled in some more soup. When I come back, Sister Geneviève was sitting up. She'd pulled up her dress and was examining the fine bandaging job the farmer had done. Not a drop of blood on them white strips, but that had to be on account of my needlework. She had also lowered her hood.

"Thank you, Señor de la Cruz." She sounded

perfect French again. "My leg feels so much better."

She give that old gent a look that no nun I'd knowed had ever give me. I could practically see de la Cruz's beard melt. I even saw his smile. The farmer had forgotten all about that gun she'd stuck in his face, all about my lies, all about everything but just what a beautiful woman she was.

"As I said, Sister, it was nothing."

"But it was!" She said that with pure emotion.

"Well, it was the least I could do, Sister. Will you tell the priest at Anton Chico to remember me?"

"Most certainly. And I shall never forget you."

Me? I was seething. Them two talking like I wasn't in the room. Her praising him for all his kindness and hard work, but it had been me who'd fished her out of the Pecos, had stitched up her leg before she bled out like a stuck pig. I pulled the crucifix from my vest and gave it to her. "Sorry it broke."

She took it, but didn't look at the pin I'd snapped off, didn't look at nothing but that giant farmer.

"We'd better be on our way," I told her.

"Pardon me," Jorge was saying. "But your leg should rest. You should spend the night here then leave in the morning. Already, the day is late, and Anton Chico is twelve miles or so downstream. Please, rest here for the night. I know it is not much, but . . ." Shrugging, he grinned like a teenage schoolboy.

Finally, Geneviève Tremblay sought out my advice.

"I heard the train just now," I said, all conversational-like. Hoping she'd get my drift.

She didn't. Or if she did, she ignored it.

"Heading to Las Vegas," I said.

She ate more soup.

"Wonder if Sean Fenn's on it."

She kept right on eating.

I got her meaning. Turning to Jorge de la Cruz, I said, "I reckon it would be good to rest here. Maybe I can catch some trout in the river. Cook some up for supper."

It is what I done.

Didn't get thanked for that, neither.

Here's one of the first mistakes—not counting falling off the train and into the Pecos River— Sister Geneviève made. She smiled too often at Jorge de la Cruz. Oh, not that he got any manly notions, not as old as he must've been, but he just couldn't let that lovely nun out of his sight.

Next morning, after cooking us a fine breakfast, he insisted that he would escort us down to Anton Chico. It was too far to walk, he said, for a woman of the cloth with such a fresh wound to her limb. So I saddled the two mules that I'd had to unsaddle the previous night, and the big farmer helped Geneviève Tremblay into the saddle, practically barreling me over to do the deed. Made sure she was comfortable, handed her a canteen of water and a sack of tortillas and *cabrito*.

Yep, they rode, and I walked. Twelve miles south. Having spent the night in the lean-to with that farmer, who snored like a dozen damned howitzers, keeping me awake all night. Twelve miles down the river, and Jorge de la Cruz didn't shut up once, just kept talking to Sister Geneviève the whole day.

Anton Chico ain't nothing but a village in the Pecos River Valley, but it was a mighty important one—a million-acre land grant full of cattlemen, sheepherders, freighters, and the like. The Spanish colonists had built it like a fort when they was settling here in the early 1860s. Homes of stone, and high walls, a church built stronger than the Alamo.

They rode right through the village, the Sister and the farmer, with me walking behind them, hat pulled low and head bowed, just in case any of Felipe Hernandez's men was watching.

We passed a nice stone building with a barn and corral, and there was plenty of good horse-flesh in that corral—which caught my fancy.

"Look at those horses, Mister Bishop," the nun called out. "Are those the kind of horses you have expressed an interest in purchasing?"

They was sure worth stealing, but I didn't answer.

"Sister Gen." The farmer had trouble saying Geneviève, so he'd shortened it to Gen just how Sean Fenn had done and how I did on occasion. "That is the home of Demyan Blanco, surely one of the finest caballeros in the Río Pecos Valley."

"Does he sell horses?" she asked.

"But of course." Jorge de la Cruz turned to give me a look I'd seen plenty of times before, like when waiters and hostelers was wondering if I could pay my bill. "But he is a tough one to haggle with, especially over horses."

We went on to Abercrombie's Store, which was right next to the San José church, but the bells was ringing in those twin towers by the time we got there. It had taken us all day to ride and walk to Anton Chico on account that de la Cruz insisted on traveling like a snail so not to wear out Sister Gen, and we'd stopped for a noon meal that had taken a coon's age to finish on account that even while eating, the farmer couldn't shut up.

Geneviève swung off Lucía, and tested her leg. "It is Mass. We should attend."

"*Bueno*," de la Cruz said. "Afterward, I shall introduce you to Padre Guerra."

"Gracias," she told him, and leaned against his massive body so he could help her inside the church. "But it would be much better if you could introduce Mister Bishop to Señor Blanco."

He shouted something, belching out a laugh, saying that he would be much happy to do that, and that Demyan Blanco was his cousin.

So I went to Mass. Sat squirming on the back pew, all that Latin and all that kneeling and such bringing back to mind my years at the Sisters of Charity orphanage. I knowed I couldn't partake of any of the doings, since I'd never been confirmed, and knowed if I done something only Catholics could do, I'd be struck dead by lightning and sent straight to Hell. So I squirmed, and got to thinking about Sister Rocío and the Valley of Fire. But I couldn't think of nothing that one-armed hag had told me, nothing that made sense, nothing that would explain why a nun would bust me out of jail. I couldn't think why a nun like Sister Geneviève would stay with me and insist on finding something buried in a bunch of lava rocks, or what a nun knew that would interest Sean Fenn.

Every once in a while, I'd catch myself praying, coming up with the right responses to something the priest said, but mostly I wondered if Felipe Hernandez, or Sean Fenn, would be waiting for me once I stepped out that front door.

They weren't. Maybe God listened, though I doubt if He cared a whit for me.

It was nigh dark. Anton Chico was about to go to sleep, but we headed to Abercrombie's Store, where Sister Geneviève pulled out her purse and paid for supplies. Coffee and tortillas, grain for horses, canteens, bedrolls, jerky, enough grub to last a week or so, I figured.

"How about this here Winchester?" I hefted a big old Centennial model, a big caliber baby that would be sure to stop buffalo, which we wasn't gonna run into, or Sean Fenn, which I was certain we would see.

"No firearms," the nun said. "The Lord will provide."

Easy for her to say. She still had that little derringer, which wouldn't stop Sean Fenn, and maybe not even a scrawny jackrabbit.

She spent her last coins on the stuff, then said we'd be back to pick up our supplies after we'd bought some horses and tack from Señor Blanco. The merchant was glad to wait on her. The cad wouldn't give me the time of day. Then we wandered off to see Demyan Blanco.

Blanco, indeed, proved to be the best haggler in the territory. Only he didn't haggle. He set his price, and stuck with it, on account, I reckon, that he saw how desperate we was. Even de la Cruz couldn't persuade him to lower his price, which wasn't even close to being fair. I had half a mind to walk away, then come into his corrals later that night and steal some. In particular, that fine blue roan that I knowed could go across the desert like a camel. That was a fine piece of horseflesh, but even that gelding wasn't worth $200. A hundred, maybe.

"Señor," Sister Geneviève pleaded, "all we seek are two horses, and you have many, and perhaps a pack mule, but the prices you stick with are—"

Angry, de la Cruz interrupted the Sister, yelling at his cousin. "Perhaps I shall ask Father Guerra to read your name in Mass, Cousin."

I figured they were distant cousins, or just didn't like one another.

Demyan Blanco grinned. "Did you see me at Mass tonight, Cousin?"

Sister Geneviève had to step in front of the big farmer to stop the fisticuffs before they begun. "We are a civilized people and we are Christian."

"I am a freethinker," Blanco said.

"And you shall burn in Hell for your wickedness," the farmer roared.

The nun stared, giving Blanco her best, most un-nun-like smile, her eyes twinkling, but that Demyan Blanco was the hardest rock in a county of hard rocks.

"How much for the roan?" the Sister asked.

That had taken me for surprise. I'd been eying that fine gelding, had casually asked about him, but directed most of my bartering and haggling and questioning at a bay mare and a piebald gelding.

"As I told your amigo, two hundred dollars, American. Gold preferred. Ten dollars for the saddle and bridle. I have a sidesaddle that I can let go—"

"No sidesaddle. We have hard country to ride across."

That stopped Blanco, who wet his lips, and reevaluated the nun.

"How do you ever sell any horses?" I asked. "If you don't give and take?"

"I give," he said, opening his palms in a gesture of gentility. "I give horses. I take money. And I even lower the price when it suits me. It does not suit me now."

"You are—" de la Cruz started, but Sister Geneviève hushed him.

"I will take the blue roan"—she shot me a quick look—"for me. The paint horse I will pay no more than fifty dollars for, and you will throw in the saddle for Mister . . ." She had forgotten the name I was using. Hell, so had I. "For my guide."

"Let him ride bareback." Blanco was a nasty man.

"You will throw in the saddle or we will walk away."

"As you wish." He bowed.

"And the mule over there." She pointed to a big mule. "How much for him?"

"Ten dollars."

That was fair.

"And a pack saddle?"

"Twenty?"

That wasn't.

"Then I owe you two hundred eighty dollars."

By grab, she had done all that ciphering in her head.

"American." Demyan Blanco smiled. "Gold preferred."

"But, of course." Sister Geneviève was smiling herself. "I spent my last eagles at Abercrombie's." She reached into her habit.

I stepped back, ready for her to pull that little pepperbox pistol and watch Demyan Blanco wet his britches.

But that ain't what the nun pulled out at all.

What she held in her hand almost made me piss in my pants.

Chapter Nine

It wasn't big. Pressed thin, it probably didn't weigh more than six ounces, but, damn, it was beautiful.

Sister Geneviève held it reverently, even seemed to be holding her breath, then she extended her hands, balancing the ingot on her fingertips.

There was all sorts of delicate designs on the top, including a square stamp on the left end, with a small *o* above a large capital *M*. Next, you could see what appeared to be a crown, a fancy *V* and some pretty and peculiar designs. The ends was curved. Demyan Blanco's eyes glazed over. The farmer's lips parted. I kept waiting for him to drool.

"Is that . . . ?" The horse trader couldn't finish.

I started to touch it, but the Sister handed it to the farmer, who gripped it in them sweaty hams he called hands, and he staggered back against the corral post.

"It is a gold ingot, most likely assayed and minted during the reign of Philip IV."

"How much is it worth?" Blanco asked.

Sister Geneviève pointed at the *V* with her index finger. Demyan Blanco moved closer.

"That symbol is the Roman numeral five, which means it equals five Spanish ounces. An old Spanish ounce is slightly larger than how we measure an ounce today, but not much. So I'd say you'd be safe in saying this weighs almost six ounces."

Señor de la Cruz tested the weight of the ingot, lifting it up, lowering it, lifting it, his head bobbing all the while.

"Now," Sister Geneviève said, "as a nun, I do not know what the current price of gold is—"

"Eighteen dollars and ninety-four cents," I said.

They all looked at me.

I shrugged. "You play poker, you know them kinds of things," I said, but hell, the price of gold hadn't changed much in thirty years.

"Eighteen ninety-four an ounce," Blanco repeated.

"A troy ounce," the nun corrected.

"Sí," he said, as if he had any idea what a troy ounce meant.

"Which," Sister Geneviève said, "would convert this piece to a hundred and thirteen dollars and sixty-four cents . . . if you were measuring it by its weight alone."

She'd done that ciphering in her head, too. Didn't even have to slow down to think on it any.

"But this"—she plucked the ingot from the farmer's hand, and the gold bar disappeared inside her habit—"an ingot minted more than two hundred years ago, must be worth three or four times its weight."

"Sí," the farmer and horse trader harmonized.

"Would you . . ." With great hesitation and deliberation, the ingot reappeared in her hands, and she held it out, letting the farmer pick it up once more. "I hate to ask. I'm not sure I should. But would you be willing to take this for the horses, mule, and tack?" She asked that awful timidly.

"But of course." Demyan Blanco jerked the ingot from de la Cruz's fingertips. It slid into the rear pocket of his duck trousers. "If you step inside my office, I will give you bills of sale for the animals, and Jorge will be happy to saddle the animals for you. Please. Come with me. I believe I have a fresh pot of coffee on the stove."

His tune had changed, and pretty soon we were

sitting on his portal, while he filled in the bills of sale, sipped coffee, and made polite conversation.

Polite conversation my arse. He was fishing.

"Sister, may I ask where you happened to acquire such a wonderful relic from our past?"

The nun give him the dumb look, and I mean to tell you it was perfect. I had to bite my bottom lip to keep from laughing. When Blanco looked up, he saw that expression, and explained, "The ingot?"

"Oh." Sister Geneviève smiled. "I am so ignorant. It was a gift from a dear friend."

"You have no more?"

"We Sisters of Charity have little need for gold ingots, señor."

"That is true. So how did you happen to have this one?"

"As I said, it was given to me by a dear friend."

"Another Sister of Charity?"

"In fact, she is."

He began working on the next receipt. "Do you know where she got it?"

"Alas, I cannot say."

"I do not mean to pry, Sister. It is just"—he looked up, shrugged, signed his name, and rose to bring us the receipts—"such a piece of history, so unique, such a beautiful treasure."

"Yes." She sipped her coffee. "I am glad you now possess it, for carrying such an item of value made me uncomfortable."

I could tell that Demyan Blanco had no problems with that hunk of metal in his rear pocket.

We finished our coffee, shook hands with the swindler, then mounted our horses, me holding the rope to lead the pack mule, and rode back to Abercrombie's. The clerk at the store said we could bunk in the stable, or the priest would be delighted to give us shelter for the night, what with Geneviève being a woman of the cloth and all, but the nun said we had some ground to cover.

It was blacker than the ace of spades when we left Anton Chico. We rode, following the road that paralleled the Pecos River, like we was bound for Puerto de Luna and Fort Sumner, then easing off the road, and splashing through one of the little tributaries or ditches.

We kept riding till there wasn't no more water, but we still followed the dry stream bed, twisting around and about like some miserable side-winder, the hoofs of the horses and mule clanking on the rocks, our stomachs growling, the wind blowing. When the arroyo split, we turned left, heading south and west. We didn't stop till it was nigh midnight.

While the nun massaged her feet and rump—riding and walking were things she hadn't done much of—I picketed the livestock, grained them, and scooped out a hole in the moist ground till water started seeping in, giving them something to drink. I rolled out the Sister's bedroll, left mine on a rock, then climbed up a slope to study our back trail.

"I would dearly love some coffee, Mister Bishop," she said.

"No coffee," I said. "No fire. Just water and jerky. Or you can have a tortilla and some of that goat meat."

"Would you care for a tortilla and some *cabrito*?"

"I'd rather have that .45-70 Winchester."

I could hear her chewing and swallowing.

"You don't think they would follow us, do you, Mister Bishop?"

"Yes, ma'am, I do."

"Why?"

"It's what I'd do."

She snorted. "I said I have no more ancient ingots."

"I heard you. So did they."

"You don't believe me?"

I climbed back down, helped myself to a cold supper. Couldn't see a damned thing what with all the clouds and no moon. Sound carried too far out in this country. I didn't want Sister Geneviève talking too loud.

"Where did you get that ingot?"

She swallowed and uncorked her canteen. Didn't answer me.

"Would have been smarter to let me borrow them horses, Sister."

"You have forgotten the Eighth Commandment."

"No, ma'am, I ain't. Thou shalt not steal."

She looked impressed. She looked amazed when I next told her, "You would have done better if you'd recollected the one right after that. Thou shalt not bear false witness against thy neighbor."

"I did not lie."

I considered that for a spell. "That's the only ingot you got?"

"It is." She went back to massaging her feet.

"They'll come after us," I said.

Her hand stopped.

"Just to make sure. You should have bought that Winchester. Your Ladies Companion ain't gonna help us much. Well, it ain't gonna help you, anyhow."

I wolfed down my supper, washed it down with water, and headed to the piebald.

"I mean to thank you for buying this horse for me, Sister." I threw the blanket back on its back. "Most cowboys in these parts frown upon paint horses. Think only Indians ride them. But I ain't that particular. Especially now."

"Mister Bishop." There wasn't no panic in her voice, which partly surprised me, but mostly didn't. "Do you plan on leaving me in this wilderness? Alone?"

"You can get back to Anton Chico," I told her. "Just follow the canyon back to the road."

Behind me, the hammer clicked on her pepperbox. I kept right on with the saddle, tossing the stirrup up, and reaching for the cinch. I could hear her standing up, moving closer.

"I wouldn't shoot me, ma'am. Like as not, you'll have need of all five rounds in that little popgun when Blanco and de la Cruz show up. Them guns have a peculiar habit of shooting all five chambers at once. Wouldn't want you to blow off some of your fingers."

"And if I blow off your head?"

"Then you'd be breaking the seventh commandment," I told her.

"Sixth."

I turned around.

"It's the sixth," the Sister said. "That's 'Thou shalt not kill.' The seventh I have no intention of committing. Not with you, sir."

A grin stretched across my beard stubble. "Oh, yeah. The seventh's that one. Not that it matters. I ain't married, and unless the Catholic church gotten mighty free-spirited since last I heard, you ain't, neither."

It was dark, but I could tell she was pointing that pepperbox in my general direction. As I rose to tighten the cinch, I told her, "But if you fire that gun, you'll have more problems than I'll never know." I threaded the latigo through the loop, pulled, did it again. "Your roan and the mule ain't tethered no more. They hear a shot, they won't stop till they're drinking water in Demyan Blanco's trough."

The hammer eased down. I moved around the horse.

"So you plan to leave me here. In the wilderness." She wasn't asking, she was telling. I didn't say nothing, but that was exactly my intention.

"Sticking around here ain't my idea of a good plan, Sister." I tugged on the horn, and the saddle felt good, though I'd tighten the cinch again before I mounted. "I got Felipe Hernandez to worry about, and I figure I can make it to Texas or Colorado if I get lucky. Now, thanks to you and that nugget, I'll have to dodge Blanco and de la Cruz, too. There ain't nothing here for me."

"There's that ingot," she said.

"Which you ain't got no more." I looked into the shadow I assumed was her. "Or you was lying?"

"No." Her voice seemed resigned. "No, that was the only ingot Sister Rocío gave me."

I had the reins in my hand, and was ready to lead the paint horse a few rods before I swung into the saddle. My brain told me to start walking, but my legs didn't obey.

"Rocío?" I blinked.

"She gave me the ingot."

I thought about this for a spell, then laughed. My legs obeyed, and I was walking away. "Sister, I always knew that blind, one-armed crone was older than dirt, but she wasn't around two hundred years ago."

"She wasn't. But she knows where the rest are."

I stopped, turned, ran my hand over my beard stubble. "The Valley of Fire." I wasn't asking, either. It made sense.

"Yes."

"She told you that."

"She did."

"She said I knowed how to find it?"

"She said you were the one who could find it."

This I considered, then shook my head. "She's lost her reason." I was walking again. "Crazy as a loon. I don't know what she's talking about."

"She can tell you herself."

"No, thank you, ma'am." I eased into the saddle. Have to admit, I kept expecting her to fire that pepperbox, to see that I'd lied, as was my habit, and hadn't bothered with the tethers to the mule and her roan. "I'm not going back to that orphanage in Santa Fe."

"That's too bad. Then we must go to Gran Quivira."

My hand held the horn and reins. All I had to do was tug on the reins, kick the piebald's side, and light a shuck for parts unknown. But I stared into the darkness at Sister Geneviève's voice.

"Gran Quivira?" Maybe she nodded, though I couldn't tell. I just assumed the nun wasn't lying to me. "There ain't been nobody at them ruins in ages."

"If we hurry," she said, "we should find help there."

"Help? Your help or mine?"

"Ours."

"I don't—" I caught myself, figuring out that she was correcting my grammar, which made me angrier. If a body kept correcting my speaking, I'd never get nothing said. "Who's there? Rocío?"

"Rocío? I certainly hope not."

"Your friends? Or Sean Fenn's?"

"Friends of the faith."

I done some more studying. Finally, I shook my head. "It's a long ride to Gran Quivira, but you might make it. Then it's another ungodly ride to the Valley of Fire. You might find some water north of Rattlesnake Hill, but don't drink it. Salt water. It'll kill you."

The piebald was tired, didn't want to leave his companions in the middle of the night, but he moved deliberately, like me. I had gone ten yards, when Sister Geneviève called my name. She added a few words, too, words that caused me to rein up.

"How you gonna make this worth my while?"

"There were twenty mules carrying ingots like that one I used at Anton Chico," she said. "Do you know how many six-ounce ingots twenty mules can carry?"

Ten minutes later, the piebald was unsaddled, tethered, and happy, and I was wolfing down more cabrito wrapped in a tortilla, massaging my own smelly feet.

Sister Geneviève was sitting across from me. "Sister Rocío told me that it happened something like this. . . ."

Chapter Ten

"In the Year of Our Lord 1598, Juan de Oñate led the Spanish colonists to the place that would be called San Gabriel northwest of Santa Fe—four hundred men, including roughly one hundred thirty soldiers, another one hundred thirty wives and children, seven thousand head of horses, cattle, goats, and burros, eighty-three carts, and ten Franciscan friars.

"The friars came to convert the savage Indians to Christianity. Soldiers came to kill and conquer. The colonists came to establish a new land. They all, even the friars, came for silver and gold. In fact, Governor Oñate himself came from a wealthy mining family in Zacatecas and brought mining equipment with him. The settlers spent more time looking for gold than farming along the Río Grande.

"Pueblo Indians gave their allegiance to the Spanish Crown, and to God, or rather, the friars.

At the confluence of the Río Grande and the Río Chama, the first capital was established in New Mexico, San Juan de los Caballeros, then moved to higher ground and rechristened San Gabriel. A church was built. And soldiers, colonists, and friars went off looking for gold.

"One family, one friar, wanted more than San Gabriel had to offer. So they moved east into the mountains, finding a fertile valley. They called the place Mora, after the mulberry trees.

"They found more than mulberry trees. In the rugged mountains somewhere between Mora and Santa Fe, they found gold. Tons of it. They found Indians, too. The priest became more interested in the gold mines than in the salvation of pagan Indian souls.

"The colonist went back to San Gabriel, and returned to Mora with a dozen soldiers. They enslaved the Indians to work the gold mine. They grew wealthy. The mine seemed as if it would never play out. It was like they had found the Seven Cities of Cibola—all in one place.

"The mine's location, they kept secret, known only by the colonist, the friar, the soldiers, and their families.

"Eighty years passed. The descendants of the colonists inherited the mine. The children, then grandchildren of the slaves, worked the mine. A new friar took over, bringing with him a mold to make ingots, stolen from Mexico City. Two other friars joined him. Life was good, for the colonists, the Spaniards, the friars.

"But in the early summer of 1680, the gold became scarce. Finally, the mine was playing out.

"When dawn broke on August tenth, some fifty to sixty Pueblos revolted, killing every Spaniard they could find. Word reached the mine. The friars and the families forced the Indians there to pack sacks and sacks of gold ingots onto burros and fled. They hurried south, past Santa Fe, joining hundreds of fleeing Spaniards. The miners made it to Gran Quivira. And that's the last anyone ever heard from them. Other colonists, soldiers, friars, fled back to Mexico. Spanish rule would not return to New Mexico until 1692, when Diego de Vargas reestablished Spanish settlements.

"By then, the priests, the soldiers, and the colonists who had fled the mine near Mora were all dead, or had no interest in returning to the mountains of New Mexico, even for a fortune. The treasure was lost."

While Sister Geneviève had been talking, she had started shivering. Like I said, even in summertime, the nights can turn chilly in this country so I decided to chance a fire, gathering dry wood, keeping it small. She kept talking, inching closer to the fire.

Her face glowed, and even though she still wore that hood, I could see the flames in her dark eyes.

Such a pretty face. Damn, it sure was wasted on a nun.

When she got to the part about the treasure being lost and all, I tossed some more wood onto the fire. No smoke, and what with us tucked down in the arroyo, I didn't think the fire could be seen by anything other than owls and nighthawks.

She fell quiet, extending her hands, warming them over the fire.

"Sister," I told Geneviève as gently as I knew how, "that is an interesting tale. But your nun friends raised me to know better than waste my time gallivanting across the New Mexico desert chasing lost mines."

"Not a lost mine," the nun said. "Especially one that was played out two hundred years ago. You saw that ingot. That's what we're after."

"It's still lost. Same thing. Gold that ain't been seen for two centuries."

"You saw it."

"I saw one ingot."

"Sister Rocío saw twenty mule-loads of ingots."

I laughed. "She's blind."

"She wasn't in 1848."

I let her keep talking.

"After the Mexican War, Sister Rocío, then a nun in her mid-thirties, arrived at Gran Quivira at the Salinas Mission ruins with two priests, an historian from the newly-founded Smithsonian Institution, and two Mexican guides. They weren't looking for gold, just wanted to see the old mission.

"What they found behind one of the walls startled them—bones of Indians, skulls crushed, bodies hacked to pieces, and one of those ingots clutched in a skeletal hand. That got them looking, exploring, digging.

"Scientist James Smithson had founded his institution to help increase and diffuse knowledge among men. Well, the scientific-minded historian with the party studied the scene and then guessed what had happened—the friars and colonists had made it to Gran Quivira—especially after one of the old Mexican guides told them of the legend of the lost Mora treasure.

"The historian wasn't sure if the Pueblo was part of the 1680 revolt, but those Indians had been murdered, and the ingot in one hand seemed to say that they had been killed in or around 1680."

"The priests," I said, and shuddered, which I hardly ever do, especially in summer. "They . . . murdered those slaves."

The nun's head bobbed. She no longer looked me in the eye. "Most likely. Sealed them in a tomb for almost one hundred seventy years."

"And that old nun, that scientist, those priests . . . they found the gold."

She looked up at me again, her head still bobbing slightly. "All of it. Well, most likely, all of it. It took them months. It was January before they had it all.

"They loaded the treasure on twenty mules, and moved quickly south, staying away from the trails to the east, staying well away from the Jornado del Muerto to the west."

I kept trying to do some ciphering in my head. Twenty mules. All of them couldn't carry gold, not if those fools knowed anything. They'd need to pack food and water. So let's make it fifteen mules carrying gold. A good mule can carry maybe twenty percent of its body weight. Say the mule weighs eight hundred pounds. That would mean . . .

I gave up. "Sister, what's twenty percent of eight hundred?"

She looked at me as if I was an idiot.

"One hundred and sixty."

"So . . . times that by fifteen . . . and . . . and . . . ?" I asked her again.

"Two thousand four hundred."

I nodded. Then it struck me that that was pounds. There are sixteen ounces in a pound, so that made it . . . ?

Another question.

She give me another answer. "Thirty-eight thousand, four hundred."

I give her a stare, then grinned. "You don't have to do no scratching, no carrying, none of them kinds of things."

"It isn't that difficult." She was smiling, not looking at me like I was a fool and criminal, which I was. She smiled like she liked me.

Sort of.

"Let's say gold's twenty dollars an ounce," I suggested.

"It's more than three-quarters of a million dollars," she said.

"You don't know the exact figure?"

"That might take me a while to do in my head."

But I knowed. Not the exact figure or nothing like that. But she was lying. She knowed exactly how much money it was. She could probably tell me at $19.84 an ounce. Troy ounce. But $750,000 was a nice round number. That's all I needed to know.

"So they took off south, probably bound for Mexico to one of the port cities. And had to go through the Valley of Fire."

Sister Geneviève said that's what happened and resumed her story.

"It's hard to keep seven hundred fifty thousand dollars a secret. They had to go for supplies, for burros and mules to carry the gold. Someone, probably one of the guides, told a friend, who told a friend. Finally, Sister Rocío's party left, moving south. By the time that pack train had reached the Valley of Fire, they knew they were being followed. They pretended to bed down for the night, making a big show of fires, then sneaked out, moving south. Quickly. Desperate.

"Two days later, the bandits caught up and attacked. But the party managed to hold out, at least until nightfall. That night turned cold, bitterly cold. One priest was dead, but Sister Rocío was determined not to let these killers get the gold. To her way of thinking, the gold belonged not to Mexicans or Spaniards or scientists with the Smithsonian Institution, but to those murdered Pueblo Indians. Definitely, bandits did not deserve the fortune.

"The priest, the scientist, the guides agreed.

"That night, the young nun and a guide named Cortez led most of the mules away from camp, turning toward the mountains to the east."

Just like that, the story ended.

Oh, I was certain-sure there was more to it. But the nun wasn't talking no more. She was staring. Staring right behind me. Slowly, she raised her hands over her head. Even slower than that, I turned to stare down the barrel of that big-ass .45-70.

They stood at the edge of the arroyo, up on the slope. I couldn't see past them where it was pitch black, but the light from the fire reached them two sorry cusses.

"*Buenos noches*," Demyan Blanco said. Beside him, holding two damned quiet horses, stood the farmer, Jorge de la Cruz. I looked around for others, but, like most folks, Blanco and the farmer was greedy sorts. They hadn't told nobody about the ingot. They'd just come chasing after us.

Blanco knelt, to give me a better look at that Winchester Centennial.

Me? Without looking back at the nun, I told her, feeling right proud of myself, "Sister, I told you we should have bought that damned rifle back in Anton Chico."

Chapter Eleven

"Sister," Blanco said, "you and your compadre are far from the road. Far from civilization."

"One gets closer to God while alone in the wilderness."

The horse trader laughed. "I would not know. Since I do not believe."

"I will pray for you."

"You should pray for yourselves!" This, surprisingly, came from the massive farmer, who led the two horses down the slope and into the arroyo, while his cousin, the horse trader, stayed up top, covering us with his Winchester. "You should pray for yourselves!" Jorge de la Cruz repeated.

It's hard to figure a fellow sometimes. I mean, twenty-four hours earlier, this farmer had shown his gentle nature, had helped fix up Sister

Geneviève's leg, practically acting like he was smitten with a woman of God. Just this evening, he had lashed out against his cousin's haggling, or refusal to haggle, and had come close to getting into a row with Demyan Blanco. Now, he ground-reined their two horses, and pulled a pistol from his waistband. One of them Dean and Adams five-shot affairs, English made, old-fashioned. Not a small gun, but it looked like a toy in that big oaf's hand.

"We do not believe that that piece of gold is all you possess," he said. Unlike that outburst a moment earlier, his tone sounded almost apologetic.

That big pistol sure didn't look it.

Sister Geneviève struck a Christlike pose, holding her arms out, her voice soft. "You may search us if you desire."

De la Cruz went about gathering some more firewood with his free hand, while his right hand kept that Dean and Adams on me. He built up the fire real good and stepped back.

Finally, the horse trader came down the slope carefully, keeping that cannon of a rifle aimed at my chest. With the rifle's barrel, he motioned me to stand closer to the nun, and I obeyed. Criminy, I had half a mind to stand behind the Sister and use her for a shield, as menacing as that Winchester was, but I knowed something about guns. A .45-70 slug would tear right through Sister

Geneviève and then blow me apart as well. So I done the manly thing. I stood in front of the Sister.

Blanco spoke in rapid, angry Spanish. Jorge de la Cruz slid his pistol back inside his pants, and pulled a coal-oil-soaked torch from the back of his horse. They had come prepared. He stuck the end of the torch in the fire, then carried his light toward our horses, jamming the bottom in the soft sand, and went to work. He sure made a mess of that fine packing job the clerk at Abercrombie's had done, throwing sacks and cans every which way, startling the mule, then ransacking my saddlebags that had come with the saddle. That didn't take long. Didn't have a damned thing in them. Blanco just stood there, cradling that Winchester, staring at us.

Wasn't too long, since we hadn't packed too much stuff, before an angry "*¡Maldita sea!*" exploded from that burly farmer's mouth. He rose, drew his revolver, and stepped around the torch. "There is nothing of value!"

"I told you as much," Sister Geneviève said demurely, "when I bought those horses and mule."

"*Bastardo*," Jorge de la Cruz whispered, then spoke again in Mexican at his cousin, who shook his head.

Blanco took over the interview. "You said the ingot was given to you by another nun."

Sister Geneviève nodded. "That is so."

"And you do not know where she found it."

"As I told you back in Anton Chico—"

The Centennial rifle came up to Blanco's shoulder. "Then why do you travel with this rapscallion, Sister? Why do you leave the road and hide in this arroyo? Why is it that Felipe Hernandez rode into our quiet village shortly after you left?"

That got my attention. I stared into the night, wondering if Hernandez was out there waiting.

"He says that you helped this miserable gringo escape from jail. He was sentenced to hang." Blanco was grinning when I turned back, figuring if Hernandez was out there, I'd already be dead. "There is a nice reward for your return to Las Vegas, señor."

"Where's Hernandez?" I asked.

The rifle lowered, but just slightly. I stuck my hands behind my back, palm out, hoping Sister Geneviève would get my intention and place that little Ladies Companion in it.

"I sent him to Puerto de Luna," Blanco said.

"Señor." Jorge de la Cruz said. "Step away from the Sister of Charity. Do so now, amigo, or I will kill you both."

"Do as he says, Mister Bishop."

The way she said it, I knew it wasn't a suggestion, and all them years in that orphanage run by nuns must have made me obey her. I moved closer to the fire, and turned around, half-expecting to see that nun gun down them two boys with that pocket .22, but she just stood there.

"Where is the gold?" Blanco asked.

"If it is not with those horses," the farmer said, "it must be on their bodies."

"You dumb son of a bitch," I told the fool. "You think we'd carry gold on us? Heavy as gold is?"

"Those are small ingots, señor." Blanco nodded at his massive cousin.

The cousin stepped in between Sister Geneviève and me. "Take off your clothes."

Blanco grinned.

Now, being truthful and all, this being likely the last testament of Micah Bishop, I admit that I had wondered just what that nun looked like under all that black wool and white trim, had done some picturing in my mind my ownself, but there is a limit to what even a rapscallion and horse thief and cardsharp will tolerate. Nuns had practically raised me and all. I might be what you call lapsed or a backslider, but there was some things you just did not do.

"What kind of men are you?" I snapped, and took several steps until that Winchester barrel was right at my sternum.

Blanco's eyes didn't blink. I could hear Jorge de la Cruz turning around, figured he had that pistol aimed at my skull.

"She's a nun!" I yelled.

"Felipe Hernandez has put a price on her head, too," Blanco said. "Nuns do not help outlaws."

"There was Sister Blandina!" I said. "She helped Billy the Kid up in Trinidad."

"She was not my nun. Nor is this wench."

Now, here I was, an inch from a .45-70 slug ripping through my chest, had gotten the attention of them two ruffians, and all Sister Geneviève had to do was pull that pistol, put a slug in the big man's back. That would distract Blanco, and I'd knock the rifle aside, jerk it from his hands, beat his brains in with the Winchester's stock.

That's what I was hoping would happen. I mean, that nun had shown no qualms about shooting me after she'd busted me out of jail. I'd even suspected her, since she had partnered with Sean Fenn, of not even being a nun, but now she acted so sweet and innocent.

"You must not harm him." She didn't shout that. Just said it like she was telling a toddler, pretty please, that he needs to hush.

Blanco shot her one mean glance. I contemplated knocking the rifle aside, but then decided I was in no hurry to get to Hell.

"You will do as my cousin says. Take off your clothes." That mean horse trader must have been picturing her as I'd been doing.

"No, señor, I will not do that. You may kill me. Do as you wish. You may even kill Mister Bishop."

That wasn't what I wanted to hear.

"But then you will never find more than three-quarters of a million dollars in ancient Spanish ingots."

Both of them thieves whispered a stunned, "*¡Joder!*" Then they got quiet, staring, dreaming of all that beautiful gold.

Things stayed that way for the longest while, them cutthroats practically salivating over their newfound riches that they hadn't found yet, the nun just standing there, hands nowhere near that pepperbox pistol in her habit, me realizing that I really needed to empty my bladder, and the horses swishing their tails.

"Where is it?" Demyan Blanco had finally found his voice.

"It is buried," she said, pausing, "at the mission ruins at Gran Quivira."

I bit my bottom lip. She, a nun, had just cut loose with a shameless falsehood. Or had she? Maybe she had lied to me. I mean, she told me the gold had been buried at Gran Quivira, but now was buried somewhere in the Valley of Fire.

"Gran Quivira?" Blanco pursed his lips. "There has never been gold there," he said after a moment. "There is nothing near those old ruins but salt . . . and . . ."

"*Fantasma.*" Jorge de la Cruz spoke in a whisper so soft, I could just manage to hear.

Well, them cousins went at each other again, barking in Mex, gesturing at each other. A good time for Sister Geneviève to pull that .22 and start the ball, but she remained an unmoving angel.

"There are no ghosts!" Blanco finished his argument with a flurry.

For a moment, I thought he might turn that Centennial rifle on the big farmer, but, alas, that wasn't in the cards. His giant cousin kicked some sands, hunched his shoulders, and glared.

"I would not discount the stories of their presence," the nun said.

Blanco spit and snorted. "I thought you would only believe in one ghost, Sister, the Holy One."

"I believe in angels," she said calmly, "and what is an angel but a ghost, a specter, an apparition." She give him one of her charming smiles. "It is said that before the Revolt of 1860, four hundred and fifty poor souls starved to death and were buried in a mass grave. That is why there was nothing there but ruins when the gold arrived during the revolt."

I could see Blanco's eyes doing some mental figuring. He knowed that piece of gold had been made during the reign of King Philip Something or other, and I doubt if he was that caught up on his studies of ancient New Mexico, but it must have struck him as being reasonable.

"The gold arrived in 1680?" Blanco asked.

"Yes. When the Pueblo Indians revolted."

Blanco shook his head. "Sister, the Pueblo Indians were revolting. So why would those dirt-diggers at Gran Quivira not kill the priests and soldiers there?"

"The *Northern* Pueblo Indians revolted," she corrected him like a child.

Reminded me of my schooling back at the orphanage, only she said it right pleasantly, and didn't crack no knuckles with her ruler.

"Not the Pueblos in the Salinas region. Besides, by that time, there were few of *Las Humanas*, as the Indians there called themselves, left at the pueblo and mission. As I said, most had died during the terrible drought in the years before. The survivors—the Spanish survivors, I mean—in Mora where the gold was mined fled for Mexico, or at least to what is today known as El Paso."

"And, naturally," Blanco said, his voice accented with sarcasm, "they took all that gold with them. They loaded down their burros with a fortune in gold. *As they fled for their very lives?*"

"Wouldn't you? Three-quarters of a million dollars worth of gold?"

That shut the bastard up.

"Why did they not come back?" Blanco asked. "When de Vargas returned years later?"

The farmer just blinked with stupidity. I reckon he hadn't studied much history.

"*¿Quién sabe?*" She shrugged.

Blanco chewed on this for a spell, carried on a quick conversation in their native tongue with his cousin, gesturing at each other, voices rising every so often, one pointing at me, the other at the Sister, then to the south a long way toward those ruins, then north back to Anton Chico.

They got quiet again, but only because the Sister had started talking.

"That much gold is too much for the Sisters of Charity. As I said, another Sister in our order revealed the story to me. We are humble people. All we desire is to help those in need, especially the children. If you can take me to the ruins at Gran Quivira, and we find the gold, you may have most of it. All we ask, as the Sisters of Charity, is enough to improve our school for girls, our orphanage, and our hospital. Is that too much to ask?"

More of that harsh Mexican lingo, more pointing, then both men nodded.

"Jorge is a faithful Catholic. He agrees with your terms, Sister. We shall take you to Gran Quivira. But we do not need this *norteamericano*." Blanco rammed the barrel into my stomach, knocking the breath out of me, and when I doubled over, the sneaky fiend tried his best to hammer out my brains with that barrel.

I hit the ground hard, rolled over, wheezing, just managing to see through tears of pain that Centennial's barrel which Blanco had planted on the bridge of my nose.

Chapter Twelve

"No!" Sister Geneviève wasn't talking so sweetly now.

That's my girl! I thought. *Start shooting these bastards.*

But she just said, "You must not kill him."

Now, you got to understand that I couldn't see too clearly. Not with a rifle barrel between my eyes, and all them tears welling in them from getting my head bashed in, but it seemed to me that Demyan Blanco didn't care one whit about the nun's demands.

"You fool!" Once again, Sister Geneviève sounded like that madam up in Colorado. "You kill him and we'll never find that gold!"

He looked up, but his finger was still tight on that Winchester's trigger.

"He knows where the gold is. I don't!"

The finger slipped out of the Winchester's trigger guard. I closed my eyes. Might have even mouthed a prayer. The pressure left my nose, and when I opened my eyes, and blinked away all them tears, Demyan Blanco had stepped away from me, moving toward the nun. I sat up, went right back down, rolled over, and heaved *cabrito* and tortillas and coffee and water onto the ground. Got so dizzy, I dropped into my own vomit.

Almost immediately, I got out of that wretched muck. Then I fell right back into it, and watched, and welcomed, the world turn black.

Gran Quivira lay maybe eighty-five miles southwest of Anton Chico. Eighty-five miles of rough travel, especially once we reached the Estancia Valley. If we reached it . . .

Felipe Hernandez would find that we wasn't in Puerto de Luna, might have already got there, and he'd come back, madder than that feller had been in Jacksboro when he'd figured out that I was using a marked deck, and he'd broke my nose, and likely would have broke some more things if Big Tim Pruett hadn't bashed his head with a whiskey bottle.

I always liked Big Tim. Wished he was riding with me right then.

Drums pounded inside my head, flattening my brains, and my stomach felt as if I'd swallowed a gallon of bile. I feared my bowels would loosen, and I'd embarrass myself in front of Sister Geneviève, but God was smiling on me.

So was that damned sun.

They'd let me sleep in my own vomit, then splashed water on my face, the fools—I'd rather have had them urinate on me rather than waste good water—jerked me up, tied my hands with leather cord, and boosted me in the saddle.

Breakfast had been tortillas and water, but I

didn't eat. My stomach wasn't up to food right then. They had decided to run a cold camp and get moving quickly, before the sun turned the country into a furnace. Or maybe they decided Felipe Hernandez might be on his way back toward Anton Chico.

All morning, we rode, the nun in front of me, Blanco taking the point, and de la Cruz, pulling the mule, bringing up the rear. It wasn't so bad, not at first. The morning dawned fairly cool, clouds helped, and we rode in the arroyo, twisting this way and that, till the dry creek bed ended, and we climbed out into rugged plains.

By that time, them clouds had blown away, the sun baked us, and the wind blew hot and dusty. Finally, we started climbing, maybe a thousand feet in elevation, and Anton Chico's probably at least a mile high. That was good. I mean once we started climbing, the piñons and junipers provided us some shade, and blocked most of the wind.

We didn't stop for noon. Didn't stop for nothing, except when the horses, and once Sister Geneviève, had to answer nature's call. Them two cousins made some hoarse whispered comments while the nun did her business in the bushes. I didn't like the way they looked at her. Come to think on it, I didn't like Blanco and his cousin none at all.

The trees grew too thick, branches slapping at us. Well, slapping ain't the best term. They knocked the hell out of us, leaving both arms with scratches and welts. The mule got stubborn, locked his hind legs like anchors, causing de la Cruz to cuss and torment and pull. The big oaf had to climb off his horse, and pull and tug and cuss some more. I had stopped, turning around, watching the fight from my saddle. Demyan Blanco came riding back, yelling at his cousin, yelling at the mule. Then he rode behind the mule, and jerked the Winchester from the scabbard.

For a second, I thought Blanco was going to shoot the poor beast. But, no, he done something even dumber.

He jacked a cartridge into the chamber and aimed. Realizing his intentions, I grabbed a tight hold of my reins. That big cannon boomed, the bullet slamming into the rocks between the mule's hind legs. Oh, that got the mule moving all right. It also sent de la Cruz's big buckskin horse cutting through the timber, heading to parts unknown.

I ain't no cowboy. Never claimed to be, never wanted to be. That piebald did a little bucking, and the only reason I didn't lose my seat in the saddle and wind up tasting gravel was because I'd hemmed the gelding in pretty tight between them piñons. The roar of the Winchester echoed loudly. A limb knocked my hat off, caused my head to pound some more, and I caught a glimpse of the mule hightailing it, heard Blanco cussing, and in the corner of my eye, I saw de la Cruz running after his frightened mare. My gelding calmed down, just enough, that I craned my neck, just in time to see the mule slam into the blue roan, and send Sister Geneviève sailing. The mule stopped. The roan rolled over, and I was off my horse.

"Dear God!" I prayed, which ain't nothing I do often. Feared the roan had rolled over the nun, and a Sister who weighs a hundred pounds after a heavy rain ain't no match for a nine hundred pound gelding.

"Stop!" Blanco shouted at me, but I paid him no mind. The roan gelding was coming up, and I snagged them reins. That horse was like a jackrabbit dodging a hawk. He reared, them front hooves coming close to braining me. He backed up, jerked me to my knees, dragged me a few feet, then his butt hit a juniper branch, and he come right at me.

I was up in an instant, still holding the reins tightly, biting back pain as the leather burned my palms. The roan just missed running over me, but I pulled the reins, started hushing and sweet-talking him. The mule brayed. Blanco cussed and come running at me. I heard him jack another shell into the Centennial.

My head was throbbing again, dust stung my eyes, the reins had left welts on my palms—should have bought a pair of gloves back at Abercrombie's—and my knees was skinned and pants ripped—should have bought some chaps, too.

The blue roan snorted, but started to calm down. I felt Blanco's rancid breath on my neck, but I wasn't in no mood to put up with that horse's arse. Turning, I thrust the reins at him and snapped, "Here. You hold him."

Leaping over a dead tree, I found the nun laying on her back. Her hood was down. She held a handkerchief under her nose.

I knelt beside her, and when she started to rise, I put my hand on her shoulder, gentle but firm. "Don't move."

She sank back to the ground, removed the handkerchief, sighed at the blood, and placed it back, sniffling.

"Anything busted?" It taken a moment before I could find the words. My heart was still racing, and my breath came out in short bursts. It sorta hurt to breathe.

"I don't think so."

My hands, still bound with that leather cord that bit into my wrists, touched her left ankle, then I eased up her leg, not touching the skin, nothing like that. Just on her skirt. She lowered the bloody piece of cotton underneath her nose, which had stopped bleeding, watching me. I looked at her, then moved my hands to her other leg, seeing if she flinched, touching her ankle, calf, lower thigh. Didn't go no higher.

Using her arms, she pushed herself up. I decided her wrists and arms wasn't broken.

"Take a deep breath."

She obeyed. Didn't gasp or nothing.

"I don't think you busted anything"—I smiled— " 'cept your nose, and it ain't broken."

"I'm glad to know that." But she tested it with her fingers, just to be certain.

We just stared at each other.

Crazy. I mean the first thing I noticed about her, with her hood down and all, was her eyebrows. They were perfect. Well, it ain't that I'd ever noticed any woman's eyebrows or nothing like that, so I can't say I'm an expert. But they looked perfect, thick then tapering in this perfect curve. Her eyes were a light brown, not too dark, not too light. I reckoned they was perfect, too.

Her dark hair, which hung to her shoulders, was kinda matted and sweaty and coated here and there with specs of dirt and piñon needles. I mean, it was a hot day, and she'd just been rammed off a horse and over a dead tree, so you couldn't expect everything about her to be perfect.

She started to move again, but I shook my head. "Just sit there for a minute. Get your breath back. Make sure you're really all right."

"I'm all right."

"Just listen to me, Sister. For once."

Her face softened, and she sank back a bit,

relaxing. Oh, I knowed she wasn't hurt too bad. I just wanted to look at her some more.

It was a round face, not too tan, not too pale, the neck long, lovely. Made me wish I could place a string of pearls over them, then I remembered I'd broken off that crucifix she had worn. She smiled. Lovely smile, showed me that her teeth was white. She had all of them, near as I could tell, unlike most of the women I'd knowed. The lips was rosy, narrow on top and thick on the bottom. Her smile pushed her cheeks up, and she was so lovely there, with blood above her lip, and her hair all messed up, and her habit dirty and ripped.

She looked like an angel.

I could have stayed like that for another hour or so, but I heard Demyan Blanco panting, heard the mule bray and then start urinating. Then Blanco was yelling, not at Sister Geneviève and me, but at his cousin, who come panting and cussing and groaning.

No longer smiling, Sister Geneviève decided that it was time to get up, and I moved over to help her, then saw something else almost as lovely as that young nun. I did a kind of stumble, dropped to a knee beside her, and caught myself with my bound hands. Snatched up that little .22, which the good Sister must have lost during her spill, so smooth that none of them b'hoys knowed I'd just armed myself. Have I ever mentioned that I am mighty good at palming cards, too?

With a little laugh, I stood, saying, "Lost my balance there," and slid the hideaway gun into the pockets of my trousers.

Blanco and his cousin was too busy cussing each other to notice. Sister Geneviève didn't see my slight of hand, neither.

I helped the nun over the dead tree, and she sat on it. I started to do the same, but decided I'd better go fetch my hat, check and hobble my paint horse.

Them two cousins, staring at me as if I was to blame for all this unnecessary excitement, looked mean.

"Where's your horse?" I asked Jorge de la Cruz.

He answered in a tirade of Mexican profanity.

Chapter Thirteen

It's a damned fool idea to travel across this country with four people and grub for two. It's even dumber to keep going with three horses and make some poor, dumb son of a bitch walk.

Naturally, that poor, dumb son of a bitch was me.

The big farmer's horse had skedaddled, likely loping back toward Anton Chico. All of us hoped that that big buckskin would break his leg in a prairie dog hole and feed some ravens and turkey buzzards, and not make it back to the little village.

Folks would start questioning things, and one of them folks might be Felipe Hernandez.

That wasn't the worst of things, neither. Sister Geneviève's blue roan had cut up his left rear leg pretty bad, and he shouldn't be going nowhere for a long while. That left the mule, which wasn't going anywhere if she didn't feel like it, my paint, and Blanco's black. That horse, which looked to be part Arabian, might have been able to run down de la Cruz's buckskin, but Blanco wasn't about to leave me and the nun alone with his dumb cousin.

So they decided they'd do without.

Damned fools.

I should have shot them right then and there.

But the more I studied on it, the more I looked at Jorge de la Cruz, I started to understand just why the Sister hadn't opened the ball earlier. Like I already mentioned, a Ladies Companion ain't much of a gun. I mean a .22 is a handy little pistol when you're shooting at barn rats or maybe rattlesnakes, if you're close enough. But I didn't think a .22 would get through de la Cruz's muscles and into any vitals. Like as not, even if I emptied all five rounds into him, it would just make him madder—like a hornet sting or something. And I'd still have Demyan Blanco to consider. So I kept the little pistol in my pants pocket.

Sore and tired and more than a trifle mad, we made camp in the woods. Blanco did consent to some coffee, and we fried up some salt pork for supper, finished the *cabrito*, and went to sleep.

Next morning, our merry little group resumed our trek, even though I argued that if the Sister rode that roan too much, he'd go lame. Maybe even die.

They didn't listen, didn't care. Gold fever had struck both of them mighty hard. I figured it to be a fatal case . . . for them, for Sister Geneviève, and for me.

Still, I reckon we had made twenty miles that first day, pretty good considering the country, and the fact that Jorge de la Cruz, big farmer that he was, couldn't ride worth a damn. Sister Geneviève was better on a horse that he was.

Ask me, the farmer was the fellow who should've been walking.

Instead of me.

Me afoot cut our speed down considerable. We dipped into a draw, and followed it. I tried to keep Pedernal Mountain in my sight, but the trees often blocked the view. Around noon, we come to a water hole, and, man alive, did that water taste good. We drank, filled our canteens, soaked our feet, let the horses get their fill.

Blanco offered me a quid of tobacco, but I shook my head. He bit off a chaw, worked it with his teeth, then nodded his head southwest. "How far?"

"We ain't halfway there."

He kept chewing. His Winchester had been left in his saddle scabbard, but the cousin was staring at me across the little pool of water, and his hand stayed too close to his ancient five-shot revolver.

"I am not used to this country," Blanco said. "It is rough."

I told him, "You ain't seen Hell yet."

He looked at me, waiting for some explanation.

Sighing, I swept my hands around the country we was in. "In case you ain't noticed, we've already started climbing down. This is high country, where we're at now, plenty of shade, plenty of water. We gotta follow this draw, and then the country's gonna flatten out and dry up. It won't turn hospitable till we're near Gran Quivira, and that ain't very hospitable."

"How do you know so much about this country?" Blanco had worked his tobacco up enough to spit. Damned fool spit into the water.

"Didn't spend all my youth playing cards and . . . selling . . . yeah, selling horses."

"You were a horse trader?" I'd gained some stature with Blanco.

"More or less."

"So what did you do, to learn about this country?"

"Scouted some for the Army," I said.

That was gospel. You'll find me on the muster roll of civilian scouts at forts Stanton and Craig. We'd chased some Apaches now and then.

Thankfully, all we done mostly was chase. Rarely found any. My duties was usually riding dispatch between Stanton and Craig, but shortly before I decided it was time to desert, they had started sending me up toward Bascom. That wasn't a fort no more, but the Army was using it as a sub-post. Anyway, you ride through that triangle, you cover a lot of ground, get to learn the country. I'd crossed the Valley of Fire many a time. Had I knowed there was a fortune of gold buried underneath them black rocks . . .

I reached my bound hands to my chest, touched it, felt something that kinda reassured me for a moment. Then I cupped my hands full of water, away from where Blanco had turned it slightly brown, and washed my face again.

Those Army days brung back fond memories. That time I'd bluffed Sergeant Ernest Sadler with a king high, not the flush, to his three queens showing. One time, our patrol had even found some Apaches not too far from Gran Quivira, and I'd managed to hide and escape. Brought two soldiers back, deader than dirt, and everybody at Craig called me a hero. Wasn't no hero. I was just smart enough to hide. And I'd been lucky.

I'd also hid out in these hills, even used the ruins at Gran Quivira as a hideout. Like that time when they'd caught me passing that counterfeit bill at Grzelachowski's store in Puerto de Luna. Or when Jim Greathouse took umbrage over my winning streak. Or when Sergeant Sadler led a patrol trying to catch me as a deserter—or because he'd learned how I'd bluffed him out of two months' pay. Yes, sir, this was good country to hide out in. Not fit to live in. But hiding out, many outlaws considered it tops.

Yes, sir, some of this country had been good to me.

Sure wasn't now.

I reckon we'd covered ten miles that day coming into McGillivroy Draw and heading into the valley. Exhausted, we camped again in the draw, finishing the tortillas, wishing de la Cruz's buckskin hadn't made off with the farmer's canteen. I checked the roan's leg, put another mud poultice on it, patted him, give him some extra grain.

Next day turned worser. Pedernal Mountain lay behind us. So did the trees, the shade, the higher country. We descended into the Estancia Valley.

Some Mexican once told me that *estancia*, in Spanish, means "place of rest." Permanent, I figured. We came out of the piñon and juniper and into a vast bowl of blowing dirt.

Oh, there was some desert scrub here and there, grass that already looked overcooked by the sun. I had to pull up my bandanna to keep from swallowing a pound of dust, kept walking, head bent low, hearing the horses laboring behind me.

We didn't talk. Couldn't.

If we was lucky, we'd cover maybe two or three hundred yards before we stopped to rest. One time, Sister Geneviève kneed her roan close to me, and without speaking, unhooked her canteen from the horn and handed it to me.

I shook my head.

Her mouth moved. Her lips were chapped. I reckon the hood of her outfit had gotten ripped up during her horse wreck, but she'd fashioned it into some kind of bonnet, which protected her a bit from the sun and wind. Her face was turning red, and her eyes was bloodshot.

My lips was sore, and when my tongue touched them to moisten them, they burned like hell.

"Drink."

This time I heard her.

I also heard Jorge de la Cruz guzzling his water, like we had plenty to spare, like we had five miles to travel instead of fifty. He started cussing again, and Demyan Blanco was too tired, or maybe too disgusted, to cuss back.

"Save your water." My voice sounded foreign, cracked, ugly, thirsty. Hell, I wanted that water she was offering me, but I knowed better than to drink it. We'd need it. Need a lot more than we had.

"*Vámanos*," Blanco ordered.

After motioning for the pretty nun to hook her canteen back on the saddle horn, I resumed my march.

Late afternoon, I noticed the clouds. At first they appeared over the Manzano Mountains, way off to the west, but soon I knowed they was bound our way. The wind picked up, hot at first, wicked, gaining fury. The mule began getting stubborn again.

"*Por Dios*," de la Cruz said, almost begging. He seen them dark clouds, too. "Maybe it will rain."

All that powdery lime-colored sand had turned Blanco's black horse practically white. We was all dusted, filthy. The Sister's roan was lathered with sweat, which the sand had turned to mud. The wind howled.

Monsoons strike this country hard and furious, but usually them frequent afternoon thunderstorms don't start till July or thereabouts. June was a mite early, but I decided I wouldn't mind a good, soaking rain, even though a cold rain could leave a body shivering to death. From how them clouds looked, this storm promised to be a regular Old Testament, fire-and-brimstone, come-to-meeting kind of storm. Already, I could see the purple curtain stretching in the distance from those black clouds to the drab earth.

"We should find cover," Blanco said. He had trouble keeping his horse in line, the black jerking his head this way and that, fighting the bit.

I laughed. "Where?"

The wind turned into a gale, then into a hurricane, then became the wrath of God. I could smell the rain, could practically taste it. I was moving closer toward Sister Geneviève and the blue roan, which was practically dragging his injured leg. The mule jerked free of de la Cruz's grasp and took off. The farmer tried to make my piebald go after him, but the horse suddenly did an abrupt turn, his back to the wind, to the storm. Blanco screamed as his black did the same. Even the nun's almost lame animal turned so he wouldn't face the coming storm. They refused to go.

I knew why.

"Get off!" I had to shout like hell so the nun could hear me. "Off!" I repeated, and she slipped from the saddle. I tried to help her as much as I could with my hands tied and all.

"What is happening?" de la Cruz yelled.

With my hands numb from the tight rawhide, I pressed Sister Geneviève close against the lathered horse. Taking the reins, I brought my arms over the nun's neck and pressed against her as tight as I could, sandwiching her between my body and the roan.

"What are you doing?"

I could just hear her. Before I could answer, the hailstones hit.

Chapter Fourteen

The only baseball game I ever saw occurred the summer before last down in Silver City. A local saloon sponsored a team and give its players uniforms with beer mugs embroidered on their shield-front shirts. Every boy on the saloon team's starting nine topped two hundred pounds. Called themselves the Fat Fellows, they did, and that they was. Fat. The game I attended, the Fat Fellows was playing a bunch of boys who championed those newfangled velocipedes. I doubt if any of them weighed much more than Sister Geneviève. They called themselves the Slim Jims. Wasn't much of a game. The Fat Fellows trounced the Slim Jims, 20-6, then bought beer for all the spectators and even them bicycle pedalers.

The reason that game comes to mind is on account that most of them hailstones that pounded us was the size of baseballs.

Not at first. The first stones come down by the thousands, stinging my shoulders, bending the brim of my hat, bouncing off the ground, off the roan, but no bigger than a thumbnail. Before long, those stones looked like white walnuts, only harder than a walnut shell. The roan lowered his head. When the stones kept getting bigger, I eased Sister Geneviève to the hail-covered ground, moved her and me underneath the roan's belly.

When that hail had reached baseball proportions, even over the noise of the stones pounding the earth, the wind roaring, and Sister Geneviève's praying, I heard Blanco screaming. It was hard to see, what with me under a horse and trying to shield a nun, and hail coming down like the walls of Jericho, but I could just make out Demyan Blanco, standing by the black's side, trying like the dickens to get that Winchester Centennial out of the scabbard. Then he went down, knocked to the frozen earth by a hailstone.

Didn't think I'd get a better chance. Couldn't see the big farmer, but even that giant would be smarting after getting cannonaded by hail.

"Stay here!" I told the nun, eased my tied hands over her neck, and leaned into the storm.

Hail bruised my back and almost knocked me to my knees. I slipped on the icy earth. The wind tried to blow me down. It did once, but I got up, prying the pepperbox from my pocket. The crown of my hat absorbed blows that otherwise would have cracked my skull. Still, one ball slammed into my shoulder, and down I went to my knees, groaning, fighting back pain, as more stones pelted me. One glanced off my forehead, and fire shot through my head. I saw orange dots. Hadn't been knocked that silly since Tin-Nose George give me a concussion with a bung starter whilst I wasn't looking.

I knowed I couldn't keep on seeing orange dots. I made myself stand. Made myself look. Made myself walk.

The black was gone. Without a rider on his back, without a man holding its reins, Blanco's horse skedaddled. I dropped into a crouch, trying to see, trying to protect myself, trying to find Demyan Blanco in order to draw a bead on that sorry excuse for a horse trader.

Just like that, the hail stopped. Like someone had turned off the spigot. But the storm wasn't over. Far from it.

Rain fell in icy, smarting, abysmal streaks. Those drops weren't the size of baseballs, but they stung something fierce. My clothes got soaked. Water cascaded off my hail-battered hat brim like I was standing under a waterfall.

I tripped over Demyan Blanco.

I stopped myself from planting my face in the frozen ground with my hands, which still gripped the Continental .22, pushed myself up, and turned.

Blanco's forehead, just above his right eye, was bleeding. Even with all that cold rain, I could see that. Cold rain falling in his face, and he wasn't moving. That's how out he was. Or maybe . . . maybe he was dead.

The Winchester wasn't near him. I didn't know if the horse had run off with that big rifle still in the scabbard or what. But it didn't matter. Blanco was out.

I brought up the pepperbox. Aimed at his throat.

Something groaned beside me, and it wasn't the wind. Seeing something moving, I turned, flinched, and just managed to avoid Jorge de la Cruz's boot. Instead of knocking my teeth down my throat, his heel caught my shoulder. The little popgun fell onto the icy stones the rain was quickly melting.

I fell the other way.

But didn't stay down. I rolled, heard a gunshot that the storm's wind and rain muffled. Maybe I heard the bullet slam into the ice, or maybe I just imagined that. Didn't matter. I rolled and rolled. Another bullet come close, so close I felt I could smell, even taste, the sulfur.

Diving behind a clump of bush, I quickly came up, wiped rain from my eyes and face, tried to breathe, tried to see.

I couldn't see nothing. The rain had turned into a wall, and the sky got blacker than the ace of spades. Couldn't hear. Couldn't see. But I knowed this monsoon wouldn't last.

Storms like these had a tendency to bleed out real quick, like that fellow who got his neck sliced by Big Tim Pruett in that dram shop up in E-Town back in '79.

There was another shot, I think. Couldn't tell for sure. I knowed I should have been counting bullets, but didn't think to do that when somebody was trying to gun me down. I was cold, wet, and miserable, and then it started thundering.

Lightning flashed so close that I squeezed my eyelids tight and saw orange again. The thunder accompanying it came instantly. Before my ears stopped ringing, I was moving, low in the rain, back toward where I thought Demyan Blanco was still laying, where I thought I'd find that .22.

I got there, but stopped. It seemed to be the place, had to be, and then I knowed it was the spot because I found the Continental. What troubled me was that I didn't find Demyan Blanco.

After cussing, I moved for the .22. Almost got to it, then the big farmer caught me from behind, grabbed my shoulders and pulled me up, leaving the .22 in the rain. He whipped me around, sent a fist into my stomach that practically drove all the way to my spine.

Breath whooshed out of my lungs. I gagged, spit out rainwater, and felt myself being hurtled back toward that clump of shrubbery.

Another flash of lighting ripped across the sky, and I spied de la Cruz, his face and hair wet, eyes wild. For a moment, I thought of myself as Jack and the farmer as Goliath. No, that ain't right. Jack wasn't the name. I think it was Daniel.

Didn't matter. I was in the den with a couple lions and a giant. And I didn't have no slingshot.

"Kill him!"

There was a moment, just a moment, when the wind quieted, and it sounded like a gentle rain shower. That's when I heard Demyan Blanco shouting. I saw him. He had that Centennial and was running toward me.

"Kill him!" Blanco shouted again.

I coughed and gagged, and I tried to tell them fools that if they killed me they'd never find the gold, even if that was a lie.

Can't figure fools. Either they decided this gold-chasing was fool's play, or maybe they come to the conclusion that they could find the gold without me, maybe even without the nun. I'd hate to imagine what those two boys would do to Sister Geneviève if that was the case. Maybe they was just idiots to begin with. Or perhaps the rain and hail and wind and desert had driven them to madness.

The Centennial roared. I saw the flame and smoke in the dark and through the rain. The bullet didn't come close to me, but it struck something solid. That much I could hear. That and whatever it had hit was falling to the ground.

Blanco worked the lever, came to a stop. I was running, but the brute named de la Cruz ran into me. Knocked me to the ground. The farmer's momentum kept him going, and he slipped in mud or ice, and plowed a furrow in the ground as he slid a good five or ten yards.

Still short of breath, still cold and tired and aching all over, I managed to come up, but only into a crouch, and I froze, knowing I was too late.

Blanco had stopped, maybe ten, fifteen yards in front of me, and he was bringing that rifle to his shoulder.

Something roared, and my eyes exploded. My face felt blistered. Heat. All around me was heat. My ears started ringing. I smelled something awful.

Figured that Lucifer was welcoming me to Hell.

Rain—cold, blessed rain—brought me back to my senses. I pushed myself up into a seated position. I'd been knocked to my back more than a rod away from where I'd been waiting to get blowed apart by a .45-70 shell. The rain had slacked, and I blinked till I could see clearly. Aching all over, somehow I stood, weaving in the rain and wind. I saw something over in the distance, not moving, but big. The roan. The roan horse. I couldn't tell if Sister Geneviève was still hiding under his belly.

My hair felt wild, full of electricity, and my face was hard, my ears stinging, my body numb. And there was that smell. Part metallic. Part brimstone. Mostly like . . .

Burned meat.

Blanco was gone. At first, that is. I didn't see him. Then I did, and wished I hadn't.

That rifle barrel was mostly melted, and Blanco lay on the earth, still holding what was left of the Centennial, sticking up like a dead cholla. No, that ain't right. It was more like the rifle's ruins had molded itself into his arms and hands and fingers. His whole body kept smoking in the rain, blackened, his eyes empty holes, his face black and red and purple. The only thing white was his teeth, and some bone showing beneath the blackened body.

Now, I have seen many bad things, many things that had turned my stomach, but I ain't never seen nothing like that. I stared, my lungs working like crazy, the rain washing over my body but not cleansing a thing. I just stared at what was left of Demyan Blanco. Didn't want to see, but couldn't look away.

Then Jorge de la Cruz knocked me back into the muck and cold.

Just as the rain stopped, he stood over me. He had found the Sister's pepperbox, which looked like an extra little finger as he aimed it at my head. I kept hoping lightning would kill him, but, well, there's that saying about lightning never striking twice.

It didn't.

He pulled the trigger. Tried to, anyway. And I learned something else. I learned why Sister Geneviève hadn't tried to gun those boys down. She had bluffed old man Evers back in the Las Vegas jail, she had bluffed me as bad as I'd done Sergeant Sadler.

That gun's hammer was busted. It wouldn't fire. Wasn't good for nothing other than a paperweight.

With an enraged curse, he flung the gun at me. Even if the .22 had hit me, it wouldn't have hurt, not a gun that tiny, that worthless. But it landed a good yard to my right.

I came up. The farmer charged me. I didn't know what had happened to his English-revolver, but I figured either he had fired all five rounds, or the Dean and Adams, being an old cap-and-ball relic, had gotten its powder or percussion caps all fouled, and he'd dropped it.

Crouching, I waited for de la Cruz to reach me, then I dived at his knees with my whole body. It knocked the breath out of me, but the farmer went flying, landing, cussing. I was up, running at him. As he pushed himself into a seated position, I kicked him full in the mouth. Blood and teeth—what few he still had—went into the air.

He fell back, and my right boot came down, but he turned his head and all I crushed was the remnants of hail. His arm connected with my calf, and now it was me going down. Before I could move, that big cur was atop my chest, spitting blood and bits of teeth into my face, then them hams he had for hands grabbed my throat.

The storm had blowed over us. The air became pleasant, and I didn't even smell Blanco's burned body no more.

Jorge de la Cruz cussed me in Spanish, in English. He cussed God. He cussed his dead cousin. Again, he cussed me, and his miserable luck. His fingers wrapped around my throat, the tree trunks he called thumbs pressed against my Adam's apple.

I couldn't breathe. Couldn't move. Couldn't do nothing but close my eyes and die.

Chapter Fifteen

Here's the moment I fell in love with Sister Geneviève Tremblay.

My eyes was open, and her face slowly come into focus. Light brown eyes staring down at me, all pitiful like, but all forgiving, too. Her slender fingers brushed back my wet hair. Her own hair was heavy and flat from the rain, but the sun was shining just behind her head, and she smiled at me. An angel's smile, part sad, but mostly lovely.

She wasn't wearing that makeshift bonnet, and her black dress was soaked from rain. She didn't look like a nun. We had just endured a couple days of hell, so she just looked like a tired but beautiful young woman. Well, it ain't every day that you wake to something like this, your head resting in a woman's lap, her stroking your forehead with perfect hands, the air smelling fresh from rain, the sun coming close to setting, and you realizing that you ain't dead.

That is what I said. "Hey . . . I ain't dead."

She almost laughed. "No. . . ." Her voice trailed off.

I started remembering things. Lightning striking Blanco. Jorge de la Cruz strangling me. I turned my head and saw the giant lying on his side.

The Sister, kind soul that she was, pushed my head back so that I looked into her eyes. "Don't look at him. Please don't look at him."

Her voice didn't sound like an angel, didn't sound perfectly French, nor did it sound like that always angry Colorado madam who was a walking whiskey vat. This angelic girl's voice sounded slightly nasal, but with a charm to it. I obeyed her. I adored her. I didn't look at the big farmer. I just stared at her.

"Where you from?" I asked.

It was like she had to think, not coming up with a lie, or nothing like that, just trying to remember. "Carbondale," she finally answered. "It's in Illinois." Her hand stopped stroking, and she reached for something beside her. "And you?"

I didn't have to remember. I was an orphan. I could only shrug.

"Oh, That's right. Here." She held a canteen, opened it, lifted my head so that I could drink.

And drink I did.

"Not too much." She took the canteen away, corked it, and set it on the ground.

See, that's another thing that made me love her. She knowed things, things a nun might not know, although the Sisters of Charity did run the hospital in Santa Fe. I guess she had probably done her share of nursing and maybe even doctoring some.

"What's your name?" That's a rude thing to ask, but . . . well, I had always been known for rudeness.

"You know that," she said.

"I know it's Geneviève, but I don't think you was always a nun."

"Tremblay."

That's not only when I fell in love with her. It's when I learned her name, too.

"I like that name."

She almost giggled. "Well, I like Micah Bishop."

"Really? I had been considering finding another handle to go by."

"Like what?"

I shrugged. I had used John Smith, but, hell, who ain't? And Big Tim Pruett, after the real Big Tim got rubbed out. For a while, after that incident with that egg-sucking dog I'd killed in Sedalia, I'd gone by Wichita Eddie Colter till I reckoned the law had lost interest in Micah Bishop and had forgotten the man he had killed in Missouri.

"Ben Franklin," I said.

She smiled again. "And what does your almanac say about today, Mr. Franklin?"

I didn't answer. Didn't know what she meant. Still don't. One of these days, though, I might learn. Well, no, I reckon I won't, since I'll be hanging by the rope till I'm dead in a few hours.

Our conversation played out. I went back to staring. She went back to rubbing my head and hair.

"I'm—" She stopped herself, looked up, not at de la Cruz or even toward Demyan Blanco, what was left of him, just stared in the distance, toward Perdenal Mountain, but I don't reckon she saw anything. She was just thinking, remembering. Still not looking at me, she said, "I'm sorry I got you into all this."

I give her a short chuckle. "You didn't get me into nothing. You got me out of a hanging."

"Yes . . . well. . . ." She give me the canteen, and I drank again, set the container down my ownself, and pushed myself till I was sitting beside her, though I guessed I could have laid in her arms the longest while.

The dizziness passed quickly. The wind blew, cool, calm. The hail had melted.

I didn't want to ask her. You know what I mean. How come I wasn't dead? How come Jorge de la Cruz lay on his side beside me, the back of his head a bloody pulp? I ain't the sharpest knife around, but I ain't as dumb as Blanco and the big farmer had been. I knowed things. Or I could make good guesses. While the farmer was choking me to death, she, the good Sister, had come up behind him, holding a rock. She had slammed it down against his head.

Slowly, I took her right hand in my own, and looked at those fingers, scratched and skinned. There was even a small scratch on her palm. She had struck de la Cruz more than once.

She let me hold her hand.

Reluctantly, I let it slip out of my grip. I wet my lips. "You all right?"

Her smile held no humor, but warmth. "I fear I might be sick."

"Nothing wrong with that."

Truth of the matter is, I'd felt sick after I'd sent Gomez to meet his maker, even if he had been trying to deliver my soul to Satan. I had lost my supper after I'd killed that drover, but had he gotten his knife a little closer to my stomach, it would have been me who was killed. And that bad man in the Indian Nations who had tried to bushwhack me—me, carrying only sixty-three cents and riding a stolen burro—he sometimes still visited me in nightmares. It hadn't been me who had killed Blanco. I looked at that as the Good Lord's doing. But seeing him fried and burned and that Winchester destroyed made my stomach do some dancing right then.

She taken a deep breath, let it out slowly, and I seen the lips start trembling, felt the weight of the world on her shoulders, and next she was crying, just bawling. It taken me a moment before I could make my arms work. They wasn't tied no more. I reached over, took her shoulders, pulled her close, and let her sob and heave and moan and pray close to me.

"It's all right. He would have killed me. Then he would have—" I knowed enough to stop. "You cry. Cry as long and as hard as you want, Sister."

"This . . . wasn't . . . supposed . . ." The words came out between gasps and tears. "It wasn't . . . it wasn't . . . sup . . . supposed to be . . . like . . . this."

"It's all right." It became my turn to stroke her hair. "It's all right."

But as I looked around, I knowed that wasn't true. Not by a long shot.

Her blue roan still stood, head down, heart broke, sides ripped and bleeding from hail. That bum leg of his was swollen and ugly. The mule and de la Cruz's big buckskin was long gone, and I had figured out what Blanco's shot had struck, recalling the sound of something falling somewhere behind me. He had killed his own black. Accidental, of course, but the horse was lying in the dirt, dead.

The sun would be down in another hour, maybe less, and we was both soaked to the bone. No way I could get a fire going, not with everything wetter than a fish in the ocean. I could see forever, and forever was a big emptiness. More than forty miles to the railroad and what might pass for civilization along the Rio Grande, and that included the Manzano Mountains blocking the path. East was even worser, desert and rough country, no water, and anybody we'd meet was like to kill us rather than save us. North . . . well north was probably Felipe Hernandez. South . . .

My head shook. I closed my eyes. I pulled the nun tight.

"God," I said, mostly a whisper and to myself. "God, Sister, why did you give me that water. What was I thinking?"

Don't rightly recollect how long the Sister sobbed, but eventually, I laid her down, still sniffling, and went to work. Gagging, eyes watering, I dragged the remnants of Demyan Blanco maybe ten rods before giving up. Made no headway with the late Jorge de la Cruz, and eventually left him where Sister Geneviève had dropped him into that eternal sleep.

I went through the saddlebags on the horse Blanco had killed, but all I found was tobacco, which I don't use, and a couple boxes of .45-70 shells, which was worthless as that melted Winchester still sticking up on the prairie like a marker for the dearly departed idiot. There was a canteen, maybe half full, and I got the bright idea to loosen my bandanna and squeeze a few drops of rainwater into the canteen's opening.

The other bag had only an extra shirt, under-garment bottoms, and a folding knife. I pocketed the knife, started to leave the clothes, but thought better of it and took them, too.

Corking the canteen, I rose and studied the horizon.

The problem with country like this is that it don't often hold water. Ground soaks up rain like a sponge. I didn't know how long I'd been unconscious, but there wasn't no mud holes, certainly no puddles.

Walking back, I happened upon the Dean and Adams five-shot. I wiped the sand off the cylinder, cocked the piece, and found it still worked. 'Course, there was no caps on it, and I knowed the rain had fouled any powder in the chambers. But it was a gun, even might fire, so I went back to the late de la Cruz. In one of his pockets, I found a tin of percussion caps, as well as a powder flask, even a handful of lead balls.

That was a start. I pocketed them things, too.

By that time, the sun had disappeared behind the Manzanos. Sister Geneviève was sitting up, staring at me.

I handed her the shirt and unmentionables. "It's going to get cold. These are dry. You should get out of them wet duds, put these on. It's gonna be a long night."

"What about you?"

"I'll manage."

She stared at the clothes, finally sighed, and stood, looking around at the barren country.

"I won't spy on you, Sister." I headed to the blue roan.

That about broke my heart, too. I pulled off the saddlebags, put the caps and balls and flask in one of them. The good Sister had stuck the crucifix I'd broken in one side, as well as her hollowed-out Bible, some food. The other had grain for the horse, so I dumped it all out on the ground. The roan didn't eat.

After loosening the cinch, I stopped, paused, considered breaking my word and just sneaking a peek at that nun. But I couldn't do it. Just couldn't. I finished with the saddle, and pushed it off the roan's back. Then removed the bridle, which I dropped, too.

The horse eyed me again with those pleading, tired eyes.

I stroked the side of its head with my knuckles. "I'm sorry, boy. I just can't help you."

That Dean and Adams wouldn't fire, not yet anyway, perhaps not ever, and I just didn't have the guts to try to cut the roan's throat with a pocket knife.

"You may turn around, Mr. Bishop."

Hefting the saddlebags over my shoulder, I obeyed my true love's command.

She'd had to roll up the muslin underpants, and had wrapped a sash of some kind around her to keep them pants from falling down. She still wore her shoes. Blanco's green and white checked shirt fit her like a prairie dress blowing in the wind.

152

"Dressed for the Easter picnic," I said.

She smiled.

I walked over to her, pulled off my hat, and handed it to her. "You'll need this, too, come tomorrow."

"What about you?"

"I'm used to the sun," I lied. Gamblers and horse thieves don't spend much time in the daylight hours.

She had shown the good sense to have picked up one canteen. I had the other.

We looked at each other, then she turned southwest while I studied northeast.

"I think . . ." we both began.

We stopped ourselves and looked away, but we wasn't laughing.

When she looked back at me, I pointed toward Anton Chico. "Best chance would be to head back where we come from."

"What about Felipe Hernandez?"

"He'd help you. And there's water that way."

Her head shook. "Gran Quivira," she said, stubborn again.

"That's—"

"Where help is," she finished for me, but it wasn't what I was going to say.

I wet my lips. They was already drying out, unlike my soaking clothes. "How do you know?"

"I have faith."

I didn't. "It's between twenty and thirty miles.

And this"—I sloshed the water in my canteen—"won't get us there."

"Gran Quivira," she said. "Then the Valley of Fire."

"You'll think we're already in the Valley of Fire come tomorrow."

She stared at me. I met her eyes. Finally, we both shrugged.

"Which way?" she asked at last.

"Away from here," I told her, and started walking, like a damned fool, southwest.

Chapter Sixteen

Reckon we made it two more miles before it got too dark to keep walking. Rattlers come out in the dark, and I didn't fancy stepping on one. There was some scrub and grass, and a bit of a depression, so we had something to block the wind. The earth was sandy, and I tried to scoop out a seep hole to get us some more water, but didn't get nothing but dirty hands. Would have had to dig 500 feet before finding water.

I handed Sister Geneviève a piece of jerky.

"Chew it slow," I told her. "Make it last. That's all we got to eat."

Even in this wasteland, a body could go a long time without food. Water was another matter.

I bit off a hunk, too, slipped the rest back in my

pocket, and tried not to let the good nun see me shivering. The wind had picked up, coming down from the mountains, and it was cold.

About that time, the coyotes started singing.

Sister Geneviève stopped chewing and turned northeast, toward our sweet serenade. Them coyotes just yipped and yapped and sang out.

"They ain't close," I told her. "Sound travels far out here, especially at night." The wind helped carry their yips and yaps. "And a coyot' is more scared of us than you need to be of them."

Wasn't much longer before they wasn't singing no more, but barking and snarling and fighting amongst themselves. The wind carried that noise to us, too.

"What are they doing now?" she asked.

I shrugged. "Well, they ain't always sociable." I swallowed my jerky, and kept the gall from rising up my throat.

No, sir, I thought. Coyotes ain't sociable, not when they's fighting over their supper. A supper of one lightning-struck horse trader, a big farmer with his brains leaking out of the hole in his skull, a dead horse and . . . I had to spit . . . that lame blue roan they'd likely already taken down.

"Take one sip of water," I told her. "Make it small. Make it last."

She done real good. But I seen her trembling all over.

"You cold?"

"No," she lied.

There was other sounds on the wind, night-hawks and screech owls, bugs and birds, the wind rustling through the grass. The coyotes soon had company. Wolves be my guess.

"What made you become a nun?" I asked, trying to take her mind off the feast and fighting going on two miles away.

I slid closer to her. She had pulled her legs up, wrapped her arms just below her knees, and was rocking. See, the problem was that Demyan Blanco had packed his extra duds for the summertime. Cotton drawers and a cotton shirt. The Sister was used to black wool.

"My father," she said, still rocking, "was a priest."

"Oh." I nodded, then done some silent studying. Except for that brief little Mass in Anton Chico, I hadn't been in too many churches—and no matter what the *Daily Optic* wrote, I did not steal the candles, cross, and coins from the collection plate from the parish in Socorro in September of '82. I can prove it, too. You check with the jailer in Bisbee, Arizona Territory. I spent six weeks there during that time. So I wasn't a frequent church-goer no more, but Rocío and them other Sisters of Charity had taught me some things.

"Priests ain't allowed to marry," I finally told her.

She kept rocking. "Never said he did. Marry, I mean."

"Oh."

We had another one of them long pauses. Silent. Nothing to hear but the wind and angry coyotes and wolves. Finally, the animals turned silent. Reckon they'd figured out there was enough meat there for everyone, and only the wind blowed, the Sister rocked, and I shivered, even though the wind and the walk had dried me out some. Just not enough.

"You just . . . wait." I laughed. "Wait . . . till . . . tomorrow. You'll be wishing . . . it was . . . cold . . . like now." My teeth chattered. "You just . . ." I started rocking, too.

"Mister Bishop."

I looked up.

She stopped rocking, let go of her legs, and opened her arms. "Will you . . . hold . . . me?"

See, it made sense. I mean, two folks alone in the cold desert, me in still-wet clothes, and her in nothing more than thin cotton. Made sense. I slid over to her. Taken us awhile to find a proper position. I mean, she didn't smell like lilac no more, but she sure didn't feel like no nun. Especially when my arms went around her, right underneath those breasts, and then we kind of locked together like spoons, and laid down, and, well, I mean, it's just that she was a woman, a young woman, a beautiful young woman, and she wasn't wearing nothing but a dead man's clothes, his underpants at that, and a shirt so thin it was . . .

Well, you got to consider and recall that I'd been locked up in this miserable dungeon they call a jail in Las Vegas, and been stuck in a coffin full of rats, and then in a boxcar where a goat had peed on me. And it's just that I hadn't been with no woman, any kind of woman, even that one in Dodge City who had given me some wretched little sickness that sent me to that drunk pill-roller who didn't give me no pills, but had this little copper tube that . . . Never mind. What I'm trying to write down is that I was a thirty-year-old man and she was a handsome woman, and sometimes you just can't control certain parts of your body.

"That thing's got a mind of his own, don't it?" Geneviève Tremblay didn't say that. That's what a concubine I'd knowed in Durango had once told me, and she was right.

What Sister Geneviève said was, "Tell me a story." Her voice was soft, all Illinois.

Not that I knowed what all Illinois sounded like.

"What kind of story?"

"Any kind."

"Like a Bible story?"

"If you like."

What I liked was how her body felt next to mine. It taken some considerable thinking on my end to even think of a story, most of which I promptly rejected. After all, the stories told at poker tables and faro layouts and in brothels ain't fitting to relate to a nun. And I didn't recall

158

nothing about them years before I'd wound up at the Sisters of Charity orphanage in Santa Fe.

Finally, I said, "Well, there was this woman. No, there were a bunch of women. All of them was beautiful. That's why they was all there. Hundreds of them. And they was all brought to this palace, and they was all given perfumes and great food—peaches, I reckon. I've always been partial to peaches."

"Me, too," she murmured.

Another reason I loved her.

"Well, good food and the best clothes. They could swim, and get their hair all pretty, and wear pearls and silver and gold. They did all this because the king had asked them all to come. He had to pick one of them to be his wife. Well, the king kept them there for a whole year."

I've always wondered just what that king did with them women while he was trying to pick one, the randy old bastard.

"So, finally, the big day comes, and all them beautiful women are decked out in the best duds, and they've got rouge on their faces, and pearls and diamonds and, well, they's all beautiful. But this one woman, she comes down, and she ain't wearing no pearl necklace. She ain't got on earrings. She's dressed, but her dress is real plain. And all them girls in their finest duds and with all that rouge and smelling like, like, like beautiful things, well, they all see this girl wearing just a plain white dress, and they all sigh, and I bet a few of them even cuss their luck.

" 'Cause it ain't no contest. They all knows it. The king knows it. He lifts his crown, not his crown, you know, but the crown for his queen, and he beckons the plain girl to come up. And she bows, and he puts the crown on her head, and she becomes his wife. She's wearing plain duds, but she sure ain't plain. Didn't need nothing, she was that beautiful. I bet her hair could be soaked with rain, and she could be burned from the sun and wind, and I bet she could be wearing . . . wearing . . . a man's shirt, and . . . and she'd still be the most beautiful girl in New Mexico Territory.

"Her name was Geneviève."

"Did they marry?" she asked.

" 'Course. The king of Spain—guess that's where he was from, it being New Mexico in them olden days—he tells you to marry, you marry. Had to. But she didn't mind. And you know what?"

"What?"

"The king loved her. That's why he picked her. A body couldn't help but love Queen Geneviève."

"Go on."

I obeyed.

"Well, the thing was that this queen, Geneviève, she had this terrible dark secret. She was married to this New Mexican king, and he was Catholic, on account he was Spanish. He had to be. But

160

the queen, Queen Geneviève, she come from Carbondale, Indiana."

"Illinois," she said.

"Oh, yeah." It's hard to concentrate when your arms are wrapped around this lovely woman, and you got all this desire, and you're trying to recollect a story that you ain't got no idea where you heard it or why or how come you're telling it while laying on the sand, and the wind's blowing, and bull bats are buzzing around eating flying bugs, and you know that you ain't got a chance in hell of making it to Gran Quivira.

"Illinois," I said anyway. "Then the king of New Mexico, he issues a law. It says that anybody from Illinois must die. They put them to death. Maybe it was in Southern New Mexico, what they started to call Arizona back in them times, not like where Arizona is now. That's it. It's during the Rebellion, when the rebels invaded New Mexico, took over the southern part of the territory called Arizona. That's it. So this king, maybe he's a general. Yeah, he's the Confederate general in charge down in Mesilla. Well, he says any Yankee from Illinois, male or female, granddaddy or kid, they must die. He's gonna put them all to death."

"Are there that many people from Illinois in Mesilla?" she asks.

"Passels of 'em," I tell her.

"Did he kill his queen?"

"He would have. This general, he was strict.

Martinet, that's what the boys called him behind his back. You couldn't call on him without an invitation, but Queen Geneviève did that. She knowed she had to do something. She had to be brave. Not for herself. But for all them Illinoisans living in Mesilla. So she come into his office, and she knowed that the last person who called on him without an invite wound up in front of a firing squad. But the king, I mean, the general, he just smiled at her, told her she looked lovely, which she did. She always looked lovely.

"She asked the king, er, general, if she could take him to supper. He said, yeah so they went out to eat in this place on the plaza that served really good posole and enchiladas, with the best damned green chile you ever tasted. Spicy hot, but just wonderful. So they's eating, and she told the general that she's from Illinois. She told him that he must kill her.

"And the king, he liked to have choked on his sopapilla. He just stared, and that's when his heart, which had been harder than granite, turned into mush. That's when he realized how much he loved her, how much he needed her. And he kissed her. And he repealed his order. And the Yankees went on to win the war, but the general was happy. And he and Geneviève lived happily ever after, and they even throwed a party every year. A Feast. Guess it's on Cinco de Mayo 'cause it happened on the fifth of May."

My lips touched her neck, accidentally, and I lifted my head, and whispered, "How's that?"

I didn't feel cold no more. I felt . . . never mind. None of your business.

"Her name was Esther."

"Huh?"

"She was Queen Esther. She wasn't from Illinois, but she was a Jew. Haman planned to kill all the Jews in the empire, but Esther prevented this. She told Ahasuerus that she was a Jew, and Ahasuerus had Haman hanged, instead. The celebration isn't Cinco de Mayo. That's when the Mexicans celebrate the victory at their battle of Puebla. The celebration is the Feast of Purim. It's on the fourteenth day of the Hebrew month of Adar. I think."

Think. She knowed.

"But I loved your story," she said so sweetly, and she reached over and squeezed my arm, which was asleep from supporting her.

A moment later, she was asleep. And there was me, wide awake, trying to remember when in hell I'd heard that Bible story that I'd gotten all mixed up. And she was asleep. And I wasn't. What I was doing, wide awake, was staring at her face, so beautiful, even though I couldn't see nothing in the darkness, but I didn't have to, because I knowed. She was more beautiful than Esther. And I really wanted her to be awake and I wanted . . .

163

I laid my head down. Taken in her scent. Closed my eyes, but I knowed I couldn't sleep.

It was the worst night of my whole life . . . in some ways. But in others, I reckon it was one of the best.

Chapter Seventeen

"Drink this." Just speaking them two words took effort. I held the canteen to Sister Geneviève's badly cracked lips. Sand coated her face, her eyes was closed, but when she smelled that water, hot and awful as it was, she like to have gone crazy, behaving like some wild animal. This time, I had to warn her. "Not too fast. Not too much!" I pulled the canteen away, unfortunately spilling a decent swallow. She lunged, caught herself in the sand, panting, heaving, my hat falling off her sweaty head.

After I corked the canteen, I eased her back against a brush that gave us some shade.

"Rest." I leaned next to her, wanting to drink from that canteen, too, but knowing better. "We . . . rest."

"How . . . long?"

"Toward dusk. Then we'll go as far as we can." I pointed. "See that mesa?"

She rose up just enough, squinted, shielding her eyes from the sun. Even out yonder, where things look closer than they really is, that purple ridge looked a million miles from where we was.

"Is there . . . water . . . there?"

"Uh . . . no. But that's where we're headed."

That night, after she'd gone to sleep, and I was all restless, I'd spied the north star. Drawed me an arrow in the sand pointing toward it. When dawn broke, I found north, then turned around and figured out southwest. That's where we was headed. That was the way to . . . to . . . ? Taken me a while before I could remember.

Anton Chico.

No no, that wasn't it. Gran Quivira.

"Beyond that's Gran Quivira."

She sank into the dirt. So did I.

If you play cards, you get to be fairly passable at math. Counting cards. Figuring the odds. Things like that. A person could last maybe three weeks without food. But water? Three days. At the most. I figured we were, say, thirty miles from Gran Quivira. There would be water there. That's why folks had settled there. But that drought had come and water had dried up. People had starved. Left. That was higher up, and there was trees, and where they was trees, you could find water. Besides, Sister Geneviève said she had faith that we'd find help there.

I had faith in that nun.

But thirty miles. That's a long way to cover on foot, in the desert, without much water, and only a couple bits of jerky for food. 'Course we still had water. I figured we had enough to get us till . . . tomorrow.

I studied west, and shook my head. Yesterday, we'd been visited by the biggest, meanest, wettest turd-float of a storm ever I'd seen. Today, nary a cloud in the sky. Just a hot wind, kicking up blinding dust and stinging sand.

She started to say something, Geneviève did, but stopped, wising up to know she'd better conserve her strength.

It strikes me now, as I sit in this dungeon, that if you can spend most of a day, in the company of a beautiful woman . . . and you don't try to talk to her, and she don't try to talk to you . . . well, that's a good sign that you must be in love. I mean, that you don't feel the need to talk. Like that strumpet over in Roswell was always doing. Talk, talk, talk, talk about nothing and about everything and she didn't know nothing. She just liked to talk. And I ain't got no interest in nothing she has to say, and conversation ain't why I'd paid her a whole dollar.

But Geneviève didn't say nothing. We just sat there, enjoying each other's company. Sorta. I mean, the sun broiled us, and the wind practically tore the skin off us. Our lips were chapped beyond recognition, and our tongues would have strangled a bobcat.

The furthest we moved was to inch over to find

better shade as the sun shifted positions. I found a pebble, put it in my mouth, trying to drum up some water in my mouth, but it didn't help none. Just tasted like dirt is all. I spit it out, and wished I hadn't. Took too much effort, and I had spit out some precious saliva.

Well, when the sun got fairly low, and the wind died down, I rose, slinging them canteens on my shoulder, reached down, helped the Sister to her feet.

"Which way . . . again?" she asked.

Taken me a long spell to remember. That's how much the sun had fried my brain. I looked west and even north, but finally got my bearings, got my head cleared, found that mesa. I pointed. "That . . . way." I wet my lips, taken her arm, and led her in the general direction.

Conserve the water, I kept telling myself. What little we had. It had to last us three days. Maybe more, considering the slow time we was making. Three days. Three days.

We was out of water by next morning.

Can't say I remember much after that. Bits and pieces come and go, like snatches of a dream you might recollect. I knowed that Sister Geneviève tossed her empty canteen to the dirt, and that I picked it up. Big Tim Pruett one time was reading this Beadle & Adams half-dime novel. I disremember the title, but it's the one in which Jesse

James is wandering through the desert and his canteen's empty, so he pitches it into the saquaro and keeps wandering, and Big Tim tossed that five-penny dreadful into the fireplace, saying only an idiot would get rid of a canteen in the desert, then told me what he'd just read, to which I had said, "I ain't never seen no saguaro in Missouri."

There ain't no saguaros in New Mexico, neither. 'Cause I would have been able to use that knife and carve into it and eat some of it. I think I read that in one of them five-penny dreadfuls Big Tim Pruett once loaned me. I did, however, come across some saltbrush. I picked some of the leaves, popped them in my mouth, started chewing, and plucked some for Sister Geneviève.

Tastes just like pure salt. Enough to keep us going.

What else do I remember?

No rain. Not even clouds. The sky was a deep blue. At first. Then it turned pale. Wasn't long till it looked just white.

She fell, Sister Geneviève did. Just lied down, panting, Blanco's shirt tight against her. Staring at the sky, but not seeing nothing.

I picked her up. Not brag, just gospel. Picked her up and carried her till I couldn't carry her no more. Dragged her after that, till even that was too hard. Then I was on the ground beside her, my own breath ragged.

"Let's . . . rest . . . here," I managed to say.

So we did. Baking in the sun, then freezing in the night, us huddled together, but me not getting no manly desires, not even with me spooning her like I was doing.

Another memory. Laying in the sand, it being morning, and we should have been walking, before the sun got too high, too hot, but my eyes was closed, hearing her breathing, letting me know she was still alive.

Then her saying, "What are those? Angels?"

Taken all the strength I could muster to pry my eyelids up. I looked at Geneviève, but she was just staring into the sky. I turned back, looked up, saw them angels. At first, I mean. With no food, no water, no chance, you see strange things. Mirage, I reckon you might call it.

Mirages don't last long. Your mind clears up, and you see that that pond of ice blue water is really just heat waves shimmering ahead of you. Same with them angels.

I rolled over, made myself stand.

"Buzzards," I told her, and took her hand, pulled her up, made her walk. Made me walk. I wasn't gonna feed no buzzards. Not yet.

Big Tim Pruett was walking right beside me, Sister Geneviève on his other side. I know. That was a mirage, too. Or a hallucination. Or Big

Tim's ghost. Walking, bigger than life, reading a Beadle & Adams half-dimer, laughing, saying only a fool would toss his canteen away while he was walking across desert without water.

I stopped, knocked that paperback out of his hand, and put my finger right under the scar on his chin that he'd gotten from a busted beer bottle in Tascosa when we was selling stolen horses.

"Let me tell you this, pard. You throw away the empty canteen because it's dead weight. You hear me! Dead weight. You ain't got no strength to carry the sumbitch. Can you understand that? Tell me! It ain't nonsense. It's extra weight. That's what it is. And you're dead. You been dead. And we ain't dead yet."

I realized I was yelling and pointing at a dead cholla, nothing left but its brown spines. Good size cactus. Nigh as tall as me, but nowhere near Big Tim's size.

I laughed. Then I turned and saw Sister Geneviève, maybe fifty yards ahead of me, walking. No, more like weaving. I hurried to catch up with her, and left Big Tim. No, I mean I left the dead cholla.

Somewhere, I'd also left one of the empty canteens. Because I'd been right. And so had that colonel what's-his-name who had penned that wild, fanciful story about Jesse James lost in the Missouri desert.

Dead weight. You can't carry it. Not in Hell.

She was running, and I saw why. Then I was running, too, but it wasn't no mirage. She was kneeling by the pool of water, and cupping her hands, and bringing it to her mouth, and then I tackled her, knocked her away, felt water drops sprinkle my blistered face.

Geneviève was getting up, crawling for the pool, crying.

I fell, grabbed her ankles, and pulled her back, my heart about to bust, my lungs heaving. I tried to say, "You can't . . . drink it," but if I said anything, I don't think it sounded human. Somehow I got to my knees, moved to her, leaned over, whispered because by that time that's all I could do. "You . . . can't . . . drink . . . it. Salt . . . lakes . . . water'll . . . kill . . . us."

No tears was coming out of her eyes. Kinda like the dry heaves.

Reckon we laid there an hour, then I managed to get up, helped pull Sister Geneviève to her feet, and we moved through those small lakes, arms over each other's shoulders. That's the only way we could get through, without losing our minds, our reason, and drunk up that salt water till it killed us.

Two days? Three? I don't know. I remember once I tried to make myself pee. Sister Geneviève just watched. I wasn't ashamed. Wasn't embarrassed. Managed to squeeze out a couple drops that looked bright orange and smelled so bad, like ammonia, it practically made my eyes water.

"Our kidneys," she whispered hoarsely, "are shutting down."

"There are times," I said as I buttoned my fly, "when you know too damned much." Said it clear. Thought I did. Must have. 'Cause she laughed.

I looked around, my brain thinking clear, recollecting something I should have recalled long before. "There should be . . . playas."

"Playas?"

"Seasonal lakes." I didn't have time to explain to her. That monsoon from back whenever? Storms like that filled some pools. That's how animals and people managed to survive in this country. I ran to a lake bed, but it was hard-packed earth. I ran to another. Same thing.

Sister Geneviève caught up with me, reminded me that we was supposed to be resting in the heat of the day.

"If we rest, we die." Then I sat down. Sat down and laughed. Yep. My mind was addled. Maybe gone.

"How long did Moses wander?" I asked her.

If she understood, she didn't show nothing. Nothing but fear.

On account I'd gone purely mad and grasped this round stone that could just fit in the palm of my hand. "Didn't he get water out of a stone? Do I have that right, Geneviève? Strike this stone, and water shall pour like beer through a tapped keg." I hit it with the barrel of the Dean and Adams. Nothing.

"It don't work." I looked at the blazing sun. "What's the matter, God? You'll help Moses, but not a Sister of Charity and a poor, miserable sinner?" I hit the stone again. Nothing. Didn't have strength enough to strike it hard. The pistol fell between my legs, Geneviève just stared at me, and I tossed the stone away, fell back, laughing, thanking God.

I turned my head, watched that stone roll and roll and roll, before it dropped and disappeared down a hole.

Geneviève and me both heard, clear as a bell, the splash.

Chapter Eighteen

I dragged myself across the rocks and cactus till I reached the spot where that little stone had disappeared. Behind me, I heard the Sister's footsteps. I dipped my hand inside that hole, not caring, not even thinking about the possibility of rattlesnakes, but couldn't touch no water.

My hand came up, and somehow, weak, thirsty as I was, I got to my knees, bent down, and grabbed this good size, tabletop rock that partly, I hoped, covered the hole. I grunted and cussed and strained. Next thing I knowed, Sister Geneviève was beside me, her hands underneath the sharp edge. Well, we couldn't flip that thing over, but somehow we managed to slide that rock a bit in the dirt, revealing a hole maybe six inches wide. The one canteen we had left had a diameter of seven inches. The damned thing wouldn't fit.

So we started digging and scooping, shoveling sand and dirt and small rocks like two dogs digging for a bone. Finally, we got the opening wide enough, and with scarred, bleeding hands, I shoved the canteen in the hole, gripping the canvas strap for dear life.

I shoved my arm all the way to the shoulder. Could see the nun kneeling beside me, swollen, chapped lips moving in silent prayer. When I couldn't get my arm down any farther, I almost bawled like a newborn. "It's not long enough."

I slowly withdrew the canteen, placing it on the rock. The strap to the canteen was a tad under two feet. Quickly, I took a pebble, dropped it down the hole. It splashed.

"How deep . . . is it?" Geneviève's voice was strained.

"I don't know. Can't be much farther."

Talk about pathetic, about hopelessness. Here we are, dying of thirst, and there's water maybe a foot, maybe only two or three inches out of our reach.

"Your sash!" It struck me quick, and I turned to the nun, and felt my heart break again.

"I . . . I . . ." Her fingers fell to the waist of her free-flowing dead man's shirt.

The sash was gone. She either lost it, or just chucked it. Dead weight and all. Remember?

Without no shyness, no discomfort, she said, "Here!" and pulled that dirty piece of cotton over her head and arms, practically flinging it to me, and just knelt there, topless, and dropped onto her hands, staring into that small, dark hole, as my tired, battered fingers tied one sleeve to the apex—I think that's the word—of the canteen's canvas strap. Tied it good. Then holding the other sleeve, I lowered the canteen through the hole. I felt the canteen hit water, and sighed.

Waiting . . . then . . . heartbreak.

"What is it?" Sister Geneviève must have read the devastation in my face.

Hurriedly, I brought up the canteen, placed it between the nun and me. I could see the water on the canteen's edges, could see Sister Geneviève running a swollen tongue over her chapped lips.

"Take some," I told her, and she did, running her fingers over the drops of water, then across her lips, her tongue.

I got busy untying my bandanna.

"It won't go under," I told her. "Not heavy enough."

After unrolling the bandanna and laying the

frayed silk square on that rock, I found a fair-sized stone nearby, and set it in the center of the bandanna. Brung the ends of the bandanna up, wrapping the rock, tying it, then affixed the bandanna to the strap with some tight knots. The nun greedily snatched another finger of water before I lowered the canteen again. Didn't blame her none at all.

The canteen hit with a splash, and immediately, I heard the gurgling as the rock sank the canteen, and water, precious water, began filling it. The weight of the water strained my muscles.

"Don't let go," the nun pleaded.

"Not on your life," I told her, but I done another loop of the shirt around my palm and wrist, just to make certain-sure.

"Exactly," she said, then added, "Our lives."

Carefully, I drew up the canteen and the rock, heard the water dripping off the sides into that pool. The canteen appeared, got lodged for a second because of the bandanna-wrapped rock, and Sister grabbed one side of the strap and me the other, and we pulled that beautiful baby up.

Both of us started, quickly stopped, kinda looked at each other sheepishly.

I wet my lips. Tried to, anyhow. "You first."

"No, I had some," she said.

You know, here's the funny thing. She's standing there, practically inches from me, and her top is naked, skin all pale in contrast to her sunburned face and throat and hands, all perfect, but I didn't notice nothing. Not then.

"You go," I insisted.

She didn't need no more inducement. She reached for the canteen, dragging the shirt behind her.

I reached out to take the canteen, felt the coolness of the water on my fingers.

Taken all the courage I could muster not to snatch the damned thing from her hands.

Instead, I managed, "Not too much. Just a little. All right?"

She lowered the canteen, just so I could see her eyes twinkling. "All right," she said, and started to bring the canteen to her lips.

Just like that, she lowered it.

"What if . . . ?" Her eyes got concerned. Couldn't say nothing else.

"Poison?" I shrugged. "It don't really matter. Not now."

Her eyes twinkled again, and she drank. I feared I'd have to stop her. You know how crazy a body gets when dying of thirst. No, most likely, you don't know. So you gotta trust me.

But she was strong, real strong. She taken a little swallow, then another, then poured some into her hands, and brought it to her face.

She didn't moan. Didn't smack her lips. Just rubbed her fingers gently over her lips. After that, she passed the canteen to me.

Tasted like the best Irish whiskey I ever had. Better even than that expensive Scotch from that highfalutin place in Denver when I started a row at a poker table, and while the bouncer and beer-jerker hurried to toss me out, Big Tim Pruett reached across the bar, snatched a bottle of something called Glenlivet, and hid it inside his coat. The saloon thugs tossed me out into the mud. Big Tim followed, grinning, and helped me up, and we wandered to the wagon yard where we was sleeping, and emptied the bottle into our empty bellies.

"Tastes like iron," she said.

"Iron ain't arsenic," I told her.

"Can I drink some more?"

"Just a swallow."

We each taken another small swallow, then I handed her the canteen, and after I nodded my approval, she emptied it over her head. Like to doubled over then, moaning, then laughing, tossing me the empty canteen, then rising up, water spilling down her dirty brown locks, over her face, over her breasts. That's when I noticed them. That's when I noticed her.

"Oh, my," I said, and taken that canteen, turned around, put that canteen down the hole, filled it up with water again, brought it up, took another swallow, then emptied the water over my head.

I imagined you could see smoke coming from my hair 'cause it sure seemed that I could feel the fire in my brains getting put out by that cool, glorious water after being baked by that blazing sun.

Again, I lowered the canteen, again it filled, but this time, I corked it, and untied her wet shirt-sleeve. That took some doing, sore and aching as my fingers was, tight and wet as that knot was. After I handed her the shirt, our eyes met. Swear to God, she smiled a little bit mischievously, taken the shirt, pulled it over her head and arms, and them perfect breasts disappeared.

"What now?" she asked.

I pointed. "Let's find some shade. We'll wait here, drink our fill, get our strength back." Already, I could feel some improvement in my aching, sun-cooked body. I mean, I spoken all them words, didn't hurt none, my mouth didn't ache, and they sounded plain as day to me.

Once I managed to stand, with the nun's help, I carried the canteen. Sister Geneviève put her arms around me, and we made it to what passed as some shade on the side of an arroyo. My brain wasn't so addled that I even found that purple mesa in the distance, which didn't look so far away anymore.

I sat beside the nun and handed her the canteen. "Remember, not too much."

She took a sip and handed it back to me. I swallowed a mouthful, and run my wet fingers over them ugly lips.

Again, our eyes met, and we gave a short little laugh.

"What, er, what made you become a nun?" I asked.

She shrugged. "Fate. A calling. God's will."

"You like it?"

Even with them lips and her sunburned face, her smile made her beautiful. "Do you enjoy being a . . . a . . ."

I finished for her. "A miserable old reprobate?"

Her laugh was giddy, probably from the insanity that was slowly passing out of our heads. "You are not *old,* Mr. Bishop."

"You ain't, neither."

She reached out, and them long, lovely fingers, touched my chin. That coarse stubble of mine must have pricked her sore fingertips like needles from a jumping cholla. But she didn't show no pain. Slowly, she lifted my head. Our eyes met.

"Is that why you are staring at my breasts?"

Well, wasn't much I could do but stutter or stammer. Reckon I had been staring. 'Course, she was all properly covered now with the green and white checked shirt. Must have been remembering.

"I don't show them for every man . . ." Then she done something different, unexpected. "Micah." She called me by my given name, and she said it so softly, so lovely. 'Course, I was already smitten by her by that time. Had been. I wrote that down already.

Her arms lowered. And we just looked into each other's eyes.

"I . . . I reckon not." My voice sounded foreign, not on account of the sand I'd been eating and my tongue slowly reducing to its normal size. "I mean . . . you being . . . a nun . . . and all."

Her hand dropped into her lap. "Yes," was all she said, and she looked away.

"Sister—"

"Please call me Geneviève. Or Gen if you like." She laughed again. "Geneviève is a handle."

"It's right pretty. Like . . ." Well, I didn't finish.

Her hand reached up to one of them shiny buttons. I thought, likely hoped, she was about to unbutton it, but the fingers trembled, lowered, and she said, "I must have lost my crucifix."

"Sorry I broke it."

She begun working on them dead man's undergarments, and she pulled up the muslin cloth, revealing her calf. She had lost the bandage where me and de la Cruz, back when the big farmer had acted nice and not crazy for gold, had doctored her up. The horsehair stitches still held.

I taken the canteen, give it to her, told her to go ahead and wash it. "Don't want it . . . getting infected . . . and all," I said.

"I don't want to waste water."

"We gots plenty to spare. Now."

She undid her boots, pulled off the filthy sock, and poured water onto that limb of hers. I watched.

"Take another drink," I told her, and she did. Then I did.

I remembered something then. "Here." I started unbuttoning my own shirt, just the top, since it was one of those pullover boiled numbers, too.

"Micah . . . ?" she asked, kind of nervous, like she feared I was gonna bare my chest for her, same as she'd done earlier.

My right hand found the mescal beads, and I withdrew the heavy necklace over my cooling head. "Here." I handed her the silver cross.

She taken it in her hands, which seemed to be trembling.

"Sometimes I forget I have it on," I told her. "It's a cross of Lorraine. Not a crucifix, I reckon. Not Catholic, I guess, but maybe it'll comfort you."

She felt the warm silver, looked at the inscription on the back. "How long have you had this?"

With a shrug, I told her, "Reckon half my life. Sister Rocío give it to me. Then I run off. Must've been fifteen, sixteen."

"What's the inscription mean?"

"Oh, I couldn't tell you," I lied. "Bunch of nonsense." I stopped quickly. "I didn't mean that. I mean, nonsense and all. I mean, I kept it all these years."

"Maybe you aren't quite the heathen you

think you are." She handed it back to me. "I can't accept this, Micah."

"Sure you can. Fits you better than me, anyhow."

Again, our eyes met, held for the longest time, and I swear, tears welled in them soft brown eyes. She put the necklace over her head, slid the heavy silver four-armed cross inside that green and white checked shirt. I didn't get no glimpse of her breasts when she done that.

"Thank you, Micah." She leaned over, and kissed my cheek. "God bless you."

Then she laid down, her head on my lap, and went to sleep.

Chapter Nineteen

For two days, we stayed like that. I mean, not with her asleep with her head on my lap, and me leaning against that arroyo wall, running my fingers through her wet hair as it dried and thinking of things that would have landed me in a confessional with a million Hail Marys for penance had I not been such a scoundrel and heathen and lapsed Catholic who had never actually been confirmed because I'd been taken by the wanderlust when I was a teen.

I guess I couldn't actually call myself Catholic, lapsed or otherwise.

We kept refilling that canteen and drinking the water, slowly building back our strength.

I cleaned up the Dean and Adams, reloaded the chambers, put fresh caps on the nipples, and then God delivered us a rabbit.

It wasn't like I had been praying for one, though maybe Gen had—I'd taken to calling her that, dropping the *Sister*, as she'd stopped using the *Mister*—her having a better relationship with the Almighty and Mary, Mother of Jesus, than me. I had left Gen by the water hole, and walked along the arroyo and dried playas, just trying to get the lay of the land, see what this country looked like, and figure out what the best way to Gran Quivira would be.

From the looks of things, Mesa de Los Jumanos, which most folks had always considered the southern end of the Estancia Valley, appeared only six or so miles south. We could start climbing out of this furnace, likely find some water there, and then come into the Liberty Valley and make our way to Gran Quivira.

Sweet Mary, blessed Father, we might just make it out of this place alive.

From the old ruins, we could easily pick up a trail, make our way east to Whiskey Jim Greathouse's place, where I was sure we could outfit ourselves with horses and grub and clean duds. Whiskey Jim had been dead a few years, but the folks who'd taken over his ranch, like Whiskey

Jim, had no love for the law, but respected ladies, especially ones who looked as lovely as Gen. Yep, they'd grubstake us.

Then . . . either go after that gold in the Valley of Fire, or just forget the whole damned thing, and maybe Gen and me could head down to Mexico, live on the beach, eat shrimp all day and night, drink tequila, and live happily ever after.

That's what I was thinking.

I wasn't hunting. Wasn't expecting nothing.

And this jackrabbit hopped out of some chamisa.

At first, I mistaken him for a rangy ol' coyot'. That's how big he was. He stopped, started chewing something in the shade, and didn't even see me.

Well, I had to be no more than ten yards from him, standing in the arroyo. My knees started buckling as I slowly pulled that old pistol from my waistband and my hands got all sweaty, all clammy. That gun was just shaking in my right hand, so I had to steady it with my left.

The rabbit just waited.

With my left thumb, I reached up to thumb back the hammer, and that's when I recollected a Dean and Adams has a spurless hammer. Ain't no external one to thumb back. It's a double-action pistol, meaning all a body's got to do is pull the trigger. The cylinder rotates, the hammer strikes the cap, the cap ignites the powder, and the powder sends the ball after the target. Pretty simple. Means you can fire a whole lot faster.

'Course, I'm old-fashioned when it comes to revolvers. I like the single action, the ones you cock with your thumb, then pull the trigger. See, Big Tim Pruett once told me, right after he killed Long Dick Watson in El Paso, that double-action guns tend to pull to the right. Or maybe it was the left. I don't rightly remember all the particulars on account that when he told me, we was hightailing it toward the Mexican border to get away from Long Dick's kinfolk, of which there was a considerable number.

Anyway, the gun pulls one way or the other, 'cause you're pulling the trigger. A single-shot ain't likely to do that as you've already cocked the hammer with your thumb and just gots to squeeze slowly.

Well, I tried to keep that barrel steady, but couldn't. It was like I had a bad case of buck fever, shaking, nervous, just froze in shock, and it wasn't no deer or elk or pronghorn I was trying to kill, just a raggedy-ass jackrabbit.

But he waited, the rabbit did, and I squeezed the trigger, the British gun kicked, liked to have knocked me to my hindquarters, and . . . well . . . I don't know. Seemed to me that the rabbit jumped into the .436 ball. Got him right in the head, and he plopped dead in the sand.

Smoke stung my eyes. I shoved the revolver

back into my waistband, then cussed good and long, jerking the gun out, dropping it into the sand, and calling myself an idiot because that barrel had been hotter than it was in this frying pan.

"Micah!" Gen screamed my name.

"It's all right!" I shouted back, picked up the Dean and Adams with my left hand, the rabbit's long legs with my right, and started running back for camp, and her.

"It's all right!" I told her again.

"What was that shot?"

"Supper!"

Cooking it was another thing. Oh, I skinned and gutted it. Was so hungry, I almost tried eating it raw. You should've seen the look on Gen's face. Well, maybe you shouldn't have. I did, and meekly laid the rabbit on a hot rock, and scooped up the entrails and skin, taken them to the edge of the arroyo, buried 'em, then come back to her, where she held out the canteen and ordered me to wash my hands.

Which I done. That's a great feeling, you know, having water to spare for such annoyances as washing.

We gathered dead grass, easy to find in that wasteland, made a pile on top a flat rock at the edge of the arroyo away from the wind, and I sprinkled gunpowder from the flask over the grass. I pulled another copper cap from the tin,

187

gently laid it down, then taken the Dean and Adams by the barrel, which had cooled by then, and gripping it tightly, like a hammer, slammed the curved grip down.

And missed.

That's how nervous I was.

Gen taken the gun from my hand, which was throbbing 'cause I'd slammed the revolver so hard. With a smile, she raised the Dean and Adams, brought it down, the grip's bottom striking the cap, which exploded, the powder burst into smelly fire, and the grass started burning.

Carefully, we added small sticks to the blaze, and as they built up, we put on more sticks, larger ones, till that fire was burning hot enough to add some good big dead cholla arms, and other driftwood. Funny thing about driftwood. You'll find wood even in a treeless expanse like the hell we was in. Well, we was in an arroyo. I reckon some of them trees could have been washed down from long about the beginning of the Manzano Mountains.

Gen quickly set up a roasting stick, skewered the rabbit, and then we was turning that thing ever so gently, smelling the grease as it dripped into the fire, us both laughing.

It probably wasn't even full done when we ripped it from the fire, and I tore the rabbit in two, giving her half, and me wolfing down the meat, then sucking the bones.

Tasted better than rustled beefsteak at Panhandle Pete's place in Tascosa.

I feared we might get sick, but we didn't. Wasn't that much meat to that rabbit after all, and it wasn't wormy or nothing. After wiping my greasy fingers on my filthy trousers, I leaned back, and added another log to the fire.

"Why didn't you think of this?" Gen motioned at the fire. "Before now?"

"What do you mean?"

"Starting a fire with the powder and revolver."

I shrugged. "Didn't strike me till now. Didn't have no need to do it."

Her eyes narrowed. "These past few nights have been rather cold."

"Oh." I laughed. "Well, the powder was dry and the revolver was all fouled after that frog strangler."

She looked perplexed. "Frog what?"

"Flash flood," I translated.

She wasn't looking at me with beady eyes no more. She smiled. "I thought you just liked hugging me in the night."

Them manly notions started forming again. I crossed my legs. "Well . . ."

She crawled over to me, our backs against the arroyo, and leaned her head on my shoulder. "You were warmer than any fire, Micah."

Slowly, I tossed away the leg bone I'd been fingering, and moved my arm over her shoulder.

The sun was down by then, birds was out chasing bugs, there weren't no coyot's howling, and the wind had died down. The fire smelled good. The smoke didn't even follow me and irritate my eyes as smoke normally done around campfires.

She lifted her head, and I turned slightly, moved my arm some to get more comfortable, and we just looked at each other. The campfire reflected off her face, and her eyes sparkled. I wanted to cross my legs again, and kinda slide up some, but her left leg was over my right, and them cotton shirt and flimsy undergarments wasn't holding much back. I wasn't sure I was breathing no more, but I knowed I wasn't dead because my heart was pounding fierce, and that wasn't the only part of me that was pounding. She reached up and brushed a lock of my dirty hair off my forehead, and her finger traced a scar, the one I'd gotten when—hell, now I done forgot how I got that thing.

My hand dropped some more, and she moved her body some, and the fire was warm, and it had gotten dark, and she wet her lips, and said my name softly, and I couldn't say nothing.

Then she said, "Micah, your hand is on my breast."

I jerked that thing away like it was hot, but it hadn't been hot. Kinda firm. I apologized profusely, and tried to sit up, but I couldn't move on account that she was kinda pinning me down, despite her not weighing a whole lot.

Soon her hands was on my face, exploring me, and I was running my fingers through her beautiful dark locks, and then touching her shoulders, and then squeezing them, and soon she was just inches from my face, and it was beautiful. Her face. The night. Everything. Our lips was almost together, and, damnation, I really wanted to just pull her to me and . . . well, that could have been the best night I'd ever had.

"It's all right," she whispered.

But even though I'd never been confirmed, I just found it hard to keep on. I mean, she was a young nun, and I surely didn't want to be the cause of her burning in Hell or condemned to Purgatory or excommunicated or stoned to death.

Her eyes closed, and she got even closer to me. I knowed my hand wasn't on her breast no more, but I'd managed to put it inside her shirt, and was rubbing the soft skin on her stomach. My eyes was closed, and we was so close to mortal sin.

Still, that was a night I'd remember forever, but not because of me and Gen.

It was because just as I was about to kiss her, a voice sent the beautiful woman diving off me, and me reaching for my gun, but never getting it.

"This is quite the pretty picture, isn't it, Vern? An amorous couple in this savage emptiness, and they are kind enough to invite us to join them."

Chapter Twenty

"One more inch, mister, and you will make me pull this trigger, which the buzzards will surely appreciate, but, alas, that would deprive Vern of his pleasures. So, please, kind sir, stop and live . . . for a few moments longer." While The Voice was talking all fancy, all deep and strong, he'd punctuated that statement with a sound I knowed all too well. It was that triple, deadly, metallic click of a Colt single-action revolver being cocked. He didn't have no Dean and Adams spurless .436.

I stopped, but Vern didn't. A boot caught me in the ribs, rolling me over, and when I had the presence, or lack, of mind to lift my head, another kick knocked me right by the fire.

"Micah!" That was Gen, but the next sound wasn't.

"Your aim and timing appear to be slightly off, Vern," The Voice said. "I remember those glorious days when you would have knocked him into that fire."

"Nah," Vern said, real slow, drawing out them words. "Didn't wants him burnin' none. Till I's finished with 'im."

Since Vern hadn't meant to kick me into the flames, the fire was still going, unaware of the predicament Gen and I was in. Somebody, reckon it was Vern, added some logs to the fire, and as I slowly sat up, the fire was going real good, and I got a good picture of them two newcomers who looked older and meaner than the desert.

Vern had a dark beard down to his sternum, and railroad ties was smaller than his arms. Must have stood six-foot-six in his stockings, but he wasn't wearing no stockings. No, sir. He had on the biggest boots I'd ever seen, with mule pulls on the sides, and leather pants stuck down the stovepipe tops, but the boots was old and dusty, and one bottom was wrapped with a bunch of rawhide, and the other had his toes—no socks—sticking out.

That big cuss made Jorge de la Cruz look like a midget. He wore fringed leather pants, and a grimy buckskin shirt. Looked to be advertising a leather shop. He cracked his knuckles—sounded like chair legs being busted over some rowdy's head in a saloon tussle—and pushed up the brim of his greasy slouch hat. Then he smiled. Didn't have but three teeth that I could tell, and I only could see them because the flames reflected off the gold fillings. He carried a big machete, and started running his thumb over the blade as he squatted, then farted.

"Dear Lord," The Voice said, and laughed, before he looked down at Gen.

His left hand gripped her shoulder, and I could tell from her face that he was squeezing real hard. His right hand held that .45 Colt aimed at me. Slowly, real careful-like, I tested the knot forming on my forehead, then rubbed them aching ribs.

"This is truly an unexpected delight," The Voice said. "We were like wandering Jews, lost in the desert, and then, I asked Vern, 'Did you hear that?' And Vern nodded, and although he is really a simpleton, he said to me, 'Can't be no fools in this land.' " The Voice give a perfect impression of his idiot partner. "But I said back to him, 'Well, let us see.' " He doubled over laughing so hard, wiped his eyes with the back of his hand holding the Colt, then shook his head. "But, swear to God, never did I think we would find this. Not out here." He looked around. "What was that shot we heard earlier today? Your horses?"

Now, The Voice, he wasn't no bigger than me. Deep voice sure didn't fit his little body. He had on worn shoes, duck pants, and a striped shirt that I taken to have been issued to him by some jailer, seeing that the Territory of New Mexico had no penitentiary at the time but sent its most despicable convicts off to Kansas. These two should have been in Kansas, by my thinking.

He wore a kepi, so maybe he was a deserter from the Army, and muslin undershirt covered by a yellow brocade vest with all the buttons ripped off. He was clean shaven. Didn't even have stubble on his chin. His hair was silver. He talked like a fancy thespian, or maybe a professor. But he wasn't acting, and I didn't care to learn nothing from the likes of that son of a bitch.

"I asked you a question, kind sir," he demanded. "Where are your horses?"

That wasn't what he'd asked at all.

"Run off in a thunderstorm. . . ." I had to think, but couldn't. "Don't really know how long ago."

"Run off." The Voice sighed, then laughed right cheerful, and spouted off with, " 'A horse! A horse! My kingdom for a horse!' "

Vern stopped thumbing that machete blade and looked at his pard like it was The Voice who was the simpleton.

The Voice quit laughing. "Oh, dear, how I love *Richard III*. But back to our interview. What was that shot which led us here just in time, alas, to interrupt your, ahem, carnal desires?"

"Shot at a rabbit. Look around. You can see the bones."

"You et it all?" Vern asked.

"We weren't expecting company," Gen said, and grimaced as The Voice laughed again and squeezed her shoulder even harder.

He shaken his head, The Voice did, pushed up his kepi's brim with the gun barrel. "That is such a sweet shame. From the looks of you, you have no food, either. No money, I warrant." He sighed. "No horses. No water."

I wasn't about to tell him about that hole.

His voice hardened, as did them light-colored eyes. "No future, either. 'Tis a shame. Truly it is. For you see, we hoped that you had some horses, on account that we have none and the law seeks us."

"The law," Vern said deliberately.

I figured he couldn't talk no way else without really thinking about what he was saying.

"Law might've heard that shot, too. Might come lookin' for us."

"Vern, Vern, Vern," The Voice said in mocking rebuke. "We have crossed over The Journey of the Dead. By now, the marshal of Magdalena has likely given us up for dead." He turned back toward me. "That explains our presence in this country, but why on earth would you two be here?" He clucked his tongue. "It isn't quite the most romantic spot."

Maybe they did have some human decency in their black souls. "She's a nun," I said. "A Sister of Charity. I was guiding her to the ruins at Gran Quivira."

The Voice was staring down at Gen. He grinned. "You sure is a pretty thing, for a nun. I've never seen a nun like you. But I'm sure you will be real charitable. Real charitable for a wanderer in a wasteland who hasn't seen a woman, any woman in, well . . ." He laughed. "As Vern would say"—he did a right fine impression—"in a coon's age."

"She's a nun, damn you!" I snapped. "A Sister

of Charity." Most men, even outlaws, they ain't ones to harm women. Even if they ain't nuns. But Vern and The Voice, they wasn't men, they wasn't even human.

The Voice wasn't listening no more. He jerked Gen to her feet, then slammed her roughly against the arroyo's high bank. I heard that nice green and white checked shirt rip, heard her scream, but I couldn't move because, well, it was on account of Vern.

"And you," Vern said, leaning closer to me, putting his machete down by his side, farting again. "You'll be real charitable with me, pretty boy. Won't you?"

His breath stank like them rabbit guts I'd buried.

"I'll take real good care of you, pretty boy, just like he's takin' real good care of that"—he chuckled—"nun!"

He had dropped to his hands and knees and started crawling, licking them thin lips with his tongue, then flicking the tongue in and out like a serpent.

The Voice was laughing, deep and throaty. Now I knowed what The Voice was attempting with Gen, but I just . . . just . . . just couldn't move. Just stared at that big, ugly bearded monster crawling right toward me. I mean . . . well, I ain't sure what I mean. Wasn't sure what he meant, what the hell he was doing, and then that long beard started dragging between my legs toward my private parts, and he righted hisself, came at me on his knees, his hands working at the buttons of them leather pants. Only then did his intentions strike me like a big flaming stick of wood.

That is what I grabbed and slammed into his head.

I hit him again, and holding the torch, I smelled that awful stink of smoke and burning hair. His beard must have been thick with grease of some kind, 'cause it erupted in flames. He was screaming, beating at his face, which was engulfed in orange flame. He fell backward, his leather shirt burning, too.

Grease. Had to have been the grease. Or God's will.

Me? I was moving.

"Vern!" The Voice cried out. "Vern! Dear God, Vern!"

Too late, I understood that I could never reach the Dean and Adams. Wasn't rightly sure I could even find it, so I changed course and headed for the machete.

"Roll over, Vern! For God's sake, don't run!"

My hand latched onto the wooden handle of that big sticker, and I rolled over on my back. The muzzle flash from The Voice's big Colt practically blinded me, and the bullet carved a ditch across my side. I let go of the machete, and grabbed my bleeding, burning side. That's what you do when you get shot. What I do, anyhow.

"You bastard!" The Voice came toward me, thumbing back the Colt's hammer. "You son of a bitch." He wasn't talking fancy no more. And them's the nicest things The Voice called me. I could see that little man coming toward me, could see the three long scratches across his cheeks, and his fly undone, just as Vern's had been.

That got me boiling mad.

I made my hand leave that throbbing side, and I cussed The Voice, and cussed Vern. I rolled over and I grabbed that machete. The gun boomed, and dirt flew into my eyes, and I rolled over, flinging the machete, praying it would gut that fancy-talking, evil, evil cur, but hearing it clang across the rocks. I knowed I'd missed, and I knowed I was dead, and I knowed what them sons of bitches would do to my true love if I didn't take them to Hell with me.

Clawing dirt out of my eyes, I still couldn't see, but I made myself move, diving to my left as The Voice fired again, missing me. The Voice swore, Vern screamed, and then Gen yelled, "Hey, asshole!"

Still, I couldn't see much of nothing, but I heard The Voice thumbing back that hammer, heard him spinning, heard the Colt boom. Then I heard the crack of the Dean and Adams, and The Voice didn't sound so much like a man no more.

Opening my eyes through the grime and tears and darkness, I saw him doubling over, the Colt falling to the dirt, and him holding his groin, yelling like a girl, begging and blubbering, and the Dean and Adams barked again. That bullet must have caught The Voice right in his head, 'cause he didn't say nothing else. Just dropped headfirst into the sand. But Gen fired again, and the bullet tore into his back (I saw that later).

The next cap misfired.

And then she was standing over him. She had picked up my machete and . . . well . . . it wasn't pretty.

I made it to my feet, and as she brought that bloody blade over her head, I stopped her. She wasn't acting human. That checked shirt had been ripped, but The Voice hadn't gotten no further, thank the Good Lord. The Voice wouldn't be doing nobody no harm. Not now. Not ever.

"Eustace!"

That brought me back to my senses.

"Eustace!"

Here come Vern, his face blackened, smoldering, a grotesque mask of black and purple, illuminated by our campfire. He staggered, maybe half blind, and I could smell burned flesh and hair, which stunk even more than the lightning-struck corpse of Demyan Blanco. Big Vern held a smoldering piece of wood.

I was reaching for the Colt that The Voice had dropped, but Gen picked it up first. She calmly thumbed back the hammer, and sent a bullet between what was left of Vern's eyes. He dropped to his knees again, and Gen's next shot hit his groin, too. Only Vern didn't feel nothing by then. Gen kept thumbing back the hammer and pulling the trigger, but by then, the only noise I heard was her sobs and that clicking sound as the hammer fell on empty chambers.

Slowly, I got to my feet, tore off my bandanna—the one I'd used to sink the canteen into the pool with a stone—and shoved it across the ditch carved down my side. Bleeding like a stuck pig, I taken the gun from Gen's hand with my hand that wasn't trying to stop myself from bleeding to death, dropped the Colt by The Voice's corpse, and moved Gen away from all the ugliness. "Go."

She stared at me.

I could see the emptiness in her eyes, the remnants of the fire still burning. "We're leaving here."

She blinked.

I wasn't sure she saw me or understood. "Come on, Gen."

She tensed when I put my arm around her, and those eyes weren't empty no more, but angry, and she almost reared back and put a fist into my nose.

The blood was soaking my bandanna, and I couldn't see her, and I was falling to my knees.

She caught me. "Micah!" She pulled me close. "Oh, Micah."

She'd regained her reason.

"Get the canteen," I told her. My head jutted toward the pack one of them two bastards had dropped near the fire. "I'll get that. You get the Dean and Adams. And our saddlebag."

"Where are we going?"

I seem to recall being asked that before. "Away from here." I started for the bag, but I never made it.

We wasn't—at least I wasn't—going nowhere.

Chapter Twenty-one

It ain't the most pleasing smell. Not like bacon frying in the skillet, or a warm peach pie. When my eyes opened, I smelled flesh burning, and my side was screaming. Orange and red and green stars flashed before me, and then I saw only blackness, emptiness, a bottomless pit sweeping up to swallow me whole.

That last part, the words I underlined, I didn't write my ownself. I mean I did, but they ain't original. It was a saying I recollect Big Tim Pruett reading aloud from that half-dime novel about Kit Carson fighting Mormon bushwhackers. I always liked it. And it fit what I felt and saw to a T.

Could've been worser, though, much, much worser. It didn't stink like gangrene, just of burnt flesh. My own.

"Hello, Micah," Gen said softly.

I saw her then, as them colorful dots faded, my eyes focusing. She was smiling, but no joy in it, and clutching the ripped checked shirt with a hand stained with dried blood. When I seen that ripped shirt, my cross of Lorraine against her pale skin, and I recollected what The Voice had been trying to do, it made me hate his damned soul all the more. The blood started rushing to my head, even though The Voice was now shouting at the devil.

"Welcome back." Gen's voice settled down my blood pressure, and for a while there, I forgot all about them two dead bastards.

I laid shirtless in the shade. Must have been nigh dusk, which meant I'd been out for some time. Almost a whole day, I figured. I reached for my side, but her hand came and taken hold of my forearm, and moved it back down. "Don't touch it. I had to cauterize it with the . . . pig's . . . machete."

That I already knowed, that she'd sealed that bullet wound with a hot blade, not that she had used that big sticker. That's what smelled liked burned flesh . . . because it was burned flesh.

She turned, looking into the dusk, and her face hardened. I knowed she was looking at the two bodies. She said, " 'The day is ours. The bloody dog is dead.' " Slowly, she looked back to me, must have seen the confusion in my face, because she explained, *Richard the Third.*"

That didn't explain nothing to me, but I

nodded as if I understood. Nodded, 'cause that's all I could do.

I tried to talk, but didn't have enough spit in my mouth to form no sentence. Bless her heart, she understood, moved closer, lifting my head, pouring water from the canteen down my throat. Tasted sweet. Then she laid my head on her lap, set the canteen down, and started stroking my hair, just gentle, the way I always figured my mama would've, had I ever knowed her.

"How long?" That's about all I could manage right then and there.

"Two days."

I sighed. I'd been out two whole days. That bullet across my side must've been a lot worser than I'd imagined.

I smelled something else, too, and knowed what that stench was. We hadn't gotten far from The Voice and Vern. They must've been still lying dead in the sun, stinking their way to Hell.

I looked up, and saw sun creeping its way between slots in a roof. A roof? No, not quite a roof. I was in a brush arbor, or maybe a lean-to. "Did you build this?" I managed to point up.

She grinned then nodded, "It isn't exactly the St. James Hotel in Cimarron."

Forcing a smile back at her, I said, "It's better." Well, not really. I mean, that Frenchy who ran that place knowed how to cook, and you could get some fine whiskey, even good wines, up there.

'Course, you could also get killed, real quick, Cimarron being one of them kinds of burgs.

Oh, it was pleasant, me lying in Gen's lap, her gentle fingers on my head again, but I knowed we couldn't stay there. Them bodies was likely already bloated, soon to get worser, and even through the slots in the roof Gen had built, I could see turkey buzzards floating in the breeze, waiting for us to hurry up and leave them to sup.

"I need to sit up," I said, and started to move. Gen almost protested, but she must have seen that I could be as mule-headed as she could be, and she helped me slide up, then eased me back against the arroyo wall. Well, there was some dizziness, and I thought for a moment I'd just lose anything in my stomach, but that passed. So did the chills. I begun looking around and pointed. "That their pack?"

"Yes."

"You go through it?"

She shook her head. "I . . . couldn't."

"Bring it—" I stopped myself.

She was a nun, and she'd just come close to being violated—hell, there wasn't no *come close* to it. That son of a bitch had ripped that shirt, and she had clawed his face. She had made him pay for his transgressions. Vern, too.

"Do you think you could bring it to me?" I spoke softly, gently. "Probably should go through it, see if there's anything we need."

Trouper that she was, Gen ducked underneath the lean-to, hurried to the pack, maybe two rods away, and dragged it back into our shelter, the shelter she had built. Her fingers begun working at the rawhide cords that fastened that decrepit piece of smelly canvas. I leaned forward, thinking I might could help, but a spasm of pain sent me back against the sandy wall. I closed my eyes, bit my lip, and tried not to scream. Must have done all right, because she didn't notice. Just went right on and got them cords undone, tossed open the cover, and reached inside.

First thing she drug out was an empty whiskey bottle, which she tossed aside. Then a rusty old food pail, also empty. She tossed that away, too. Then a gourd, which she shook, and, perplexed, looked at me. "They're packing this junk? Across the desert? Were they that stupid?"

"Not so stupid," I said. "Bottle and pail could hold water. So could the gourd if they hollowed it out."

Dead weight? Right. That's what you're likely thinking. Why would anyone carry all that across the desert, after I'd even dropped an empty canteen? But The Voice had Vern to haul all that dead weight for him.

Her head bobbed. She'd be careful from now on if she come across something that she might have mistook for garbage.

Next, she pulled out a box of lucifers, and these

she cherished, setting them gently on the ground.

"How many are in there?"

She opened the box. "Almost full."

"Good."

Back to work she was, but what she taken next made her stop, and the color drained from her face. It was a lady's chemise, French-made, hand-embroidered, real fine white cloth. One woman's hose, an ugly myrtle green color, fell out.

A stocking like that would run a body a whole thirty-nine cents for a pair. I knowed that because this strumpet I'd consorted with in Denver had made me buy her a pair, just like that one lying in the sand. I done it, and left her, because even a whore should have better taste than wear stockings that wretched color.

But I saw Gen wasn't thinking about nothing like that—how could she?—but was thinking about how them two ruffians might have come to possess such items.

"They aren't ripped," I told her. "Likely found them on the trail, too."

Not sure she believed me, but she dropped them to the ground, tried to steady her breathing, then combed her hair with her fingers.

"Put the top on," I said.

She studied me real hard, uncertain of my intentions.

"Your shirt's ripped. It'll be extra protection from the sun." I smiled. "Besides, it's real pretty."

"I don't feel pretty." Her voice was hard, bitter.

"You are."

The smile came, slowly, but it came, and she pulled the ripped shirt off, not embarrassed, nothing of the sort. I saw the cross I'd give her. The chemise went on, and then the torn shirt over it. Grinning, she held up the hose for my inspection. "And this?"

"I don't know. We could use it as a bag, I reckon."

"Or a bandage."

Back to work she went, hands disappearing inside the pack, then pulling out the next item. Wasn't another hose. It was a book, its cover torn off. It wasn't a Bible or nothing, so she just throwed that away. Same with a tintype of some naked lady, which she practically heaved all the way to Pino Mountain. Didn't let me see it, neither. Only reason I know what it was is 'cause she told me two days later.

She dragged out some clothes, too dirty for any human to wear, and a top hat, with its top all smashed down. She pitched it to me, and I put it on. Even though it didn't fit too good, it would help me in the sun when we took to walking again.

Finally, out come a canteen, which she held up and sloshed around. Glory, something was in it. She handed the canteen to me, and I pulled out the stopper, tilted it, my eyes already watering, taken a swallow—and liked to have died.

Coughed so hard, I feared, and so did Gen, that I'd open up that wound in my side. I spit, and wiped the tears in my eyes, felt snot pouring out of my nose, leaned back, and finally got my breath back.

"Now I know why the marshal of Magdalena was after them boys," I said. "That's the worst whiskey I ever drunk."

"Are you all right, Micah?" Gen asked.

I wiped my eyes, my nose, then my hands on my trousers. "Will be," I said, wheezing some. "As long as I don't drink no more of that forty rod."

She held the canteen, which was covered with blue wool, one of them old Army issue ones, and for a moment there, I thought she might take a taste. Instead, she turned the canteen over, and the whiskey fell on my side.

Well, I screamed as that whiskey burned, and I cussed, and I probably would have wet my pants if I'd had enough fluid in my kidneys. Next, she was yelling like a panther, and through the tears in my eyes, I saw why. She'd poured the rest of the whiskey on that bad cut over her calf.

Finally, both of us was all screamed out, and the turkey buzzards had flown away we'd hollered so much. She put the empty canteen by the other plunder worth keeping, and reached inside the bag. She pulled out a leather pouch, pretty big, and something was inside it. I hoped it might be some greenbacks, even though we didn't have no store or café to spend money on. Ain't that just like a gambler and thief?

No. What she pulled out, she immediately dropped.

"God," I said. "A scalp."

Her Adam's apple bobbed. "More are . . . in here."

I looked at the long black hair. Now I knew what for the law was after them two scoundrels, and why they deserved what they got. I've done some pretty wicked things in my time, but never, never have I taken a human scalp.

"Indian?"

My head shook, though I wasn't certain, but it was a pretty strong suspicion. "Mexican government pays a bounty for Apache scalps, but"—I had to take a deep breath, and slowly let it out, slowly swallow down the disgust in my throat—"some men figure that you can't tell an Apache scalp from a Mexican one." I knowed something else, which I didn't let on. That scalp, the one she'd dropped in the dust, had come off a woman's head.

Dirty, rotten, miserable sons of bitches.

Gently, Gen picked up the scalp, put it back in the pouch, taken it outside and buried it. When she got back, she grabbed the pack, and figured there wasn't nothing else in that bag for us, certainly nothing we wanted to take a chance on seeing, and she dragged it as far from us as she could.

Once she was back, she sat beside me and started sobbing. First, I figured it was because of them scalps, and I put my arm around her, pulled her close.

The cries got stronger, little short, choking gasps, and I moved closer to her, despite the burning in my side, and whispered that everything was all right.

She shook her head. "I killed two men."

Now . . . it wasn't that I was trying to be funny, and it wasn't because I wasn't really thinking about what I said and all, but it was on account that, as I think I've wrote down in this here account of mine before that I do know something about math and all, because what I said was "Actually, three, counting Jorge de la Cruz."

Wrong thing to say, because she begun all-out wailing.

I pulled her to me, and let her cry on my shoulder. I rubbed her back and whispered, "They weren't men, Gen. None of 'em was even close to being human."

She wailed.

"They would have killed us," I said. "Both of us."

More wretched, heartbreaking sobs.

"This ain't the Sisters of Charity orphanage, Gen. It ain't church. It's a hard country. And to live, you got to do some unpleasant things and all."

She made herself stop bawling. That's the kind of woman she was. I felt her arms come over my head, and she pulled me close to her, and my side was just tormenting me fierce, but I didn't cry out in pain.

"Bless me, Father," she said, "for I have sinned. It has been seven years since my last confession. . . ."

Chapter Twenty-two

Let her talk, I did. What else could I do? Let her talk until she cleansed out her soul and fell asleep. Easily, I laid her on the ground, and went down beside her, putting my right arm over her, thinking about her, about me, about us, about Sister Rocío. I went to sleep. At least, I tried to.

Next day, I knowed we had to leave. Gen must've not remembered anything about her confession, about the scalps, maybe not even about the two men she had killed. Well, she never looked at them, anyhow, and didn't mention nothing about all she'd said.

By this time, gray wolves had begun gathering around, running off the coyot's. Big wolves kept snarling in the distance, waiting to get at The Voice and Vern. I wasn't gonna deprive them critters for much longer.

That stocking turned out to be a right fine bandage across my side, and I taken the whiskey-soaked canteen, the empty bottle of King Bee Whiskey, and the rusty pail to the water hole. Filled them up—rinsing out the old canteen three times upon Gen's orders—and set them aside. Well, the rusty pail wouldn't hold a drop, so we left it, but I did hollow out the gourd with that pocketknife, and it held a bit of water just fine.

"Were there any bullets in that bag?" I asked Gen.

She shook her head.

I give her The Voice's Colt, a long-barreled .45. "It's empty." I reckon she already knowed that on account that she had emptied it. "But it's a good gun. Might find some bullets for it somewhere down the line."

She shoved it into the saddlebag, along with the gourd and the whiskey bottle.

I tipped up my too-small top hat and hefted the machete, but it proved too cumbersome, too heavy. I tossed that big sticker toward the swelling, stinking corpse of Vern. Besides, I had a pocketknife and a Dean and Adams, which I had reloaded.

Gen had found me a piece of driftwood, good and hard and twisted, which I could use for a crutch to help me with my bum side and all. Once I picked up the canteens, and slung them over my shoulder, she took the saddlebags and pulled my hat down on her head. Then she walked to me, taken that top hat off me, give me mine, and put the silly battered old top hat on her.

"It fits me better anyhow," she said.

I wasn't going to argue that point. Never cared for top hats. Too dandified for me.

Her head tilted north.

Mine shook. I pointed south.

"We don't have to go to Gran Quivira. Or the Valley of Fire."

"Gran Quivira's closer," I said.

"But—"

"There's shelter there. And I should be able to find water. Or at least trails." I gestured toward the other direction. "Head back through that furnace?" I couldn't stop shuddering at the mere thought of such torture. "Six miles, no more than eight. We'll be climbing up Mesa de Los Jumanos. We'll be out of this hell."

"Micah," she pleaded, but I had my stubborn streak going.

"It's our only chance," I said.

Her head dropped, but nodded, and she taken off, with me limping just behind her.

Them wolves wasted no time once we got moving.

Bad as my side ached, we didn't make good time, but we was far from them bad men, far from them bad memories. I don't know. Maybe what I should have done was taken Gen up on her suggestion. Mayhap we should have tried to make it back north, toward Anton Chico, and rolled the dice, said the devil with Felipe Hernandez. Or we could have moved west. There was passes between those mountains as the Manzanos were well north and west of us by then. We could have picked up the Camino Real, or the Rio Grande, even the Atchison, Topeka and Santa Fe. Might could I'd even pay a visit to the marshal of Magdalena, see if he'd trust me—if not me, then Sister Geneviève Tremblay—and find out if there was some kind of reward posted on The Voice and Vern.

Might be, of course, that I was just a damned fool. Nah. Ain't no *might* to that.

On the second day, we begun to climb, sliding on them rocks, grabbing scrub, making footholds. Now, that mesa ain't nowhere near the Sangre de Cristos or Manzanos, but when a body has been walking as far as me and Gen had, gone through all we had, well, even a stroll across the Santa Fe Plaza would be a handful.

On the fourth day, we was well up the slope, even had some black cedar for shade. Seen us a couple rattlesnakes, but they seen us first. By whirring their tails, they let us know that we wasn't welcome.

"We could shoot one," Gen suggested. "Ever tasted rattlesnake?"

"Enough to know I'd rather eat something else."

Leaving them alone, we kept going.

• • •

"They called the Indians here Jumanos," I said as we kept on climbing, following what appeared to be an animal trail, cougar I reckon, maybe some pronghorns. "Means 'The Striped Ones.' See, the Indians here painted a stripe over their nose."

We stopped to rest under the shade of a lone juniper. After taking a swallow from the canteen, I offered a slug of water to Gen, but she turned up her nose.

"Is there any water in the other one?"

Struck me odd, but I sloshed our old one around, pulled it off my shoulder, handed it to her. "That one," she said, making a face at the canteen I'd drunk from, "was the one those cutthroats had. With the bad whiskey."

"We rinsed it out," I told her.

While drinking, she shook her head.

"Three times. You made me do it." I reached up and tapped the wooden bottom. Her eyes peered over the container. "Not too much. Got to last us a bit more."

After she had corked the canteen, she handed it back to me. I taken one more quick pull from mine, and didn't taste nary a hint of that rotgut, put the stopper back in it, and knelt, removing my hat, wiping the sweat from my brow.

"How do you know?" Gen asked.

"Know what?"

"About the Jumanos."

Had to study on that some. Finally, I shrugged. "Not exactly sure."

"When you were scouting for the Army?"

Done some more thinking. "Maybe, but I doubt it. Seems to have come to me earlier."

Her eyes twinkled. "I think those Tompiro Indians were before your time."

My head bobbed. "Yeah. I warrant they was. How'd you know?"

She laughed, so musical, and life just danced in them sweet eyes of hers. "Because you're not that much older than me, Micah, and . . ."

My head was shaking, so she let her words fade. "That they were called Tompiro? That's what I meant."

"The church had a mission here," she said. "That's why we are bound for Gran Quivira."

Again, I shook my head. "The Sisters of Charity weren't here."

No more laughter, no more life in her pretty eyes. "Are you interrogating me?"

I snorted and slapped my knee, which irritated my side. "No, girl. Of course not."

The smile returned, but she wasn't so certain no more. "The Catholic church, Micah, had the mission here. The Sisters of Charity are part of the Catholic church."

I pushed myself back to my feet with the crutch Gen had got for me.

On we went, chewing salt grass leaves when

we could find them, conserving our water, resting a lot, moving south.

Next morning—I think it was, but it's hard to tell. Days just run together when you're walking through desert, hardly eating, hardly living, barely surviving. Anyhow, it was morning when I knelt by a plant, and plucked a red berry, maybe the size of a marble, from it. I popped it in my mouth, made a face, then grabbed another, and handed it to Gen, who was kneeling beside me.

She ate it, and her face scrunched up, too. Gen spit hers out. "It's bitter."

"Wolfberry." I handed her some more. Indians, I recollected, boiled them, then dried them and ate them. That I had learned during my brief career as an Army scout. But you could eat some raw. If your taste buds did not object too much. And your stomach.

"I can't—"

"You got to," I said, and forced another into my mouth. "It's food, and we need food. You just can't eat too many."

She ate another. "You don't have to worry about that."

That's about all the food we had. Oh, I spied a herd of pronghorn once, way off in the distance, probably eight or ten, but I knowed I'd have no chance of sneaking up on them close enough to shoot with a revolver. And even if I lucked out, pronghorns being dumb, curious critters, I was pretty certain even if I hit a buck or doe with a bullet, I wouldn't kill it outright, and a pronghorn can run a long ways before it dies.

We made it into thicker timber, then started down, me limping right badly by that time, and fairly often cussing myself silently as the biggest damned fool in New Mexico Territory.

All this while, though, I kept formulating plans. Eventually, I'd come to the conclusion that my brilliant idea would get me killed, but I'd then start thinking of another one.

Gen fell silent, too, troubled. Or maybe she was formulating her own plans.

I hoped hers was a whole lot better than mine.

See, plans wasn't my point of expertise. Generally, as I'd told Gen before, I made things up as they come to me.

Heading downhill now, we reached the end of the timber, coming to a sea of bluestem, blue grama, and Indian rice grass, all of it tan from the sun and lack of rainfall. But the grass sure waved in the wind.

The sea didn't go on forever. I pointed to a hill.

Gen shielded her eyes and stared.

"Gran Quivira," I told her, smiling slightly.

She lowered her hands, and turned to me, mouth trembling. "Micah. . . ." she started, but I was already walking through the ugly grass.

"Watch out for snakes," I told her. "Don't want to get bit by one this close to home."

Not that Gran Quivira was home, but it might be my final resting place.

Despite my bum leg and throbbing side, I moved at a pretty good clip, heading across the little valley that separated the mesa from the old ruins. Hell, it was too hot in the day for rattlers to be out no how.

Rattlers meaning animals, of course. There is another kind.

"Micah!"

I stopped. She'd caught up with me, was walking beside me, and pointed toward the ruins, which we was just now beginning to make out. This time, it was me who had to shield my eyes. Four horses came loping down that rocky slope, and they wasn't wild beasts. Far from it. They carried riders.

"Run!" Gen screamed, but I tossed down my crutch, and raised my hands over my head.

"We'd never make it," I told her. "These them friends of yours?"

"No," she said, which was not a good answer.

Two of the riders spread out, armed with Winchesters aimed in our general direction. The other two rode right for us, sunlight bouncing off the revolvers in their hands.

Gen stepped toward them, but stopped, and slowly lifted her hands toward the heavens, too.

The two boys flanking us pulled up, keeping us covered. They must have figured us important, ornery heroes just like Kit Carson and Jesse James.

The other two riders slowed their horses to a walk, and I started my right hand for my waist, but the Dean and Adams wasn't there.

"Damn it!" I turned to Gen. "I must've lost my revolver."

She seemed relieved.

The rattler on the claybank rode up easily, chuckling, shaking his head, grinning at me whilst pointing a Colt revolver at my head.

"I'll be damned," Sean Fenn said. "I'd given y'all up for dead."

Chapter Twenty-three

A second later, Sean Fenn's expression changed. Gone was that look of delight, replaced with utter shock. "Jesus Christ!" he shouted, and swung deftly off the claybank, handing the reins to the rider beside him and holstering his gun. He took two steps toward Gen, stopped, and whispered, "My God, Gen, are . . . are you . . . all right?"

Me? I shot a glance at Gen, didn't see nothing strange about her.

"Yes, Sean," she said softly. "I am fine." Her voice betrayed her true feelings, though, and

Fenn was waving his hat at the two outriders, hollering at them to hurry in, bring some water, some jerky, and some hardtack.

As Gen got pampered, Fenn walked over to me. I didn't expect to rate such fine treatment and respect. No concern on his face when he come up to me. Instead, he sniggered. "Christ, Bishop, you look like hell." When he got closer, though, he stared at me long and hard. "Good God Almighty."

Well, he sure didn't make me feel real pretty.

He started to bend down for my crutch, thought better of it, and his hand touched the butt of his Colt. "Let's have your gun, Bishop."

"Lost it," I told him.

"Like hell."

"It's true, Sean." Gen's voice carried across the flats, and me and Fenn looked at her. Lowering the saddlebags, she knelt, opened one of the pouches, and pulled out The Voice's empty Colt. "This is all we have."

The first rider taken the handgun, pulling it to half cock, opening the loading gate, and rolling the cylinder on his arm to see that it was unloaded. Then he lowered the hammer and shoved the weapon into his waistband.

A smirk returned to Fenn's face. He picked up the crutch, handed it to me, and for that I was grateful. I leaned on it. 'Course, he still didn't trust me, so he pushed up my ragged, dirty, ripped shirt and found no Dean and Adams .436 or

Continental Ladies Companion—only the green hose that had become a bandage. He laughed.

"That must have been some time y'all had, eh, Bishop?"

I wasn't paying him no mind, though I absently drew the pocketknife from my trousers, and tossed it to him, reckoning that would make him feel better. One of the riders handed Gen a piece of bread, probably rock hard. She taken it, and just stared at it as if she'd never seen sourdough before.

"Go ahead, Gen." Fenn was looking at her, too. "Feast. You're nothing but bones."

"She shouldn't eat too much," I said. "Make her bad sick."

Back at me, he frowned. "What have y'all had to eat?"

"A rabbit," I answered. "Little bit of jerky. Some wolfberries a day or so ago."

"Since when?"

Now that took some figuring, and even though I knowed how to cipher real good, and determine odds, and things like that, I had no idea. When had that thunderstorm hit? How long had I been laid up after The Voice plugged me? How many days had we walked since leaving the water hole? Even now, I still ain't rightly certain.

Even after Fenn told me the date, I couldn't fathom a guess. Well, we hadn't been wandering for forty years, but I felt fifty years older.

"Corbin!" Fenn turned toward the guy with the bread. "Put Gen on your horse. Take her to camp. We'll feed her some of that soup. Now, damn it!" Turning back at me, he said, "But you, Bishop, you walk."

I limped past him.

"Sean!" Gen managed to call out. "He can barely walk. We've walked forty miles."

Well, the way I figured it, I'd walked a lot farther than that.

"He'll have to," Fenn said to her. "There's no way I'd ever trust Micah Bishop on a horse, especially my horse."

Even I had to laugh at that one.

Here's another reason I didn't like Sean Fenn. He had no respect for nobody but hisself. You take the ruins of Gran Quivira. He said only fools would have lived in this country, he called the Indians that had called this country home "diggers," and said while these savage Indians didn't even know about the wheel, the Renaissance was happening in Europe. And . . . the priest who had started the big church never even finished it.

"Because," Fenn reasoned, "he was smart enough to leave."

I looked at those crumbling walls, some of them thirty feet high and six feet thick, and the rotting rafters that must have weighed maybe as much as two tons—from trees that had to have been fifteen miles from here—and I had nothing but respect for the Indians who built this place.

But I reckon sentiments such as them won't be enough to get me through them pearly gates, or slip me out of a hangman's noose.

Anyhow, they herded Gen and me into a square room without windows and only a single exit in one of the smallest structures. One of Fenn's men taken the horses somewheres. There was coffee in a pot, cold, since they had no fire going at the moment, and soup in a bucket, likewise cold. They fed Gen. Told me to sit down.

Fenn had three men with him, the gringo with the bushy mustache and Texas hat, Corbin. Another one wore a sugarloaf sombrero, and I think his name was Benigno. The third one, lanky and rawboned and ugly as sin, I never heard called nothing. His face was heavily scarred, so I just thought of him as The Pockmarked Man.

Once Fenn made sure Gen was comfortable, he left her to her soup, which she could barely eat, and knelt across from me, rolling a cigarette with one hand.

The other three men stood behind him, holding their guns.

"Mind if I ask you something?" I said, all polite and friendly.

"Ask away. I'll be asking you questions as soon as I have myself a smoke."

"How'd you get off that train?"

He grinned.

To make him feel proud of hisself, I added, "Figured they would haul you all the way to Santa Fe."

"They did." He found a lucifer in his vest pocket, struck it on a rock, and got his cigarette going. "Took me all the way to the county jail."

"And?"

"Santa Fe is in Santa Fe County. Las Vegas is in San Miguel County. There's no love lost between those two jurisdictions, and not much cooperation among the legal authorities." Fenn smiled. "Besides, you've lived in this territory long enough to know that. "

Should've knowed. He'd bribed his way out of the calaboose.

"How long have you been waiting here?"

He wagged a finger at me and blew a smoke ring into the air. "You asked me some*thing,* Bishop. Now it's my turn. Fill me in, pretty please, on what happened since you left my company."

I told him what I figured he needed to know, nothing more.

"You expect me to believe that bit of nonsense?" He blew smoke in my face, but I didn't cough.

I just stared back at him. I hadn't lied. Everything I told him had been gospel.

"It's true, Sean," Gen said.

She was standing, though leaning against the rocky wall to keep from falling.

Fenn glanced at her, then leaned toward me and crushed his cigarette out on my forearm.

I couldn't just stare him down then. I yelped, slapped at the burn, then he slapped my hat off, and punched me to the ground. My teeth clicked hard against each other, and I spit a bit of blood onto the rock. One of his boys hooted. The others said nothing.

"Leave him alone, damn you!" That come from Gen.

Fenn had balled his hand into a fist, and I was expecting another hammer to my head, but he turned and saw Gen. His fingers reappeared, and he pushed back his hat. First he looked at her, then at me, then at her, then again at me, then at her, and when he turned to face me again, he was grinning.

"Were your evenings with her as pleasant as she once made mine?"

That's another thing I despised about Sean Fenn. He knowed how to hurt a person, not just with guns and fists, but words. "Go to hell, you son of a bitch," I told him.

That prompted him to hurt me more with fists, which, you might find hard to believe, I preferred to his words.

When I come to, I peeled the wet bandanna off my eyelids, squinted at the bright sunlight, and felt fingers on my forehead, fingers whose touch I'd recognize anywhere.

Gen came into focus.

"You're a damned fool," she said.

I could tell she'd been crying. That was easy. Tears cut quite the path down all the dirt on her face, but I guess she still looked beautiful to me. Over her objections, I pushed myself up, leaned against the rocky wall, and felt my right boot.

"How bad is that foot?"

"It's all right," I said, and let out a sigh of relief.

"Let me look at—"

"No!" I grabbed her arm before it touched my leg, and she jerked from my grip, my anger, my reaction.

"You ain't a nun, are you?" I said.

Her lips trembled, and she had to wipe away the tears that had begun flowing down those dirty cheeks. Her head shook. She couldn't speak.

"I figured." I spit out some blood, run my tongue over my teeth, and didn't notice none missing. Fenn wasn't hitting as hard as he once did, or maybe he realized he needed me to be able to talk.

Her head bowed. I let her sob. She choked out something, then spoke so I could understand. "I tried to tell you."

My head shook, and maybe that broke her heart. "You didn't try that hard, Geneviève." I figured it had come time to drop the *Gen*. For now. Sean Fenn called her Gen, and I didn't like nothing about Sean Fenn.

"Did I tell you . . . any . . . anything?" she asked.

She must've blocked out her confession, and I don't rightly blame her for that. I even hoped she had forgotten most of what had happened, wouldn't recollect The Voice and Vern, or, for that matter, even Jorge de la Cruz.

She was reaching under her ripped shirt, into her chemise, but my hand stopped her, gently this time, and I shook my head. "Keep that," I whispered.

"I can't."

"Please."

Her hand fell away from her chest, and I sighed with relief.

"Can you forgive me, Micah?" she asked, hopeful.

I smiled, which hurt like hell. "Already done that."

She leaned over and kissed my bearded cheek. That hurt like hell, too, but I didn't mind, didn't wince, didn't complain.

"Damn," Fenn's voice called out, "I can't leave you two lovebirds alone for a minute, can I?"

Geneviève turned around, and even beneath all that dirt, and dried trails of tear, I could see her face flaming red. "Don't you touch him again, Sean Fenn. Don't you ever lay a hand on him."

Fenn's face hardened, and he reached for his holstered revolver. "Mind your tongue. Out here, I'm God."

"We need him," she said, spacing her words out for emphasis.

"Why do you think I busted him out of jail?" He pushed her aside, and pointed a finger at me. "Think that deal in Las Vegas was for old time's sake, pard? Is that what you think?" He was madder than Geneviève. "Here's the deal, Bishop. You live as long as I let you live. You don't make love to my girl behind my back—"

"I never—"

He slapped me down. That one really hurt. Didn't knock a tooth out, but it sure loosened one of them big ones. My head slammed against a rock, and blood gushed from my head. Reckon that blow jarred some sense back into me, as instantly I recollected that I'd never been real good at planning things, and this plan—if I ever had one—wasn't turning out the way I'd hoped.

"Leave him alone!" Like a catamount, Geneviève leaped on Fenn's back, but he flipped her over his head, the wind whooshing from her lungs when she landed.

That I saw, and I came up, blinking blood from my left eye. Fenn turned, drawing his revolver, but I wasn't going after him. I was crawling to that girl, lying, eyes staring vacantly, and me fearing that bastard had broke her neck or back. Her lungs fought for breath, and I lifted her into my arms as Fenn eared back his Colt's hammer. I expected we was both dead, but one of Fenn's

230

men—Corbin, it was—stopped him from really making a mess of things.

"You best control your temper, Fenn," the gunman said. "I didn't hire on to be part of a lover's quarrel. You promised us a fortune in gold. And to hear you talk, you need that fellow there."

Chapter Twenty-four

Since Corbin had probably just stopped Fenn from killing me and Geneviève, I decided that I liked that fellow, and would regret when it come time to kill the bastard. His words somehow quieted Fenn's anger.

Once his revolver was holstered, Fenn hauled Geneviève away, and Corbin and The Pockmarked Man dragged me off to another room where Corbin stitched up my head, and wrapped a fairly clean bandanna around it.

Then he said, "Get cleaned up."

I saw an enamel bowl, a shaving kit, even a mirror.

Gingerly, I moved over to the mirrored wall. Wasn't no ceiling. No floor. Just more rock walls. After picking up the razor, I eyed Corbin. "Y'all trust me with this?"

"Don't cut your throat," he said, which wasn't my meaning.

There was even some soap. I washed my face, and, sake's alive, did that feel glorious. Scrubbed it good, though I left my bandaged forehead alone, and it was like I was in the fanciest hotel in Denver because The Pockmarked Man passed me another towel—not really a towel, now that I think on it, but a bandanna that wasn't sweaty and dirty. After drying off, I found the brush in the tin, began working up a lather.

Wasn't till I saw my reflection that I dropped both tin and brush.

Now I knowed what had shocked Sean Fenn so much when he laid eyes on Geneviève and me.

A cadaver looked better than me, and it wasn't on account of the bandage, some blood already soaking through the faded yellow silk. Wasn't because of the bruises and scratches. Slowly, I recollected how Geneviève looked now, comparing that vision to how I recalled them memories from her arrival in the Las Vegas jail . . . and the hotel room . . . and even in that boxcar.

My eyes was sunk way back in my head, and despite the stubble of beard I'd planned on shaving off, I could see how hollow my cheeks was. Carefully, I reached over and felt my right arm, staring at that bony thing, seeing the puckered mark Sean Fenn's cigarette had left. I lifted up my shirt, past the green stocking bandage, saw them ribs that brung to mind skeletons. Lastly, I slipped my hand inside my trousers, made a fist, pushed against the fabric. Criminy, if it hadn't been for suspenders, I would've been dragging them britches at my ankles.

Felt my Adam's apple bob, and had to wait till my hands stopped shaking before I could pick up the tin and the razor.

"You best hurry," Corbin said. "Fenn lacks patience, and we'd like to get moving out of this"—he seemed to shudder—"evil place."

Studied him through the mirror, I did. Big Tim Pruett once told me that you needed to know the fellow you was going up against. 'Course, he was talking about boxing and poker, but I figured that it would come in handy, too, when your life and soul depended on it. Corbin didn't seem to be the kind of gent to spook easily, but I recollected how de la Cruz—or had it been Blanco?—had mentioned that Gran Quivira was haunted.

"How long have y'all been camped here?" I spoke real casual, so they wouldn't suspicion my motives, fetching razor and cup, opening the blade and wiping it on my trousers.

"Too damned long," he said.

The Pockmarked Man shifted his legs, leaned against the rocky wall, and the Mexican come into the room, scraping his boot on a rock. Even better. I had all three's attention.

"They say many, many Indians were murdered here." I started stropping the razor against a piece of leather hanging on the wall—like this place was a regular barber shop on the plaza.

The Mexican stopped scraping the manure off his boot.

"And their bodies were sealed"—I tapped the rocks and mortar—"inside these walls."

The Pockmarked Man straightened, moved a couple steps away from the wall that had been holding him up. He started to look back, but couldn't.

"A place like this," I said, and tested the razor, "is . . . well. . . ." I shuddered. Honest. Didn't pretend to, neither. It was like somebody had just stepped on my grave. Might have been the Mexican, which would explain how come he had manure all over the bottom of his boot.

"Stop with the ghost stories, Bishop," Corbin said. "And focus on making yourself presentable."

That got my curiosity up. "Presentable? For who?"

He didn't answer. Just pointed at the razor.

Don't reckon I filled that "presentable" bill, even though I hadn't nicked me once with that razor, and it wasn't that sharp and the water was only lukewarm. I mean, my face was bruised, and a scab was beginning to form on my forehead underneath that bandage.

Still donned the miserable clothes I'd had on my back since Las Vegas. I stank to high heaven, could only imagine that I smelled worser downwind of my person. I had the ugliest green bandage on my side, my shirt was torn and ripped, my boots had holes in the bottoms and a couple in the tops, and one boot top had a three-inch slash along the seam.

When I'd made myself as pretty as I reckon the boys figured I could ever get, Corbin pointed through the opening, and I followed The Pockmarked Man and Benigno, with Corbin keeping a safe and respectable distance behind me.

We walked into another building, or part of the one they'd held me in, then ducked through a small doorway—the Indians who'd lived here must have been real tiny individuals—and wandered through a regular maze. I figured a body could get lost in here and die of starvation or thirst before he ever found his way out. At last, we reached a three-cornered room, with three small, square windows in one side. The tops of two walls was pretty much rounded, and the floor was dirt and grass and plenty of rocks. Through the windows was green shrubbery and a cloudless sky. Looking up, I spied a couple-three ravens flying around in the wind. The sky was so blue, so beautiful. Wished I could have been flying up there with them big, black birds.

What I noticed most about the room was the smokeless fire—they was smart enough to use dry wood—and a coffeepot resting on a rock, a bunch of cups next to the stone ring.

Well, that ain't altogether true, neither. What I noticed most was Geneviève. She sat in the corner under one of the square windows, the one with a bunch of loose rocks on the bottom. She looked real thin, too, and she'd always appeared to be a small, delicate woman. The bruises was showing on her face, too, now that she'd washed up, but I didn't know how many of them purple spots come from Sean Fenn, and how many come from The Voice, or maybe just from all that hard traveling we'd done across the desert.

"Help yourself to some coffee, Bishop." Fenn spoke before I seen him. He come around the empty spot where a wall stood two centuries earlier.

Bending with my leg, and head, and ribs, didn't seem such a promising venture, but Fenn was in a friendly mood for the time. He must've realized the pain I was in, so he squatted to pour me a cup. I taken it and quickly sipped some.

"Good coffee," I said. Meant it, too.

"Thank you, kindly," Corbin said.

Yep, I wouldn't enjoy killing him.

Fenn decided that was enough social talk. "What do you know about the gold?"

"Probably no more than you do."

He motioned for me to sit on a rocky ledge, and I done so, mainly because Big Tim Pruett had always said that coffee tastes better when you're sitting or squatting, not standing.

"Where's his crutch?" Geneviève asked.

"Walking's good for him," Fenn said. "A man like Micah Bishop would likely use a crutch as a weapon. Isn't that right, Bishop?"

"Can't deny that." I taken another sip.

"The gold?" Fenn said.

"Folks have been looking for gold since them Spanish con . . . conster . . . conquis . . . since them explorers was first here."

"You know the gold I mean." Fenn's voice lost that friendly tone.

"Well, what I knows goes something like this. In olden times, Spanish explorers found a gold mine way up in Mora. Mine played out about the time of the Pueblo Revolt of 1680. The Spanish tried to make it to Mexico, hauling plunder with them. The Indians they'd enslaved helped carry their riches. Made it here, and killed the Indians." I tapped the wall behind. "Buried them in these walls."

Sneaked me a look-see at the Mexican and The Pockmarked Man, but they didn't seem scared. Not yet. But I figured their nerves wasn't as strong as they made out.

"There the gold sat, buried, till some scientists come here in 1848. There was a small party. They tried to make it out with all the gold, using mules to carry it. They made it to the Valley of Fire."

"Fires."

I craned my neck to see the Mexican. "Beg your pardon," I said.

He spoke in rapid Spanish, then told me, and the rest of our merry group, that the proper name was the Valley of Fires.

"What's the difference?" I said.

"Singular and plural," Corbin answered, him being smarter than most gunmen.

"The map the fellow in Socorro showed me had it 'Fire,' " The Pockmarked Man said. "I can show you. It's in my war bag."

"A gringo," Benigno said. "*Norteamericano. Imbecíl.*" He waved his hand. "I know this country. It is my homeland. It is the Valley of Fires."

"I've heard tell of a Valley of Fire in Nevada," The Pockmarked Man said.

"And if you combine the one in Nevada to the one south of here you'd have two," Corbin said lightly.

"Making them the Valley of Fires." The Pockmarked Man nodded his head as if that was the final word on the subject.

It wasn't.

"Or the Valleys of Fire," Corbin said.

"Gringo," Benigno said. "*Norteamericano. Imbecíl.* I tell you, it is Fires."

"Who gives a damn!" Sean Fenn had the last word on the matter. He gestured angrily at me. "What happened in the Valley of Fire?"

I shot Geneviève a glance. See, all this story I'd heard from her, but then Blanco and that big farmer from along the Pecos River had come upon us, and she hadn't finished the story, but I made me a good guess. "It was buried there."

Had to be. They seemed to think I knowed where it was, but I didn't know nothing. Excepting what Geneviève had told me, and she hadn't finished that tale.

"Where?" Fenn demanded.

"In the Valley of Fire."

"Fires!" Benigno said, determined to prove his case.

Fenn shot the Mexican the meanest look I'd ever seen him give, and Benigno promptly decided that it didn't matter one way or the other what anybody called it.

"Where in the Valley of Fire?" Fenn asked me.

"How the hell should I know?" I decided to make them do some talking, instead of me.

"Here's why." Fenn jumped to his feet, his face reddening once again.

That man needed to do something about that temper. He was liable to have his whole head just blow up from all that blood rushing to it.

"I'm in Santa Fe, minding my own business, when some damned Mex named Felipe Hernandez barges into the saloon, yelling that he is going to hang Micah Bishop the day after tomorrow, and everyone is invited to see the killer of his cousin—I forgot the dead man's name—swing. I laugh, even consider taking the northbound up to Vegas to watch you jerk. But almost immediately, I start hearing stories about this nun. This old crone of a nun with one arm and blind as a bat. The stories that reach me at the faro layouts are that she must save Micah Bishop.

"Now, I could care less, but then there's another story making its way in Santa Fe. That burg has more gossips than a Baptist church. I start hearing crazy things. About a fortune in ancient ingots. Buried in the Valley of Fire." He glared at the Mexican, just daring him to say something, just give him a reason to blow his fool head off. Benigno kept quiet.

"So . . ."

I finished for Fenn. "So you sent her . . ." I tilted my head toward Geneviève. ". . . to the Sisters of Charity orphanage. Had her make a quick friendship with an old blind nun. Get the story from the nun herself, find out if I was really worth saving. Something like that, Sean?"

"You aren't as stupid as I remembered," Fenn said.

I kept looking at Geneviève, waited till she raised her head to look at me. "How'd you manage to fool the Mother Superior, get inside, find Sister Rocío?"

Geneviève lowered her gaze, wrapped her arms around her knees, begun rocking back and forth, staring at the dirt.

"They were expecting a nun to join their cult," Fenn said. "Figured Gen could play that part for a day. Got her all dandied up, sent her on her way."

"Yeah," I said, "but the Mother Superior—"

"She was almost a nun." Fenn cut me off. "Almost. Till she met me. Ain't that right, Gen?" He spoke vindictively.

"Don't call her that," I said.

"What? Gen?"

"Yeah."

He laughed. "Pardon me all to hell." He laughed at Geneviève, still rocking, not saying nothing, not crying, just rocking.

I drawed a deep breath, let it out, and shrugged. "Well, I don't know what Sister Rocío told you. Don't know how I can help you fellows. You should ask the nun herself."

"An excellent idea!" Fenn laughed.

Geneviève stopped rocking, and looked at him with the most hatred I'd ever seen in a pretty woman's eyes.

Chapter Twenty-five

"You brought her here?" Geneviève came to her feet, shaking with rage. "You pathetic bastard! You brought a seventy-year-old nun, blind and frail with a bad heart and dying of carcinoma?"

That hit me like a .45 slug in the chest. My breath come up short. Sister Rocío was . . . dying?

"Well, it wasn't quite as romantic as your little excursion here," Fenn said, all snug, all snide. "We took the train from Santa Fe to Socorro and rented some horses. The old biddy said she'd only ride a burro, but I am always one to please. We compromised on a mule. A small mule."

"And brought her here?" Geneviève's arm swept across the crumbling rock walls.

"Yes, damn it." Fenn wasn't so snug no more. He was angry. "But you two are to blame. When the train pulled into Santa Fe, you two weren't on it. You'd flown the coop. I didn't know where or how. Didn't know if you were dead or alive. And three-quarters of a million dollars worth of gold ingots . . . well . . . what did you expect me to do?"

He jabbed a finger at me. "She, that damned old, blind nun, she said you were the only one who could find it." Fenn had to stop, put his hand on the rocks.

I was praying that he might drop dead of apoplexy right then and there, but, no luck.

When he looked up, when his mouth started moving, he wasn't shouting no more, but speaking evenly, softly. "What I did know was that here, Gran Quivira, was the starting point. If you were somehow still alive, you would get here with Bishop." He was grinning, a mean-spirited smile. "Or maybe, I thought, just maybe, you might decide that Bishop was a better pard than ol' Sean Fenn. Maybe you might decide that all you needed was Micah Bishop to lead you to all them riches.

"I guess that's about what happened."

She spit in the dirt. I shook my head.

"Either way, I figured you and him. . . ." His gesture at me wasn't so gentle. Fenn had to catch his breath again, steady himself, get some control back. "You and him would have to start here, too."

"Why here?" I asked.

"Don't play me for a damned fool, Bishop!" He spoke with such forcefulness, I spilled what was left of that coffee on my shirt, even slid back some.

Son of a bitch was crazy.

"You know why. That nun said we had to start here. So you'll guide us to that fortune, Bishop. Or I bury you and your lovely concubine here."

"And the old nun?" Geneviève asked.

"Well, that's why I brought her here." Fenn smiled. "In case you were dead, or caught, or lost.

I thought maybe I could persuade the nun to let me find that fortune." He clapped his hands. "But let's go ask her. Shall we?"

The first Spanish mission went up at Gran Quivira in 1629. At least, that's what the *Santa Fe New Mexican* reported after I was back in the Las Vegas jail. They let me read newspapers while I waited to see if any judge would allow my lawyer's appeal, which, of course, as you already know, didn't happen.

The second church, the real big one, they begun to build in 1659 when the new priest, Father Diego de Santander decided to put up a bigger one. 'Course, they never finished this one. It was all over by 1670, ten years before the big Indian revolt. They just stopped building the church and left Gran Quivira.

Read that in the *New Mexican*, too.

We wandered back through the maze, me and Geneviève following Benigno and The Pockmarked Man, Corbin and Fenn dragging behind. We crossed more rocks on the slope and come to the unfinished, but mighty impressive, walls of the second church. The sun made these walls look almost white, like the biggest tombstone ever made, and I was glad to step through the opening and into the shade.

My heart skipped some, because there she was, sitting on the massive rock windowsill, her one arm resting on what must have been left of an old viga from the roof, staring at the blowing tan grass, the cholla, the juniper trees, and across the emptiness, and on toward the mesa. That country looked real pretty from there, and not as Geneviève and me had seen it up close and dying of thirst.

'Course, the sad part about it all was that I knowed that Sister Rocío couldn't see a thing.

"Sister," Sean Fenn called out, all polite and respectful and charming and as deadly as a sidewinder, "that gallant nobleman Micah Bishop has finally arrived." He pushed me toward her. "And Sister Geneviève is here with him."

I heard Geneviève walking behind me.

The old nun turned. She wore her habit, same as Geneviève had been wearing when I'd first seen her. Her eyes were dark, empty, as I remembered them, but she held out her hand, and smiled. She had no teeth, but I remembered that she'd only had two or three—and one of them was black—back when I'd been a kid.

"Micah," she said, her voice old, fading, but just as I remembered from them times at the Sisters of Charity orphanage. She muttered something in Spanish, crossed herself, and asked almost hopeful, "Is it you, my son?"

I gripped her hand, worn and rugged as old leather, squeezed it, and sat on the ledge beside her.

"What's left of me," I told her.

Then I couldn't help myself. I embraced her in a deep, strong hug, and she give me a good squeeze herself with that one arm of hers.

When we separated, I had to dab at my own eyes, cussing the dust and the wind.

Softly, she said, "Your voice has changed, Micah."

"It's been a hell of a bad week," I said.

The fingers unfolded and she slapped my face, which got the tooth Sean Fenn had loosened to aching and the gums bleeding again. Sternly, she chastised me. "Watch your mouth, Señor Bishop. Ten Our Fathers—*muy pronto.*"

What, fifteen, sixteen years had passed, but she moved real quick, still packed a wallop, and didn't need no eyes to find my face.

"How long has it been, my child?" She was all quiet and kind, again.

I told her. She sighed. "It feels much longer."

"I feel older," I said, which weren't no lie. Felt about as old as she was.

She fell silent, thinking back all those years. After a long moment, she said. "If my memory has not failed me, you were not confirmed before you . . ." She had to pause again, thinking of the right word. "Before you . . ."

"Ran away."

"Sí. That is what you did." Her head shook, but I thought she was smiling.

"When was your last confession?"

I smiled back at her, though she couldn't see

me. "Rocío," I said. "I wasn't confirmed. Remember? I ain't Catholic. I'm pagan."

The fist connected again. "Don't be disrespectful, Señor Bishop. I am *Sister* Rocío."

"Yes, ma'am." I tested my jaw.

"You say you have not been to confession?"

"No, ma'am, I haven't."

"You have not repented? You are still as wild and as wicked as you were when you first arrived at the orphanage?"

"Probably even wilder."

"So you are telling me, Sister Rocío, a dying woman who will not live to see many more sunrises, you are telling me that we shall not walk the Streets of Gold together?"

I wet my lips, hated to answer, but I didn't want to get knocked in the jaw again.

"Probably not, Sister."

Another long, sad pause.

So long, it got to be awkward, so I broke it by saying, "I'm sorry."

Her head bobbed. "It is probably for the better, my son. Who would want to be in Heaven with evildoers and whoremongers and gamblers and wicked, wicked men like you?"

I waited. The fist didn't strike.

At last, a grin made its way through the pits and crevasses of her deeply browned face. "It is a joke, Micah." She patted my arm. "You may laugh."

As I obliged her, she squeezed my arm.

"My son, you are nothing more than bones. Do you have the carcinoma as the doctors say I have?"

"I hope to hell—" I took a deep breath, rethought, and said, "I don't think so, Sister Rocío."

"You are not ill?"

I shrugged, considered the bullet wound across my side, the stitches in my forehead, the rawness of my left calf and ankle, the bruises and scrapes and aches throughout the rest of my person. "Well . . . I've felt better, but I ain't sick or nothing."

Those fingers turned into a wheelwright's vise, digging into my arm. "Must I correct your grammar?" Again, she fired off something toward God and Mary and the Holy Ghost in Spanish. "*¡Ay, caramba!* English is my second language, and I speak it better than this wayfarer."

"I'm not sick," I corrected myself so blood might flow to my hand and fingers once more. "Not sick or nothing."

"Or *anything*."

"I'm not sick or anything."

"And Geneviève." She turned, must have felt Geneviève's presence. Her hand left my arm—to my joy—and reached toward the Sister who wasn't a Sister. "Sister Geneviève, you are here as well?"

Geneviève took the old woman's hand in both of hers, squeezing. "I am here, Sister Rocío." She sounded perfect French again.

"My new friend . . ." Rocío patted Geneviève's arm, causing the pretty young fraud to bite her lips because of all those bruises and scrapes on her person. But you couldn't fault the blind nun none, since she couldn't see how she was hurting Geneviève. And you had to respect that pretty girl, because she didn't let Rocío know no better.

"You found the prodigal son," the old woman said. "I am much happy."

"I am happy I found him, too." Geneviève was looking at me when she said it.

"He is everything I told you he was?" Rocío asked.

Geneviève's smile seemed genuine. "Everything and more."

That was all Sean Fenn could take. "Sister Rocío, I have brought Micah Bishop to you. You want to find the gold, and you say he's the only one who can do that. Well, he's here. You said we should start our journey here."

"To pay our respects to the dead," the nun said solemnly. "To pray for God's forgiveness."

"Well," Fenn said. "We probably should get a move on."

The wind started picking up, and I checked the sky, but didn't see no rain clouds.

"Sister Rocío," I said gently, putting my hand on

her shoulder, giving it a nice squeeze. "You told these people that I could find the gold. But . . . well . . . I don't know anything about this."

"Yes, my child, you do," she said, and for a moment there, I thought she could see, blind as she was, I thought she could see not only me, but right through me. "And, yet, you don't." She turned toward Fenn's voice, and told him, "It is not the gold I seek, but you may have what you find."

She begun her story.

Chapter Twenty-six

She started at the beginning, which is where most stories begin, even though we knowed—or thought we knowed—all about how the gold was found in Mora, how it got to Gran Quivira, where it got rediscovered in 1848. Sister Rocío repeated all that, but I knowed a lot better than to interrupt her.

On the other hand, Sean Fenn didn't.

"We know all that!" he snapped. "Where the hell's the fornicating gold today?" Actually, that ain't exactly what he said. He used another word, one that caused the rest of us who'd gathered around Sister Rocío to hear her story to cringe. I mean, even nuns and priests swore a right healthy amount, but there's some words that you ain't supposed to say in polite society.

She just stopped, pursed her lips, and turned toward Fenn's voice. "Young man"—she spoke to him like she would a child—"using profanity simply shows one's ignorance. If you'd care to hear my story, I will tell it in my own way. If not, you may leave and go fornicate yourself."

Nobody interrupted the old nun after that.

After about an hour and a half, she reached the part just before Geneviève had stopped when she was telling me about the gold and all. That's when the giant farmer from the Pecos River and that bastard of a horse trader from Anton Chico had interrupted our evening, and started us both on the road to Hell.

Started us both on the road to Hell.

That ain't bad. If I had more time at this writing thing, I might could find me a job writing for the *Illustrated Police News*. I always loved to look at them pictures.

Anyway, Rocío and the gent from the Smithsonian had found the bodies of all them poor dead Indians and the ingots. They had sent for supplies, fetching burros and grub from Socorro. They brung back something else, a fact Geneviève had left out or forgotten.

The guide named Cortez returned with five nuns.

According to Sister Rocío this is what happened next.

"Why on earth did you bring these women with you?" asked the gent from the Smithsonian Institution, who called hisself Doctor Erskine Primrose IV, all haughty and offended.

"They are bound for the mission at San Elizario," Cortez told him.

That is right near El Paso. I know, on account that there's a jail there that I've spent some time in. It wasn't a bad place to be because it's right close to the mission. Those bells sounded mighty pretty, but not as pretty as when the choir or congregation started singing. It was some of the best music I've ever heard whilst in jail. Almost as pretty as that deputy sheriff who clawed the banjo so fine in Ouray, Colorado.

"That is the way we planned to travel, is it not so?" Cortez pointed out.

Dr. Primrose said, "Yes, but—"

"But," Cortez said. He was pretty good at making plans.

Well, maybe not that good, since he was soon to be dead, but there wasn't nothing wrong with his plans.

"But," Cortez said, "if we are merely transporting five nuns, six including Sister Rocío, who would think to rob us for a fortune in gold?"

Primrose grinned. He liked Cortez's thinking, which is how come he'd be dead, too, within a matter of days.

Sighing, Sister Rocío stopped her telling of the story to inform us, "I should have spoken out. I should have warned the five young nuns that they should have stayed in Socorro, followed El Camino Real to El Paso." Her head dropped, and she crossed herself and fell to silent prayer.

Fenn got impatient, waiting for her to talk some more, but he didn't say nothing. He just tossed another piece of wood on the fire The Pockmarked Man had started.

Back to the Sister's story.

Right before they lit a shuck for El Paso, a norther blew in, dropping the temperature into the teens. It was a veritable blue norther—wet, mean, ugly.

They bundled up, the nuns sang songs, and they journeyed south through the Pinatosa, where there ain't nothing to block the wind. By the time they reached the Malpais on the edge of the Valley of Fire, ice covered them badlands.

That was where the bandits hit.

"Because one cannot keep such fortune a secret," Rocío said to us. "One of the guides must have let a friend know."

Once Rocío, Primrose, Cortez, them nuns and all was pinned down, bandits sent word that they would let everyone go if they left the gold. Nobody believed them. Cortez asked if they would at least spare the lives of the six nuns. The bandits said they would consider it, which meant, no. Primrose asked if they would spare him. Rocío slammed her fist into the back of his head; she had two good hands back in them days.

They didn't give up, and everybody tried to prepare for the long night ahead of 'em.

Night turned even more bitter. A priest had already been killed with a bullet through his temple, and two burros were lying in the ice, frozen stiff, shot full of holes. The nuns prayed for deliverance. Sister Rocío decided that the gold should go to the Indians, not to the Mexicans, not to the Smithsonian, but especially not to bandits. The menfolk decided to stay behind, sacrifice themselves, and send the nuns and the gold south with one man. Cortez drew the short straw, which meant he'd leave with the nuns—and the gold.

All of the men built up a big fire that night, made a show of their camp, then, with the wind howling and clouds blacking out the moon, Cortez and Rocío led the five other nuns, the burros, and the gold into the Valley of Fire.

A country full of lava rocks ain't easy to cross in daylight. But in bitter cold? With ice coating the ground? Being pursued by bandits with murderous intent?

It was a miracle they made it as far as they'd done.

As dawn broke, Sister Rocío couldn't feel her fingers no more. Hurt so bad, she couldn't even rub her rosary.

Dawn brung light, but no heat. A freezing fog swept across the rugged trail, coating giant lava boulders, turning the grass—what little there was—into fingers of icicles. Even the packs, the harness, the hides of her burro got frosted. She figured the other nuns and their burros ahead of her was suffering just as bad.

That's a crazy thing. Freezing fog. You wouldn't expect to find it in country like this, but it happened. Once, Big Tim Pruett and I was in eastern Colorado, and the fog got so thick, the two of us was lost for a whole day. It wasn't freezing, of course, on account that it was early August, but I imagine it could've been that White Death—that's what the Indians called freezing fog—had we been out in February.

Sister Rocío flexed her fingers, then began rubbing them furiously against her woolen habit. That, too, was coated with ice. So was a bandanna she'd tried to turn into a muffler.

Ahead of her, a burro snorted. She could barely see it through the thick fog.

Her own burro shook its head, sending particles of ice everywhere. At least they was moving, Rocío thought. Stop, and they'd all die.

As if God heard her thoughts, Cortez called out something far ahead of her in that killing fog. The mules stopped.

Instantly, she felt colder.

She removed the bandanna just long enough to shake out the ice, formed on the outside by the fog and on the inside by her freezing breath. After she had rubbed her cheeks, Sister Rocío checked her fingertips. No frostbite. Not yet.

It hurt to breathe. She had no idea how cold it was. Ten below zero? Colder?

Hard to believe it could get that cold in Hades.

I watched Sister Rocío flex her fingers as if she was still on that burro in the freezing fog. She took a deep breath, rubbed her cheeks, and looked down at the fingertips on her one hand. This here is more of her story.

"Sister Rocío." Out of the fog, Cortez appeared. Ice coated his clothes, his mustache and beard. Speaking in Spanish, he asked if she was all right.

Somehow, her fingers fashioned a knot on the bandanna, and she pulled it over her throbbing nose. "Sí," she answered. Even that hurt.

"We should not be here," Cortez said. "This is the errand of a fool."

Cold had muddled his memory, too, I reckon. It was his idea.

"How much farther?" she asked. Her teeth ached.

"*¡Qué chinga!*" Cortez railed. "Forgive me, Sister. I do not even know. In this whiteness, I am not even sure where we are."

Sister Rocío pointed south. Ahead of her, the nuns begun singing, anything to stay warmer, but they stopped when they heard a muffled report, echoing off the lava, the canyons, the mountains off to the east. Another shot. Then a cannonade, sounding like rolling thunder in the distance.

Sister Rocío lifted her head, her fingers brushing against her rosary again, then her crucifix, and she turned to look down the trail toward the sound of the gunshots.

"Those pigs!" Cortez spat. "They have resumed their assault." He fell silent again, listening.

"Sí." Again, Rocío made the sign of the cross.

"Primrose was a fool," Cortez said, "but the priests, my amigos, they were good men."

Cortez got mighty forgetful. Primrose had stayed behind, dying for them freezing nuns.

"God will welcome them all with open arms."

Behind Rocío, burros had their whiskers frozen, their ears coated white, and their breath like smoke. Icicles hung from their harnesses and packs, too. The animals looked as miserable, as near death, as Rocío imagined that she must appear.

Cortez spat at his feet. The saliva froze before it reached the icy ground.

"We must hurry," Rocío told him. "Before they come after us. After the gold."

"I should gladly let them have the gold. And you, as well, Sister. They might let me live."

Their eyes held. She said nothing.

Cortez grinned. "That much gold. It is enough to tempt even a priest. Or a nun. Even six nuns."

"You must do what your heart tells you to do."

"*¡Maldita sea!*" Cortez shook his head, checking the rope, harnesses, and packs as he made his way forward, speaking to the young nuns.

The rope connecting her mule to the one in front of her grew taut, and the leather creaked, icicles broke, and they was moving again. She looked behind her at the miserable beasts following. Beyond that was just the fog's icy whiteness. Wasn't no gunfire no more.

Turning to look ahead, she prayed. Not for herself. Not for Cortez. Not for the gold, or for her mission. She prayed for the souls of Primrose and them others, all dead. Or about to be murdered. She prayed for the dead Indians them Spaniards had murdered at Gran Quivira.

Despite the rising sun, the White Death, that freezing fog, showed no signs of burning off. The mule train followed the trail, or what might pass for a trail. Soon, it turned even colder. Every breath burned her nostrils, her throat, her lungs. She shoved her aching fingers inside the coarse wool habit.

They climbed a rocky slope higher. The trail got narrower, and she glanced down the steep side. Frozen rocks stretched down. It looked like they was in the ocean way up north, and the sea was filled with icebergs.

Breathing that cold air almost doubled her over in agony.

Ahead of her, Cortez swore bitterly. Behind her, a burro snorted.

Slowly, painfully, she brought numb fingers toward her face, to work on the knot to her bandanna. Ice crumpled as the cloth loosened. Somehow, she managed to shake it as the burros plodded along.

A shadow in the fog moved wildly, toppling over the edge of the trail, landing on the jagged slope. A nun's piercing cry followed. Almost immediately, another shadow fell over the edge. Then one from behind. And another.

More cries.

"Sister Rocío!"

She could just hear Cortez's voice over screaming burros and young nuns.

"Jump, Sister. Jump!"

Her own burro was braying, and suddenly she could see, could understand.

Slipping on a patch of ice, a burro had plummeted over the edge. Roped together, it had pulled the animal ahead of it over, and the one behind it, as well. Like dominos, one after another, the burros, their packs, their riders, were jerked into the abyss, into eternity.

Her own mount, braying and trying to use its hoofs as brakes, was being pulled over the edge.

Sister Rocío sucked in a deep breath. She didn't hear Cortez no more, heard only screams —her own—and an avalanche of lava rocks below. Her burro was yanked into the carnage, and she barely cleared the harness.

But she was too late.

She found herself in frigid air, as if frozen in time, then saw the white rocks rush up to greet her, felt the sharp stones slam into her side and legs and arms, and she was tumbling, rolling, screaming, bouncing, swallowing icy dust, while more burros got jerked and crushed.

She molded into the avalanche of harnesses, and ropes, and rocks, and burros alive and dead and dying, and packs, and a crucifix, and a rosary, and the hood of her habit.

Rolling downhill, sliding, tumbling out of the White Death.

And into Hell itself.

Chapter Twenty-seven

"I do not know how long I lay there, unconscious," Rocío told us. "Hours perhaps. *¿Quién sabe?* When my eyes opened, Cortez was gone. I was alone. The other young Sisters . . ." She crossed herself and bowed her head.

"All of them?" Geneviève asked softly. "Dead?"

"Sí. So young. So innocent." Rocío's gnarled finger rose to brush a tear before it fell into one of the crevasses of her ancient face."

"The mules?" Fenn asked. "They were dead, too?"

"Not mules, my son," Sister Rocío corrected. "Burros. But, sí, they had died, too. Except one, whose front legs were broken. He was braying in terrible pain and would die before nightfall."

"Cortez?" That was what interested Fenn right then. "How many mules did he manage to save? How many didn't fall into that gorge?"

"Only three. I did not see this, for I was busy falling and being knocked unconscious, but it is my belief that our guide managed to slice the rope that bound our burros together at the last second, thus saving the three with which he fled."

"He didn't try to save you?" Geneviève asked angrily. "He didn't even check on you or the others? He just left?"

"Likely," Rocío answered, "he thought we were

all dead, or soon would be, and he had much fear. He thought the banditos would come soon."

"Three burros." Fenn done some ciphering hisself, trying to figure out how much weight they could've taken in gold.

Rocío grinned because she knowed exactly what he was doing. "One of the burros carried water," she told him. "Not gold. Another carried food. Only one burro was loaded with the weight of the devil."

Fenn spit. It sizzled in the fire. "You expect me to believe that this Cortez just left all that gold down there?"

"It was freezing. It was terribly windy. And there were two dozen banditos behind us. I think it was prudent for him to do as he did, but he should have kept going south for El Paso. Alas, he was found frozen to death in the Capitan Mountains. He must have turned east, unsure of where he should go. Perhaps he was lost. It was very white, very foggy, terribly cold."

"What about the gold with him?"

She laughed. "I have always imagined this burro, wandering around in the Capitan Mountains, chewing on grass in the spring, drinking from the bubbling rivers, just packing ingots with him, oblivious to the fortune he carried. It is a good vision, is it not?"

"It is very good." Geneviève reached over to pat Sister Rocío's thigh.

The Pockmarked Man refilled everybody's coffee cups. Sean Fenn went back to ciphering how much gold was left behind. Corbin brought up the question about those two dozen banditos. "You were the only one left alive—"

"Except for the poor burro with the two broken legs," Sister Rocío interrupted him with a correction.

Smiling, nodding, Corbin said, "Except for the poor burro with the two broken legs."

"But he was dead soon," Rocío said, and crossed herself.

"Yes. I'm sure he was." Corbin sipped some coffee. "But there were bandits coming your way. And they would find you, the dead mules, the dead nuns."

"That is what I thought," Rocío said. "It is what I feared."

"So you moved the gold." Fenn had figured it all out.

Rocío let a sly grin crease her face.

"All of it?" The Pockmarked Man didn't seem to believe it. I mean, he was looking at Rocío as a seventy-three-year-old blind woman, forgetting that this had happened back in 1848.

"One finds strength to do what others find impossible," she said. "The Blessed Mother guided me.

"I dragged the bodies of my young, beautiful, gold-hearted nuns away from the rocks. I blessed them. I kissed their foreheads. Many ingots had fallen out of their packs. All I needed to do was pick them up, follow the canyon—"

"Over lava rocks?" Fenn asked.

"No. The lava had not flowed here. That is why there was a canyon. This was earth, though covered in great sheets of ice. I looked up. I saw Mount Ararat."

"Ararat?" Fenn asked, interested again. "Where's that?"

Even I remembered that much from all them Bible readings and talks and sermons at the orphanage. "In the Old Testament," I told him.

"Sí," Rocío said. "I saw the Ark. It was my beacon. I went down a canyon, then another. I found what passed for a cave. The cave, of course, was in the great bed of lava. The ingots could be placed there, into the darkness. I went back to the burros and the packs and those poor, dead, pitiful nuns. It was very sad."

"Yeah," Fenn said, who wasn't grieving none of nuns dead and gone for thirty-eight years. "That had to take you a good long time."

"*Es verdad.* I worked well into darkness. By then it was very cold. By then my fingers had . . . how is it said?"

"Frostbite," I said.

"Sí."

"But what about the bandits?" Fenn asked.

With a shrug, Rocío said, "Perhaps they never

showed up. Anyway, I never saw them. Poor Cortez. Had he not fled when we were all pulled down from the trail, he could have helped me bury all the gold, and he could have returned to find it and dig it up and become very wealthy instead of very dead in the Capitan Mountains."

"So once you got the last of the ingots in that cave," Fenn said, "what happened next?"

"I had to seal the cave's entrance. I did not think of it as burying a treasure, but sealing a tomb. Keeping those dear, grand nuns away from vultures, ravens, and coyotes."

"Lava rocks are heavy," Fenn pointed out.

"Not as heavy as gold. One was loose. I thought if I could pull it down, other stones would follow, and, if such was God's will, return at some point. Find the nuns. Bring them home. They deserve a fitting burial. That is my wish now."

"After forty years?" Fenn asked, getting all snide again.

"Thirty-eight," Rocío corrected.

"We'll come back to that point," Fenn said. "You sealed the cave with the gold and dead nuns in it."

"And almost myself."

She kept talking, this time without interruption for a long, long while. This here is more of what she told us.

The freezing fog was gone, but so was the sun, and no moon shone. With a bent but sharp machete from one of the burro's packs, Sister Rocío worked on the loose boulder, and finally, it gave way. She tried to get out of the path, but the black and red rocks came pounding after her. She slipped on a patch of ice and landed between the brutal rocks. A boulder fell on her arm, pinning her there. A blinding flash of pain, bitter cold, and then she fell into blessed unconsciousness again.

When she awakened, she had to claw her way out of nine inches of snow. Dawn had broke, and it wasn't so cold no more, but still freezing. Her arm remained pinned beneath a boulder. She couldn't move.

By all rights, she should have been dead already, but, in case you ain't figured it out for yourselves, Sister Rocío was a tough old bird, even back when she was thirty-five. But she couldn't survive much longer. Another night would drop them temperatures, and she knowed she'd freeze to death. Wouldn't be no snow to bury herself in, to keep herself warm enough to live. And them bandits . . . she still figured they'd come along and finish her off.

But they didn't. Likely, they'd turned back when the freezing fog hit, went back to Gran Quivira, and then back to Socorro or wherever men of their ilk hid out in 1848.

By noon, she knowed what she had to do.

"Good God!" Corbin gasped. That was the first interruption.

"Sí," Sister Rocío said. "God is good."

"How did you do it?" Geneviève asked.

Sean Fenn was too dumb to figure out what it was that Sister Rocío knowed she had to do.

"The machete was nearby. God's mercy is infinite."

"But"—The Pockmarked Man's lip trembled —"you just couldn't hack it off."

"Not the way I was pinned," Rocío said.

"Then . . . how?" But it wasn't that I really wanted to know.

"I bent my forearm backward, away from the rock. I screamed, of course. Never had I endured such agony, and never had I imagined that I possessed the stomach, the ability to afflict such pain on myself. I just kept bending my arm, yelling, crying, wishing I were dead, until the bone cracked."

I slid down a bit. Poured my coffee onto the ground. Along about that time, my stomach didn't feel too good.

"So once you broke that bone, you used the machete to cut off your arm." Fenn shaken his head and let out a part-sigh, part-laugh.

"It was not so simple," Rocío said. "It took a good two hours before I had the strength to move. I cupped some of the melting snow—melting because the sun was out, not because it was no longer freezing—and I drank some. Drank more. Wiped my brow, which was heavy with sweat that did not freeze. And then, after I had prayed and pleaded for strength—"

"You sawed off your own arm," Fenn finished for her.

But he was a damned fool.

"Feel your arm, young man," Rocío said, and then waited patiently for Fenn to feel his arm, which, of course, he wasn't about to do.

"Do you feel the two bones in your forearm? I had broken one. I had to break the second bone, too."

Corbin twisted the ends of his mustache. "The ulna and the radius." That man was full of wonders.

"The names I do not know. So again, I screamed and prayed and begged and bent back my arm. This one was more painful. This time, I knew just how badly breaking a bone in my arm hurt. It took me three times as long before the bone snapped, and I blacked out."

I was rubbing my arm. So was Geneviève. So was Benigno. The Pockmarked Man just stared with his mouth agape. Corbin tucked in his neck and bent his head down real low. I didn't care to see what Fenn was doing.

"Then I picked up the machete."

We sat silent for a long while before Rocío resumed talking.

"After I cut off my arm, I made a tourniquet, began walking, down the path, climbing over the lava, crossing the Malpais. It snowed again, turning the world white.

"The Mexican War had ended. On the next day, a patrol of *soldados norteamericanos* happened upon me. A surgeon was with them."

"You must have been delighted to see them," Geneviève said.

Rocío's head shook. "I mentioned that it had snowed again, did I not? By the time the *soldados* found me, I saw nothing. The snow had blinded me. I have not seen anything but blackness since."

We studied on that some.

"But the surgeon with the *norteamericanos* saved me. He removed more of my arm, and took me back to Santa Fe. It became my home. For years, I helped the priests, the bishops, the people in need. I tried to forget what had happened in that terrible valley of snow and ice and rocks and death."

Again, we got silent. Geneviève handed Sister Rocío another cup of coffee. "And you joined the Sisters of Charity?"

"Not until they arrived in Santa Fe after the War of the Rebellion was over in the east." The old nun smiled. "But yes, the Sisters of Charity gave me a new purpose. As they have given you, my new friend."

Them words hurt Geneviève. Her face paled,

her lips trembled, and she like to have busted out in tears.

"But you went back to being a nun," Fenn was saying, sarcastic, inconsiderate as hell. "Living the good life. Not thinking about that gold for close to forty years."

"Oh, no, my son. I thought of it daily. I waited until the right person came into my life, a person strong and wild and wily enough to find that gold."

Everybody, even that blind old nun, faced me.

"Micah Bishop became my eyes when he was fourteen years old."

Chapter Twenty-eight

"Do you remember Mount Ararat?" Sister Rocío asked.

"Maybe." I liked things a whole lot better when not everybody was paying me all this mind.

"And the Temptation in the Wilderness?"

"Uh . . . was that Luke?"

The hand walloped me. "Matthew," she snapped. "Four. One through eleven."

"Right. I knowed that."

"He is my eyes," Sister Rocío said proudly. "I knew that when he arrived at the orphanage. You see, he was found wandering in the Valley of Fire, a poor waif in rags. An Army patrol found him, brought him to the railroad, and a kind seamstress in Socorro sent him by train to Santa Fe, to the Sisters of Charity. You remember all that, don't you, my son?"

Yeah, and I even knowed why I'd been wandering in them lava rocks. I was hiding from the law and the storekeeper in White Oaks who'd gotten tired of me stealing his bread and apples and assorted sundries.

The nun kept on talking, bragging about me. Made me feel kinda proud.

"I knew he would grow up to be wild and stubborn and independent, that he would possess courage and heart, that he could find the resting place of those poor nuns. He could bring them back to be buried as they should. He could deliver the gold to the Indians, the poor slaves who deserve it."

Well, everybody was staring at me by that time, and I didn't feel too popular. I wanted to sneak into a hole and stay there for about two hundred and sixty-three years.

"But he ran off when he was sixteen." Sean Fenn had figured things out. "Is that wild and stubborn and independent enough for you, Sister? Is that how he showed his heart and courage?"

"God's will be done," Rocío said. "He returned."

"Yeah." Fenn slapped his knee. "He returned to Las Vegas. To kill a guy in a saloon brawl. To get sentenced to hang."

"But God intervened."

"I intervened." Fenn was standing now. "I'm God."

"You will not speak with such sacrilege," Rocío told him.

But Fenn wasn't listening. "So where's the gold?" he demanded. He wasn't talking to the nun no more. He stared right at me, and I knowed I was in for a sound thrashing.

"I don't rightly know," I said, and that was honest.

Fenn pulled his Colt.

"He doesn't know that he knows," Rocío said, "but he knows. I know he knows. For he has the Cross of Lorraine."

Here's the point where things got ticklish, and my heart started beating and I knowed I was sweating. Usually, I can run a pretty fair bluff, better than fair if you want to know the God's honest truth, but I was having a bad day. Rocío might have thought she knowed some things that I knowed, but what I really knowed was right then and there, Geneviève Tremblay held my life in her hands.

There I was, betting on a woman who wasn't a nun, and who had been intimate with the biggest son of a bitch I'd ever knowed. There was a silver cross beneath her torn green and white checked shirt that once belonged to a dead man, and beneath a real fancy chemise that probably had belonged to a Mexican woman who'd been killed and scalped because south of the border her hair could pass for an Apache's.

"The Cross of Lorraine?" Corbin said.

"Lorraine was the name of one of the nuns killed in the Valley of Fire, in the Malpais," Rocío said. "I took the cross from her body and kept it for years. It was a Cross of Lorraine. Are you familiar with that style, young man?"

"Well . . ." Corbin wasn't that educated.

"It's French," Geneviève said, and everybody was looking at her. Everybody but me, because I knowed better, having played cards long enough to know you never tip your hand. My right hand, though, was beginning to inch down my left leg just in case everything I figured was dead wrong.

"The Knights Templar used it in the Crusades, and the French Jesuits brought it to America." Yes, by grab, Geneviève did know a right tidy amount when it come to French crosses and all. "It is a two-barred cross. Two bars on the top. The Catholics used one version of the Cross of Lorraine to represent the archbishop."

Fenn chuckled. "You really did almost become a nun, didn't you, Gen?"

I wet my lips, and then Fenn swore, and leaped off that rocky bench. "Wait a minute!" he snapped, remembering as I figured he would, and then he charged to me, and before I could straighten or get to that boot, he jerked me to my feet, shoved me against the rock wall, and yelled. "I know that damned cross."

He ripped my shirt, just tore the front all the way in two, but the only things he seen was a bandage of a myrtle green stocking, some sunburn around and below the collar, some scars, and hair and dirt. All I'd really done was wash my face and shave. I wouldn't have called myself presentable.

"Where is it?"

Before I could answer, Fenn loosened another tooth with a mean backhand, and I was laying on the ground.

Sister Rocío was pleading, "What is going on? What is happening? What is that young man doing to my Micah?" But nobody was answering her on account they was all preoccupied watching me get the bitter hell beat out of me . . . again.

"Where is it?" Fenn demanded.

"I ain't got it no more!" I hoped he could hear me, 'cause I'd covered my head and mouth with my folded arms, praying that he wouldn't punch me or kick me no more.

Naturally, he booted me in my stomach. I rolled over and vomited.

"Liar!" he yelled. "You had that cross when we rode into Deming five years ago. You said you'd never get rid of it. Said it brought you luck. Where the hell is it?" He bent over, lifted me up.

Sister Rocío kept right on wailing, begging, pleading for mercy, but Sean Fenn was riled, and he had never listened to nothing when his dander was up. Again, he shoved me against the wall, and weren't no way I could reach my bum leg.

The plan I'd thunk up was turning out about as bad as Cortez's had done thirty-eight years earlier.

"Where is it?"

"It's out in the desert, most likely," I said.

He swore, grabbed a handful of hair, slammed me against the wall. That opened the cut in my forehead and gave me a matching one on the back of my skull.

"Where is it?" Fenn roared again.

Sister Rocío was speaking in tongue, or it might have just been Latin. Corbin was considering intervening. Benigno and The Pockmarked Man wasn't doing nothing. I was hurting, and Fenn was screaming. Then Geneviève was yelling for Fenn to stop, to leave me alone, that I was the only chance they had at finding that gold.

Finally, I heard her say, "He doesn't have that cross, Sean!"

Fenn stopped kicking me and punching me, while Sister Rocío kept on praying in Latin. Through blurred vision, I seemed to see Geneviève standing there—an angel or devil, I wasn't certain—but I knowed her next words would either leave me dead or not. I figured they'd leave me dead.

She said, "He must have lost it in the desert."

I swear, if I hadn't been gasping for breath and

crying with pain, I might have breathed a sigh of relief. She hadn't betrayed me.

Well, not yet.

"You"—Fenn waited till his heart slowed down a mite—"saw it?"

Her head bobbed.

"Of course, you did," Fenn said, all jealous, all bitter and ugly again.

But Geneviève told him, "Sean. He had it when we were on the train, and in the jail. Remember?"

Fenn likely didn't remember none of that, but he nodded as if he did. He swore, cussed his luck and his stupidity. "We should have just killed the son of a bitch and grabbed the cross."

"We didn't know about the cross then," she reminded him.

"You're sure he had it? Do you know when he lost it?"

"I'm sure he had it when we were crossing that furnace. But it was just extra weight, Sean."

She must have been listening to me, or maybe I'd said something about such things to her. Who the hell knew?

"We were walking, and fighting to stay alive. It's out there." She gestured off to the north and east. "Lost. Unless you want to go find it."

"Find it?" He cussed hisself again. "Out there? Fat chance."

"Then leave him alone," Geneviève said. "He's the only chance we have of finding those ingots."

That stopped Rocío from talking Latin. She raised her head, lowered her one arm, and said, "He is my eyes. He knows."

I pushed my way past Fenn, made it to Sister Rocío, helped her up, guided her back to where she'd been sitting.

"What happened to the cross, my child?" she asked.

I hated lying to her, but figured she, Mary, Jesus, and God would understand. "Guess I just tossed it off while crossing the desert."

She popped me hard on the top of my head with her knuckles. "Imbecíl!"

Corbin snorted, but nobody else found it funny, not with that much gold at stake.

"What's so important about the cross?" Fenn asked.

"It was a map to the graves of those poor nuns," she said.

"Wasn't no map," I told her. "Just a bunch of words. A poem or something." "

Them knuckles popped me good again.

"Jar his memory, Sister!" Corbin said, and I think he was joking, but that got Fenn asking about the cross, the poem, the words, and the map on that cross of Lorraine.

"If he can remember what was engraved on the back of the cross, we will find those poor nuns," Rocío said. "We will return them to be buried in hallowed ground."

About here is where I figured Geneviève would show her greed, because that was a hell of a lot of gold. I expected that she'd show Fenn that cross I'd give her, and her and Fenn would ride off and live happily ever after, richer than likely the entire population of New Mexico Territory combined, and I'd be feeding the ravens and turkey buzzards and coyotes that seemed to be following me around that summer.

But what Geneviève said was "He is Sister Rocío's eyes. We need him. He's our only chance. He can remember."

Like a million banshees, the wind wailed. Fenn rubbed his chin, then turned on his heel and stormed away, disappearing behind one of the walls. He yelled to The Pockmarked Man, "Tie him up. Tight. If he gets loose, you die. We leave for the Valley of Fire at first light."

Chapter Twenty-nine

That night, the wind moaned like the demons of all them murdered Indians buried inside those walls. The moon had come full, making them rocky walls glow like the largest tombstones ever put up over a bunch of graves. I don't get scared that easily, but after getting the bitter hell beat out of me, getting tied up with rawhide cords so tight they bit into my wrists, flung around like a sack of wheat, and dumped in some hole in the ground, well, my nerves wasn't in the best of shape.

Add to that the fact that my life wasn't worth squat, and my ingenious plan had turned into a complete failure—like most of my plans—well, it's no wonder that I yelled, "Jesus Christ!" when the ha'nt appeared.

It appeared on the rocky wall, a white apparition, ghostly hair blowing in the wind, and then another shadow—dark and devious and cold like old Beelzebub hisself—stood right beside it. The white ghost turned and whispered to the dark ghost, and then started to climb down onto its hands and knees, and lowered itself into the pit. The dark ghost just stood there in its shadowy form. The white ghost dropped the last few inches, and I heard the knee joints crack. It said, "Oomph," and fell on its backside, and then it yelled, "Ouch!" sounding just like a woman who'd just landed her buttocks on a sharp rock.

When the ha'nt slowly rose, rubbing its hindquarters, and started for me, I got the idea that it wasn't no ghost at all. "Geneviève?" I blinked.

The ha'nt said, "Shhhhhhhhhh!" It knelt beside me and kissed my cheek. "Don't talk."

But I didn't listen. Hell, that wind was wailing so loud, even the Devil couldn't hear what anyone said in a hole in the ground at Gran Quivira.

"Geneviève," I told her, "get out of here. If

Sean Fenn finds you here, as temperamental as he gets, he's liable to kill you."

"We're leaving." She unfolded the pocket-knife that I'd given Fenn to make him feel better when he hadn't found no pistol or other armaments on my person.

I started to protest, but she was leaning over my body, slicing—more like sawing—through the cords that bound my wrist because by that time the blade had gotten fairly dull. When I was free, before I could start rubbing my wrists to get the blood flowing again, she leaned forward and kissed me full on the mouth.

Well, I forgot all about ghosts and the wind and Sean Fenn and my aching hands and wrists. I wrapped my arms around her and kissed her back, and might could have kept right on doing that for a good long while, but it was Geneviève who pulled away. "I know where the horses are."

She was close enough and the moon was high enough and shining enough light that I could see her face was kinda bewildered but lovely.

"You knew," she said.

"Knew what?" I asked.

"That I was with Fenn, that they'd be waiting, most likely, here. You knew that. How?"

I looked up at the second ghost, still a dark, unmoving shadow and wondered if my mind was playing tricks on me. Then my brain clicked for once. "Is that Sister Rocío up yonder?"

"Yes. How did you know? About me and . . . Fenn?"

I was up, moving toward the rock wall. "You confessed."

"What?"

I climbed up a mound of rubble, reached down, pulled her up behind me.

"After . . ." Well, I didn't need to remind her about The Voice and Vern. "You must've been out of your mind. You confessed. You said, 'Bless me, Father, for I have sinned. It has been seven years since my last confession.' "

Again, she was close enough that I could see just how soft brown her eyes was, could see the bags underneath 'em, and the scars, and the scabs, and the dirt and the bruises, and them streaks from all her tears. "I wondered about that, about why a nun would confess, or even if she did confess, why it'd been seven years since her last visit. But I didn't have to wonder too much longer because you confessed everything."

She blinked. Like she'd been struck dumb. I got a handhold above me, climbed up to the remnants of a rafter, hoped it would support my weight, and pulled myself up. I reached down, taken hold of Geneviève's hand, and helped her up beside me.

"Everything?" she asked.

I tried to get my balance, almost slipped once, but found a grip on another rock, and Geneviève was holding my leg, making sure I didn't topple over.

"I don't know what all you've done in seven years," I said, "but I got the gist of things."

Up to the top, I pulled myself, rocks tearing through my already ruined shirt, and scratching my ribs all to hell. Then I rolled over, leaned down, grabbed her outstretched hands, and pulled her all the way to the top.

"But you still came here," she said, trying to catch her breath. "Why on earth . . . ?"

"It seemed a good idea at the time," I said.

She was on her side, and staring right into my eyes, still trying to find some sanity, or secret genius, to my thinking. But she couldn't. Probably on account that none of it was there.

I reached over and put my hand on her cheek, and felt the tears. She grabbed my hand and held it against her. I wet my lips, and really, really, I wanted to kiss her, but I knowed that Sean Fenn wasn't no fool. If we was going to get out of there, it was the time to go.

Besides, there was that dark shadow again, standing behind Geneviève. I looked up to tell Sister Rocío that we'd be leaving, and that I hoped to hell she could ride, but I got kicked in the head. That kick snapped me back and up, and down I went back into the pit from whence I'd clumb up.

I hit with a thud, missing the sharp pointed rock that had likely bruised Geneviève's buttocks, but the ground was hard enough to knock the wind out of me. Another thump, and Geneviève shouted a cry of pain that I could hear real clear in the pit. Then the shadow was beside me, grunting as it hit.

When I could see enough from the moonlight, I spied the original shade, the dark ha'nt that had stood next to the white specter back when I thought Geneviève was a ghost. I knowed then that there was two dark ghosts around. One was Sister Rocío, who stood silently above. The other jerked me by my torn shirt and ripped off the whole left sleeve. He shoved me over Geneviève, who he'd also flung into the pit.

"I will take that cross," Benigno said. I could hear clearly in the pit. I heard the Mexican cock a revolver.

I was on my back, slowly pulling myself up, pulling my knees up to my chest, my back braced against the rocky side of the pit. "I don't have that damned cross."

"I am not talking to you, señor," Benigno said. "It is Señorita Tremblay I address. Hand it over."

"What?" she said.

"I am no fool like the gringos I ride with, señorita. I saw the cross underneath your chemise. I noticed it because I was staring at your *pechos*, and your shirt was torn. I honestly do not see how Fenn or Corbin missed it, but they are fools. I will take the cross, señorita." He aimed the big Remington at Geneviève's chest.

The chance of the bullet getting deflected by that silver Cross of Lorraine then ricocheting and plugging the Mexican betwixt his eyes wasn't good at all.

"*¡Al demonio!* Give it to me. Muy pronto."

She sat up, pulled open her ripped shirt, grabbed the mescal beads, and there was that silver cross, reflecting moonlight.

Benigno smiled, crossing hisself with his hand that wasn't holding that .44.

"Forgive me, señorita. I hate that I must kill you both, but it is for the best. I will take the cross and find the gold. I will tell Fenn that—"

"Shouldn't you look at the directions, first, Benigno?" I asked him. He was dumber than me. "It ain't exactly—"

When he turned, I shot him right betwixt his eyes. Don't reckon he'd ever seen that Dean and Adams. Oh, he was fine at spotting a cross hanging below a beautiful young woman's breasts, but nobody had thought to look inside my left boot. I was glad to get that .436 out, as it had been tormenting my calf and ankle for so long. I was even gladder that it hadn't misfired, considering all the beatings I'd took. But I was most glad to see Benigno standing there for a good five or six seconds. The Remington slipped from his fingers—it didn't go off—then he just toppled over backward.

The muzzle flash hurt my eyes, and I rubbed

them furiously. I crawled to Geneviève, who wasn't where I thought she'd be on account she had run over to the dead Mexican. She was grabbing his Remington and pointing it up. For a second there, once I could see clear enough, I thought she was about to blow a hole through Sister Rocío, but she didn't. Then I knowed. She was waiting for Fenn or Corbin or The Pockmarked Man to come and investigate . . . and fill us with bullets.

But only the shade that was Sister Rocío stood there.

Geneviève turned toward me, and I rubbed my eyes some more, finally got to where I could see fair enough. Nobody had come. Waiting for us up top? To shoot our heads when they appeared over the earthen walls?

That's when I understood.

"The wind," I said. "They didn't hear nothing. Not with us in this pit. Not as loud as the wind's blowing."

She smiled, like luck was shining on us more than the moon, and done the damnedest thing. She lowered the Remington's hammer, and handed the gun to me.

That is when I realized Geneviève loved me. Why else would she give me a loaded revolver?

I shoved it into my waistband and went back to the rubble, I reclumb my way up to the top, helping Geneviève behind me, and when we was back at ground level, nobody killed us. All we saw was those eerie walls glowing from the moonlight. All we heard—and felt—was the violent wind.

She ran over to the shadow that was Sister Rocío, and I caught up with her. Rocío hadn't heard the gunshot that'd blowed out Benigno's brains, proving that my theory about the wind was right. She hadn't seen the gunshot because, well, she was blind.

"Which way?" I asked.

Geneviève pointed. She whispered something to Rocío, or maybe she shouted it, but I couldn't hear because of the roar. I could see because of the moon, and I followed the nun who wasn't, who led the nun who was. We ran one way then another and up over a wall, and down a hill, and there was Fenn's claybank, two pack mules, and the bay horse that Corbin had been riding.

They'd been picketed on a rope stretched between two piñons. They weren't in the mood for a moonlight ride in a violent wind, but the mule didn't seem to mind when Geneviève eased Sister Rocío into the saddle.

"You must hold on tight, Sister Rocío!" Geneviève shouted, and even I heard that. The old nun nodded. Geneviève swung into the claybank's saddle, which left me the bay, and I taken the lead rope to the other mule, the one with a pack saddle but no packs.

"Where are the other horses?" I yelled.

"What?" she shot back.

"The other horses?"

"I turned them loose! Ran them off. So Sean can't follow!"

Or couldn't. For a while. Till he caught up with them mounts. Then he'd come, and come a-killing.

He would know where we was going.

To the Valley of Fire.

Chapter Thirty

"Purgatory is suffering."

Them words Sister Rocío had spoke to me some fifteen, sixteen years earlier come back as we rode south. I figured all them levels of Purgatory lay between Gran Quivira and the Valley of Fire.

"We must empty Purgatory with our prayers," Sister Rocío said as dawn broke. We'd been riding forever, and my backside and thighs felt like we'd already covered six or seven levels of Purgatory. You recollect how many times I'd gotten my arse whupped, and how long I'd been in that desert without hardly a bite to eat, and how long it had been since I'd been horseback. We'll, I'd been doing some praying that night.

One prayer got answered. The wind had died down about 3 a.m.

We stopped in a forest of cholla, letting the horses and mules rest a bit while we drunk tepid water from canteens and chewed on jerky.

"How are you feeling, Sister?" I asked, handing the blind nun my canteen.

"Are we at the Valley of Fire?" she asked.

"Not yet," I answered. "Best drink some. You want to get off that mule, stretch your legs?"

She drank, and grinned. "I fear, my son, if I dismounted, I would not be able to climb back on again."

I taken the canteen she handed back to me and corked it. "I got a similar fear my ownself."

"Can you see Mount Ararat?" she asked. Once she'd let go of the canteen, she'd gripped the saddle horn like it was the Good Book. She wasn't used to riding, and we'd be riding hard.

All I could see was cholla and dead grass. Where we was, the land looked flat and ugly, but this country could fool a body. It resembled the plains of Kansas, except for them big cactus, but it wasn't flat. You'd come out of a dip, climb a bit, and then you'd see the Capitans down to the south and east, and off to the west, Cupadera Mesa.

"Not yet, Sister. You rest. Sure you don't want to stretch your legs, walk around?"

"I will stay where I am," she said. "For now."

After I'd put my canteen back around my horn, or, rather, the horn of the good stock saddle that belonged to Corbin, I went over to Geneviève, who was kneeling over a patch of dead grass, holding the reins to Fenn's claybank, and chewing on jerky.

"How is she doing?" Geneviève asked.

"Better than I am," I answered, but I wasn't looking at her no more. I was looking north. Didn't see no dust, and that was a good thing.

"What does she mean?" Geneviève asked, and I turned back to face her. "About Mount Ararat? What does that cross mean?"

I squatted beside her, then just sank down, and tried to massage my back. Twisted my neck one way and t'other, checked the myrtle green bandage, the bandanna over the stitched cut on my forehead, and the knot on the back of my skull.

"Do you know?" Geneviève asked. "Have you read—"

"About Mount Ararat? Yeah, I know. You do, too, if you'd tried to be a nun."

Wrong thing to say. Pain, bad memories, or some such filled her soulful eyes, and I regretted my choice. I hadn't been thinking. Before I could apologize, Geneviève recovered. She smiled, and it seemed like it was a warm, friendly smile, not that she was hiding nothing. "Yes, but I don't think Moses landed the Ark out here. Do you?"

"No, I don't. Not Moses, no how."

She looked at me for a moment, then laughed. It was a good laugh. Real girlish and full of innocence. Leaning back, she ran her fingers through her hair, shook her head, straightened, and smiled at me. "Moses. Good heavens. I must be tired. Noah. Noah didn't end his voyage here."

"May I see the cross?"

Without hesitation, she reached inside her torn shirt, pulled the necklace over her head, studied what was written on the back again, and handed me the two-barred piece of silver.

It was heavy, smooth on top despite all my travels, all the Purgatories I'd been through, and reflected the sun as I looked at it. Not a crucifix, but a cross. I turned it over and read the inscription.

> From the top of Ararat,
> We must climb down.
> Into the cañon
> Beside the King's crown,
> Where black meets the red.
> Into the second cañon,
> We walk with pain,
> Until we can touch
> The cross of Lorraine.
> Hallowed be the dead.

I read it. Read it again. Read it silently, then read it out loud to Geneviève. Twice. She just stared at me like I was speaking in tongues.

"Any ideas?" she asked.

I shrugged. "Benigno would have been mad as hell had he killed us and then read this." I pitched the cross back to her. "It ain't no map."

"You knew that. You wore that cross for sixteen years."

"Yeah." I looked south again like I expected the seas to lower, the dove to fly off, and Mount Ararat to rise up and hand over a fortune in old ingots to us.

"You never thought about what that poem was supposed to mean?"

"I'm still trying to figure out what a Hail Mary is supposed to mean."

She spoke sadly, eyes closed: "*Áve María, grátia pléna, Dóminus técum. Benedícta tu in muliéribus, et benedíctus frúctus véntris túi, Iésus. Sáncta María, Máter Déi, óra pro nóbis peccatóribus, nunc et in hóra mórtis nóstrae. Ámen.*"

The scary thing, is, once she started with the Sáncta María, I was saying it with her.

"You really did want to be a nun," I said after we'd crossed ourselves. It was a statement, not a question.

"Yes. Even now . . ." She shrugged, sighed, and sniffed.

"What happened?" I mean, now that I knowed she wasn't really a nun, I was kinda hopeful and all about me and her.

She was looking off to the south, too, and she

slowly stood, knees popping, joints aching, and pulled on that beaten all to hell top hat. "You know."

And, dumb as I was, I knowed. But I said, "I rode with him, Geneviève. Not for long, but it didn't take long to know all I needed to know about Sean Fenn. He's no good. I mean, there ain't one decent thing about him."

"I know that, too, Micah," she said, and she was walking to the claybank, and what she said next like to have broke my heart. "But we can't help who we fall in love with."

And there was the lovely young woman from Carbondale, Illinois, with brown hair and a slender body, brown eyes, and scars and pains that run deeper than all my aches. She was talking to Sister Rocío, finally patting the blind nun's thigh. She taken the lead rope to the mule and mounted Fenn's horse, sitting in the saddle and waiting for me to climb into the bay's saddle and pull the mule with the packsaddle and no packs.

It struck me then. I ain't never claimed to be no wizard, but I knowed then. Knowed all I needed to know. Geneviève Tremblay, twenty-five, twenty-six years old or thereabouts, was young and good and kind. She should have gone on to become a nun, and worked to help wild, uncontrollable waifs like I'd been all them years ago. She could have saved aplenty, and even now, she could have saved me. She hadn't, though. On account of a slick-talking sidewinder named Sean Fenn. She still loved him, or thought she did. I don't know, maybe there was still enough Sisters of Charity in her to think she could change that son of a bitch, could save his soul, could make him see the light.

She probably did care for me, and it might could that she could even wind up in bed with me, which would have been glorious, but I knowed. Yes, sir, dumb as I was, I knowed.

I loved her.

But she could never truly love me.

Well, it would have been fairly easy to turn east, head to Carrizozo and on into Lincoln on the Rio Bonito, let the blind nun and the fraudulent nun go off into the Valley of Fire. I could head over to Ike Stockton's saloon, and get good and roostered. By that time, it was really what I wanted to get. Still, I didn't have it in me. Couldn't leave Sister Rocío and Geneviève.

Late that afternoon, we reached the Malpais. We'd done some hard traveling, and I had to give Sister Rocío a ton of credit. She'd made it across that high desert, but now there was lava flows that stood real high.

The lava flows had begun some thousands of years ago. They stretched over better than a hundred sections. Forty-odd miles long, as much as five miles wide. We was in a sea of mostly black rocks that hit better than a hundred and fifty feet thick in spots.

'Course, it wasn't all black rocks. No way our horses and mules could make it across that country without breaking their legs and our necks. This was what folks called the Chihuahuan Desert, and it smelled of creosote. Every now and then, we'd see patches of mesquite and yucca aplenty, and our horses chewed on bear grass when we'd let 'em.

A roadrunner bolted out from one of them large holes, and liked to have spooked that bay I was riding into pitching me. He done some dancing, but I stuck with him, got him calmed down, then looked across this level of Purgatory.

Looking at the towering mounds of lava that rose above the grassy path we was on, I reined in the bay, and stood in the stirrups, looking for, but not finding, Mount Ararat.

"It has to be here," I said to myself, but I said it out loud.

Geneviève heard me. "We're in an ocean."

Sure looked that way. An angry ocean, but of black rocks instead of waves.

"The wine-dark sea," Geneviève said.

I nodded, thinking that I'd enjoy a goblet of Madeira. One time Big Tim Pruett stole a bottle, and we'd drunk it all. It hadn't tasted bad, and didn't leave us with no headache, but we had also emptied a bottle of mescal before Big Tim plucked that wine bottle, so it wasn't that we really tasted much of nothing.

"It's getting dark," I said.

"I know." Geneviève looked at me hopefully, but there wasn't nothing I could do except swing off the saddle and walk over toward Sister Rocío.

"We need to make camp," I told her. I wrapped the reins to the bay around a dead juniper and reached up to help the blind nun off the mule.

"Have you seen Mount Ararat?" she asked.

I shook my head, which didn't tell the nun nothing, but then said, "It hasn't been forty days and forty nights yet."

Out in this wine-dark sea of lava, it could easily take us twice as long to find what we'd come to get.

Chapter Thirty-one

Red lava. Black lava. Yellow sandstone slopes rising from the lava, and pink sandstone ledges on the ground. That's all you could see, except for the clumps of brush and cactus and the mountains looking so blue and black way off to the east and west.

"Must've been a hell of a volcano," I said, just to say something on account nobody had said nothing since breakfast that morning. It hadn't really been breakfast. Mostly some hardtack that was only slightly softer than the rocks that surrounded us, and water that tasted harder than them rocks.

I showed off how smart I was, saying them lava rocks come from volcanoes. I knowed that. Thought I did. But I reckon I should've kept my mouth shut and just listened to the wind.

"Micah." Sister Rocío sounded just like she had back at the orphanage when she was about to correct my ignorant answer or inform me that I owed her ten Hail Marys, five Our Fathers and one Glory Be. She even waited till I turned around to face her, as if she could see me. "Do you see any volcanoes around here?"

"None smoking," I said.

Nobody laughed. Seeing that stern look that told me she didn't appreciate smart alecks, I sucked in a deep breath, let it out, and said more respectful, "No, ma'am."

"There is nothing that even looks like a volcano, is there?"

The nearest mountains was the Capitans, and they looked like mountains, not volcanoes. She waited for me to look around, but I wasn't going to do that for some blind woman. I'd traveled around these parts enough to know that nothing resembled a volcano.

When she figured she had given me enough time, she said, "Of course, you don't. Because there is no volcano here. These flows were not caused by a volcano, but vents in the valley floor. The molten lava flowed, cooled, and formed these islands."

"Islands in a wine-dark sea," Sister Geneviève said, because she was still focusing on wine-dark seas.

"The islands are called kipukas," the blind old bird said.

Even Sister Geneviève turned, her face revealing curiosity and surprise, to face the old woman.

"How do you know all this?" Geneviève finally asked.

I felt more grouchy than curious or surprised, and was grinding my teeth to keep from calling the blind nun a know-it-all. A teacher's pet.

With a smile Sister Rocío explained, "A scientist —a geologist—spoke to the Sisters of Charity two years ago come September."

Me and Geneviève stared, first at the nun, then at each other.

Said Rocío, "He was quite informative."

Me and Geneviève done some more staring.

"We sponsor many such lectures," Rocío explained. "Back in '81, Governor Lew Wallace read a chapter from his stunning novel *Ben-Hur: A Tale of the Christ* shortly before he left the territory. He proved, to the thinking of the Mother Superior and myself, to be much more capable as a writer than as a governor, and though his novel had Protestant leanings, we did admire that chariot race. To my thinking, however, the best lecture was a friend of the carpenter who fixed our door who had known and ridden with Kit Carson. This person spoke about the days of the mountain men and fur traders in Taos. He was quite the salty talker."

We didn't say nothing.

"Well," Sister Rocío said with a snort, "what do you expect us nuns to do, read the New Testament and gossip about the archbishop behind his back every day?"

The two women had gotten some sleep the previous night, but I hadn't. A body doesn't sleep too good when he knows that Sean Fenn's gonna be trailing him. So I was bone tired when we ate a cold breakfast, then started scouring the Valley of Fire for a grave that only a blind woman knowed where to find it.

Morning had passed slowly as we picked our trails through the lava flows, seeing some colorful lizards sunning themselves, but nothing else. Had to be ten or eleven that morning when I eased the bay over toward Sister Geneviève and asked to see that cross again. After she handed it to me, I turned it over, read them words again, looked across the Valley of Fire, and scratched my head.

"Sister." The saddle creaked as I turned toward Rocío. "What does this mean, 'From the top of Ararat we must climb down'?"

"It means what it says. You climb down off Mount Ararat."

I give the cross back to Geneviève, looked around to study the land.

Well, if I clumb high enough up the nearest sandstone slope, I reckoned that I could see the Capitan Mountains, and a bunch of brown grass filling the Tularosa betwixt them mountains and where we was sweating. But I don't think I could see all the way to the Old Testament in the land of the Israelites.

Another memory latched on to my brain. It hit me so sudden, so hard, that I reined in the bay, and sucked in a deep breath.

You spill as much whiskey as I'd done, you ride hell-bent for leather enough to save your hide, you don't recollect all the things nuns made you do back when you was living in an orphanage. I'd forgotten all about it, till everything surged up and like to have knocked me out of the saddle.

Geneviève started, "What's the mat—"

"You used to make me draw pictures . . . back when I was a kid." I was already pointing a finger at the blind nun.

Another smile cracked through that grizzled face. "You should have stuck to art, Micah," Rocío said. "You were talented."

"At stick figures," I said with a snort.

"Yes, but your landscapes were spectacular."

She smiled, and said almost in a whisper, almost like she was coaxing something up that had been buried in my memories, "Remember?"

'Course, I'm thinking, *how the hell would a blind nun know if my drawings was artistic or not?*

"Remember," she repeated softly.

It was like Rocío had transformed herself into that buxomly lass with the turban and the silver rings and pretty necklaces who had tried to hypnotize Big Tim Pruett in Albuquerque that day. She told him to watch the gold watch she kept twirling, but all Big Tim and me could focus on was them enormous breasts of hers. She didn't put Big Tim under, but somehow Sister Rocío was doing something to my mind, my memories.

"And close your eyes."

I done, and . . . this is the strange part. Once I'd shut them eyelids tight, I wasn't no thirty-something-year-old drifter wanted for murder and stuck with a beautiful woman and a blind nun, with a cutthroat named Sean Fenn likely just a half day's ride behind us coming to kill, and maybe a fortune in gold somewhere in a hole in all these black rocks that were twisted and wavy and hard and reminded me of giant cow turds.

Instead, I pictured myself as a twelve-year-old orphan sitting in a room in an adobe building in a sleepy town called Santa Fe with a blind nun who had only one arm. It had just slammed the back of my head hard enough to make my front teeth chatter.

No. No, that ain't right, either. You see, I didn't picture myself as that kid who once was me. Instead, I was that little boy.

"You are drawing Mount Ararat," Sister Rocío says sharply.

"I don't wanna," I rebel.

Wham. My head hurts.

"Where are you?" the nun's voice asks.

"In Noah's Ark."

"You are looking for . . . ?"

"The dove I sent out."

"And what do you see?"

"Water. Black as midnight. Deep water."

"But there it is. . . ."

"Land!" I cry.

"Exactly," Sister Rocío says. "Mount Ararat."

"We sail for it," I tell her.

"What does it look like?"

"Red." I'm drawing, eyes closed, trying to figure out what it must be like to be Sister Rocío, blind and all. I only draw with my right hand. I never open my eyes.

"No, not red. There is a red trail on the ocean, but the mountain isn't red. It's more yellow. Yellow boulders, but not corn yellow. More like . . . tan."

"A jumble of boulders," Sister Rocío says. "Round?"

"Not really." I can see them, chipped, some long, but most of them flat, red, tan, probably weighing one to five tons each.

"Is it easy to climb?" she asks. "Ararat?"

"Yes. If you pick the right path."

"Vegetation?"

"Prickly pear. Some cholla. Grass. Yucca. A pine tree."

"Juniper," she corrects.

Yep, she's right. It is a juniper, twisted and mean and tough and sturdy.

"Does it smell like juniper, though?" she asks me.

I breathe in deeply and slowly exhale. Because I'm fourteen years old and because I know I'm in Santa Fe and it's dinnertime, what I should smell are roasting chiles and beans and coffee, or the sweat of an old woman coaxing me to draw her a pretty picture. But that's not what I smell.

"It smells like . . ."

"Like?" the nun coaxes.

"Creosote."

"Then there must also be . . ."

"Creosote." I feel smart. I want to turn in my desk and give Nancy Jean Dobie a smug look, but I don't . . . because I don't want to get my head slapped by ruler or fist or forced to say penances till I can hardly speak no more.

"What's at the top of Mount Ararat?"

"The Ark."

"Why?"

"Because we've landed."

"But do you still see the scene from your perch in the sea?"

My head bobs. "I am the dove. I am flying. I can see the cabin and the decks, and the animals sticking their heads from over the sides."

"The Ark has been sailing for a long time," she says.

"There is moss—"

"Mold," she corrects.

"Mold on the sides."

"What does the mold look like?"

"Green spots."

"And now where are you?" Rocío asks.

"I'm on top of the Ark."

"And what do you see?"

"Clouds."

"More rain?"

"Mountains."

"Where?"

"To the east."

"Look to the west."

I obey.

"What do you see now?"

"Just ocean. Black, black ocean."

"So east is land. Can you look down?"

"Yes."

"And what do you see, Micah?"

My horse started peeing, but my eyes remained closed. I knowed my left hand was atop the horn, and my right index finger drew an imaginary pencil across the open palm. Must've been doing that while in that trance, that vision, that whatever-the-hell-you-call-it, but it didn't feel like my finger tracing my palm. Felt like I was holding a pencil and scratching my thoughts on paper.

"What do you see, Micah?" Sister Rocío asked.

My eyes opened, and it was like I half- expected to see a painting or a map, but all I seen was my finger on my calloused palm. I turned to Sister Rocío and answered, "I see a canyon."

She smiled. "Exactly."

That crone had given me hope, which can be dangersome. Hell, I felt like a ten-year-old on his birthday. Standing in the stirrups, I stared across the valley. 'Course, I didn't see the Ark, and I sure didn't spot Mount Ararat. I didn't see nothing except one of them lizards on a giant lava cow turd, grass, and cactus.

Still smiling, I settled back into the saddle, wet my lips, and smiled at Geneviève, who, smart as she was, pretty as she was, looked at me utterly stupidly.

"You had me draw Mount Ararat." I eased my horse over to Sister Rocío. "From your memories. You told me what it looked like, but you had me drawing what you remembered. Not from some Bible illustration." I patted her shoulder and looked again.

"Do you see it?" Geneviève asked.

"I don't see a damned thing but black lava."

Sister Rocío's knuckles cracked my skull, just above where I'd cut my noggin after Fenn had slammed me against a rock.

"Ten Our Fathers, Micah," Rocío instructed me, even though I didn't have a rosary or the time to say no penance.

"So . . ." Geneviève started. "How?"

I'd turned the bay around. "Well, now I know what I'm looking for."

"Which is?"

"Tan rocks," I said. "A mountain of large but loose tan rocks."

"Could it be red?" Geneviève was suddenly excited. She jerked around, pointing to a little rise off to the northwest. "There are red rocks over there."

"That's lava," I told her. "Red lava. No, I think what I'm looking for isn't lava, but sandstone."

I could see in my mind what I'd drawed for Sister Rocío back all them long years ago.

"The sandstone was here when the lava emerged from the vents," Sister Rocío was speaking like a geologist lecturing a bunch of Sisters of Charity again. "The sandstone remained its natural color, yellow-tinted tan, on the slopes, but where the lava seeped across it, the sandstone was turned into a more pinkish hue."

"Some lecture you got there," I told her.

Rocío grinned. "Actually, I preferred the salty-tongued rapscallion who had known Kit Carson."

Pointing south, I start speaking to Geneviève. "We haven't crossed the road that leads to Carrizozo. I think we need to find it. That's where she buried those nuns and the gold."

"What makes you think that?" Geneviève asked.

"Because an Army patrol found her, took her east to Socorro." I felt good. I mean, when you feel smart, you feel good. Usually, I'm dumber than a fence post, but in a poker game—providing I hadn't drunk too much whiskey or just wasn't playing smart cards—and out in the open country when my life depended on things, I did have a brain that worked halfway decent.

"They'd be following a trail. On horseback. Wouldn't want to cross this valley except on a trail." I motioned toward Rocío. "She'd just hacked off her arm and was suffering from exposure. She couldn't have wandered too far."

Geneviève smiled, nodded, and eased her horse south, pulling Rocío's mule behind her. I tugged on the other mule's lead rope, and felt good and smart and lucky.

Till I looked behind me.

Chapter Thirty-two

I didn't tell Geneviève or Rocío about the dust I'd spied off to the northeast. No need in getting them all scared and concerned and fearful that Sean Fenn was heading our way. Way I figured things, I was scared and concerned and fearful enough for us all. Besides, that dust could have come from a herd of cattle, or some peaceable cowhand headed up to White Oaks, or just a dust devil blowed up by the wind. Could've been anything.

'Course, deep down, I knowed better.

We rode down the trail, smelling creosote and dust, that black lava rising higher and higher. I'd rein up, ease down, and climb afoot up the rocks, looking around for Mount Ararat.

Nothing that I could see resembled them drawings I pictured in my head.

Back in the saddle, I kicked the bay into a walk, tugging the mule behind me, and called out to the blind woman, "Sister Rocío, I need some help."

"Yes, son, I know," she said, all friendly, but it prompted a chuckle that Geneviève couldn't stifle.

I give her my meanest stare, which made her laugh even more.

"Well, yes, ma'am, don't we all," said I, "but,

what I mean is, this is big country. Better than a hundred sections. There are lots of little hills here and there. Could take us months to search for that hill you call Ararat, and we ain't got months."

Thinking, but not saying, *Probably ain't got more than a day.*

"What do you remember?" I reined up, turned, and waited. Geneviève stopped the claybank, and Rocío sat on the mule.

"Close your eyes, Sister Rocío," I told her, just like she'd done to me, hypnotic and all. "Think back."

She snorted. "Micah, I am blind. I don't need to close my eyes to picture anything."

Geneviève looked back at me, but I give her the look that dared her to laugh. Besides, the old woman did close her eyes. So there.

"It was winter," she said. "The land was covered in snow and ice, but I do remember . . . a bat."

"Bat?" I asked.

Her empty eyes opened. "Yes. Bat. It looked like a rabbit."

Her mind's gone, I told myself again.

"You know," she said. "Long ears?"

"Don't bats migrate?" Geneviève asked.

"Not the one I saw," she said. "It was dead. But these bats do not migrate, either. They live here. Cortez, the guide, told me this." Her head bobbed at some ancient memory. "Now, I remember. Cortez said the bats were common along the

Tularosa Valley. We had found some guano and the dead bat. How is that?"

"Fine," I said, and couldn't hide my irritation. "Now all I got to look for is a pile of bat dung, and a skeleton of a big-eared bat."

"Exactly," Rocío said.

She wasn't been sarcastic, like me. She was dead serious.

"A big-eared bat," she said. "That's what it is called. Thomas's big-eared . . . no, that isn't it. Thompson's, no Townsend's. A Townsend's big-eared bat. They roost alone. They have really big ears, and their fur, usually brown or gray, protects them while they hibernate. And they do not migrate. So they are usually around this country, even during the winter."

My mouth was open. So was Geneviève's. You don't expect to hear so much from a nun about bats, which I'd always been taught was critters of Satan.

"One of our lecturers," Rocío explained, "called himself a chiropterologist. Oh, I guess that was five or six years ago. He was on his way to Carlsbad, the deep cave there, to study the bats that call it home during certain times of the year. I forget the exact species. Anyway, he planned to stop in the Tularosa Valley to study the Townsend's big-eared bat. He gave a most inspired talk. Very passionate about 'the order Chiroptera,' as he called it."

Geneviève said, "A chi . . . uh, chiro . . . a . . ."

"Chiropterologist," Rocío completed.

"Too bad he ain't here with us." I stood in the saddle, looked back northeast, but didn't see no dust—which didn't mean a damned thing. "He might be able to tell us where to find a dead bat that was here about thirty-eight years ago."

"You are being silly, Micah. We do not look for a bat skeleton. But near a cave. When I saw the dead bat and its giant ears—poor creature, he must have frozen to death—poor Lorraine, she feared it was an omen. That bats were instruments of the Devil. Those French, they have some strange notions. But Cortez said they were common here, and he pointed south and west. He said the big-eared bats often hibernated in a cave. He said we would soon be near the cave, and suggested that we hide there from the banditos. Alas, we never made it there. But I remember—" She paused, thinking back. "But we were near there. We must've been."

"Crockett's Cave," I said.

"What?" Geneviève asked.

"Yes," Rocío said. "That was the name Cortez used. Crockett's Cave."

"You know of it?" Geneviève asked.

I nodded. I'd hid in that thing, dodging them boys from White Oaks. Didn't know its name till I got found.

"We need to go west some," I said. "And south a bit."

Nudging the bay into a walk, I tried to find a way to cut through the massive black wall of lava. It would take some doing, but I was already doing some figuring, and remembering. Through my head, that poem ran over and over again.

> From the top of Ararat,
> We must climb down.
> Into the cañon
> Beside the King's crown,
> Where black meets the red.
> Into the second cañon,
> We walk with pain,
> Until we can touch
> The cross of Lorraine.
> Hallowed be the dead.

I tried to recollect something near that cave that fit that description. And then I started swearing under my breath.

You're that close to a big cave, Rocío. Why couldn't you have found it, stashed the gold and the bodies in that? Instead of sticking everything in a hole and burying it all with black lava?

Like she read my thoughts, my mind, Sister Rocío said, "Purgatory is suffering."

And we was about to suffer.

Oh, I reckon we got farther than I really expected us to get on horseback in that country, winding this way, then that, coming to a dead-end, doubling back, finding another trail . . . till the trails played out. After checking the sun to determine the best direction, I dropped to the sandstone grit, and began unsaddling the bay. "We walk."

"What about the horses and mules?" Geneviève asked.

There was grass and some shade. I mean, it wasn't like that livery stable in Dodge City where Big Tim Pruett and I once spent three weeks—I mean to tell you, that stable was better than some hotels we'd hung our hats in—but considering where we was, it was right respectable for two horses and a couple mules.

"We'll water them before we leave, tether them. They should be all right. If we ain't gone too long."

She moved closer to me, Geneviève did, put a hand on my arm as I was taking off the bridle, and said in a whisper, "And what about Rocío?"

With a shrug, I answered, "She comes with us."

"Micah." Her head tilted back to that mountain of black. "Over that?"

"We ain't got much choice," I told her. I mean, if we headed back north, then cut west, we'd likely run into that dust I'd seen. This way, Sean Fenn would have to come looking for us. Given the size of the Valley of Fire and just how many nooks and crannies we'd already uncovered, well, it might take him a passable amount of time.

Once I got the horses on a picket rope, giving

them plenty of room to graze and all, I taken the canteens, a sack of jerky, and biscuits. "We find the place first," I told Geneviève. "Then we come back for the horses, the gold—"

"And the bodies of Lorraine and our other Sisters," Rocío said, her ears just as sharp as they'd been during lessons.

"Yes, ma'am," I told her, and moved over, put my arm over her shoulder. Being all encouraging and the like, I said, "Sister, I'll need you to hold my hand. Don't fret. We got to climb, find a good trail up this hill of lava. I'll tell you where to step, what to avoid, things like that. And I won't drop you. Won't let go of your hand, no matter what. Think you can do it?"

"Of course, my son. Our Father, our Blessed Mother, will guide my way."

I led her past the horses and on toward Geneviève, who was looking at me like I was out of my mind. As I passed her, I had to remind her, "I didn't drop you from that train, did I?"

Didn't drop old Rocío, neither, though it did get kinda ticklish there.

First off, there weren't no trail up the lava. Had to climb a good twenty, twenty-two feet. I got a hand hold, felt my way up a bit. Reached down, taken Sister Rocío's hand, told her what to do. She got up just fine. On the other hand, Geneviève had mountain goat in her veins. She scurried up one way, then t'other, leaning forward, leaping. She made it to the top and called down to ask if she should toss down a rope. 'Cause she'd taken the pack of supplies (biscuits, jerky, rope) up with her.

"We'll make out fine, Sister," I told her. No way she could pull either Rocío or me up, thin as she was.

I seen a yucca over some sharp rocks a ways up, so I told Rocío, "Sister, this is gonna be like a dance of some kind. I'm gonna slide up a bit, then you slide up beside me. I'll have your hand the whole time. Ready?"

She nodded, and I ripped my pants. Damned embarrassing, but nothing could be done. She slid up easy. Then we done it again. And again.

"This is hard on one's buttocks," she said when we rested by the yucca.

"Too bad you never had no buttocktologist lecture at one of your meetings," I told her.

"You never were very funny, Micah," she said.

Up we went.

She slipped once, but I didn't drop her. We swung over a deep crevasse. I put my other arm around her to steady her, then squeezed her shoulder.

"I was almost flying like an angel," she said, and grinned. "This is exhilarating."

"It scares the Jesus out of me," I told her.

She would've skinned my head with her knuckles, but I held her hand. Instead, she told me to say ten Hail Marys, which I done on the last leg up the hill.

'Course, up top, I seen a real problem. We was sky-lining the country. Sister Rocío wore black, which would make it hard for even a person with spyglasses to see, but me and Geneviève had on light-colored duds.

"All right, Sister," I said, finding a canyon. "Now we go back down."

They didn't question me. Seemed to accept that I knowed what I was doing, where we was going, none of which was true.

"There's a jumping cholla about ten feet to your left, Sister," I said as I eased her down. "Other way. Other way!" I had to swing her, lessen she get a mouthful of cholla spines. She hit hard. Geneviève gasped. I almost let go of the blind woman's hand.

"Are you all right?" me and Geneviève yelled at the same time.

First, she tried to cross herself, but couldn't on account that I gripped her one hand with all the muscle I had left in me. She made the motions with the stub of her other arm, shook her habit, which had gotten kinda askew from bounding off lava, and said, "I will be, if Micah ever learns the difference between right and left."

Well, we made it down into that canyon, with Rocío getting three, four more bruises, and me with ripped pants. We moved through that trail, climbed up again, and kept right on going.

We climbed up a hill, not Ararat or nothing like that, and looked west. All you could see below was black, broken by juts of piñon and yucca and cholla. It appeared to stretch all the way to the Rio Grande, but I knowed it didn't.

"The, uh, Crockett's Cave"—I pointed—"is off that ways a bit."

We rested. I opened the bag of biscuits, handed the two ladies some water. Sister Rocío went off to nature's call. Even nuns have to potty here and there.

"Micah." Geneviève's voice was quiet.

"Yeah." I was looking at all that awful country, trying to figure out where the hell Crockett's Cave was. Hell, I hadn't been near that hole in the ground for better than half my life.

"I didn't want to mention this, didn't want to scare you or Rocío, but . . . well . . . earlier . . . I saw dust."

"Yeah." I was resigned. Seemed to have become more Calvinistic or Presbyterian in my thinking. What happened, happened. A sinner and mortal like me couldn't stop it.

"You saw it, too?"

"Yeah." I looked north. No dust. Just more black.

"Micah."

I looked at Geneviève. She pointed east. "I saw dust . . . that way."

That could've been what I saw. I mean, Sean Fenn could have kept riding. Geneviève had spied the dust long after I'd seen it off to the northeast.

"When did you see that dust?" I asked.

She might have answered, but the only thing I heard was the gunshot.

Chapter Thirty-three

The bullet clipped a sprig off a juniper as I grabbed Geneviève's arm and pulled her down on top of me. Another bullet left a white mark across a chunk of lava. Rolling off me, Geneviève screamed out Rocío's name, and when I sat up, clawing to get the Dean and Adams out of my waistband, I seen the blind nun just standing there, a yucca on one side of her and a long drop to the ground on the other.

"Geneviève, Micah!" the old woman called out. "What is going on!"

"Get—!" Stopped myself. I was gonna tell her to get down, but if she went into the yucca, she'd get sliced to ribbons. If she went the other way, she'd likely break her neck. Had to be an eighteen-foot drop down to nothing but more black rocks. So hero that I was, I was off and running, telling Geneviève, "Cover me," and hearing her say, "What?"

I heard two, three more shots, but nothing hit me. No bullet whined off rocks. Old Rocío stood fingering her rosary, opening her mouth to ask another question when I grabbed her by the waist and brought her down, twisting my body so she landed on my stomach, and liked to have broke my backbone. I think she did crack a couple ribs.

"Micah!"

I groaned.

"What is going on?"

I made myself sit halfway up, turning to peer down the edge of the ridge we was on. Them boys was shooting uphill, so it'd take a might fine shot to plug one of us. Didn't see no smoke from carbines or rifles, but I heard some cussing, the voices bouncing off the rocks so there was no chance to tell where they was hiding.

"Micah," Rocío said again.

"Jesus Christ!" I snapped. "Are you deaf, too? Didn't you hear them gunshots?"

"There is no call to take the Lord's name in vain, Micah Bishop."

"There ain't no call in me getting my head shot off, neither, trying to keep you alive." I wasn't in a forgiving mood. "Next time you hear a gunshot, you duck. Something goes ka-boom, just fall to your belly no matter what. You savvy?"

For once, she didn't try to brain me with her knuckles, or give me some penance. She merely nodded.

There was another shot, this one high, but Rocío ducked. Just flattened herself on the rock.

"Good girl," I told her. But to them boys doing the shooting, I wasn't so polite. "You damned miserable sons of bitches!" I yelled, and heard my profanity echo across the Valley of Fire. "That's an eighty-year-old blind nun you're shooting at, Fenn!"

A few more shots, and when the last bullet whined off a boulder higher up the hill, Rocío pointed out, "Micah, I am not eighty years old."

Damn a woman's vanity. Even a blind nun's.

Then a voice spoke. "I have learned not to trust nuns, amigo. At least, I do not trust nuns that travel with the likes of you, *cabrón*."

Son of a bitch. I'd almost forgotten all about Felipe Hernandez.

"What the hell!" I said, more to myself. Had Hernandez been waiting all this time for me to turn up in the Valley of Fire, miles from nowhere?

Actually, checking the copy of the *Las Vegas Daily Optic* that I ain't used for privy paper yet, I read that the "Roving Territorial Reporter" learned that Hernandez followed a cold trail from Las Vegas to Anton Chico to Puerto de Luna to Fort Sumner to White Oaks and finally to Carrizozo where he had spent some time in a house of ill repute before giving up and deciding to follow the trail from Carrizozo to San Antonio (New Mexico Territory's town, not the Alamo burg in Texas). According to a *chica de la noche* whose charms Hernandez had admired, the son of a bitch had given up on ever seeing me, Micah Bishop, dead. He and the two cousins who hadn't given up on what they considered a forlorn chase, happened upon me, Micah Bishop, by pure, accidental luck.

'Course, none of that I knowed certain-sure till my trial and conviction. All I knowed then was that I was in a peck of trouble.

Geneviève come crawling on hands and knees through a natural depression, bringing the sacks with her. As long as she kept her head down, she was pretty much safe. For now.

"I tell you what, amigo!" Hernandez called up to us again. "I will let the nun go free. On my word as a gentleman, I guarantee that she will not be harmed."

One nun. They'd seen Rocío, but not Geneviève. who had just reached us.

I helped her out of the little ditch, handed her Benigno's Remington, and told her to make sure Rocío didn't draw no fire from them boys down below.

"Are those gentlemen after the gold ingots, too?" Rocío asked.

"They're after my arse," I said, not loud enough for even old elephant ears to hear. "They don't know a thing about the gold, Sister."

I then repeated it to myself, out loud, just to

make sure that I understood what I'd just said. "They don't know a thing about the gold."

My eyes met Geneviève's, held for a moment, then I turned back to look down the slope.

"You can't trust them," Geneviève said.

"I know that."

"They'll kill you just as soon as they can."

"Most likely. But I don't think they'll shoot Rocío." I met her eyes again. "Can't say the same about you. You did club the jailer when you busted me out, and Felipe Hernandez's reputation stinks like a week-dead coyot'."

I taken me another deep breath, studied things over some in my mind, and finally decided to strike up a conversation with the boys down below with guns. "Felipe!" I called out. "How did you know it was me up here?"

"I didn't, *cabrón*! Until you told me."

"So you just fired on a nun?"

"I'd fire upon my own mother to see you swing. Gomez was my favorite uncle's son."

I wet my lips. Rubbed my chin. Bit my bottom lip. Finally decided to take a risk. You gotta do that when you're playing cards. Sometimes that risk will prompt the guy with the winning hand to fold.

"Felipe!" I shouted. "What if I told you that I knew the general whereabouts to a fortune in gold?"

"I would say," Hernandez said, and he said it.

I had no idea what he was saying because of all the echoes and the fact that my Spanish wasn't that good. "Speak English!"

"Then I would say that I cannot trust this Micah Bishop. And that I own a hotel, an emporium, I have real estate and investments in the train depot, two hotels, a grain mill, a gambling parlor, the local mortuary, a sawmill and a farm and a rancho in the country. And much, much more. I would say that I do not need to go chasing a dollar or two in gold at every drop of the hat."

So I yelled back down to him that $750,000 ain't quite the same as chasing a dollar. I looked on the ridge we'd clumb up. It was sandstone, and it ran a few hundred yards, then dropped below the black lava, but I could see that it was something like an arroyo. It would make a pretty good trail for mules and horses, maybe even a wagon.

There was some talking among the cousins and Felipe Hernandez. Finally, Hernandez yelled that he would never, ever trust the likes of me, and that I should say my prayers and send my confession to one of the nuns, because he was done talking and was ready to avenge Gomez's death.

"Seven hundred and fifty thousand dollars in ancient Spanish ingots!" I yelled. "Buried not more 'n a mile from here! Ingots made for King Richard III."

"Philip IV," Geneviève corrected.

"It don't matter." To them killers below, I

hollered, "Remember the story of the lost gold mine in Mora? This is where most of the ingots will be found." So I give them the story as best I could.

"I do not want gold," Felipe Hernandez snapped once more. "I just want you, Micah Bishop, and I want you dead."

There was more cussing echoing across the rocks, and then there was a gunshot, and it didn't bounce off the country so good on account that it had been muffled. As if it had been fired at a target fairly close.

"Señor!" a new voice said. "I have killed my cousin Felipe. My cousin Carlos and I never cared much for him anyway. If we come up with our guns holstered, will you talk to us more about this gold?"

I lifted my head up a ways, wet my bottom lip, and wiped my palms on my pants legs. "Step out in the open. But remember, I've got a Sharps Big Fifty, and ain't never missed with it." Because I'd never shot a big buffalo rifle. Didn't have it with me on this little expedition as I hadn't never owned one.

They stood above some boulders, probably sixty yards down the ridge, one in a black, wide-brimmed hat, the other wearing a tan bowler. They kept their hands out from their sides, palms facing me, and started walking toward us.

When they got closer, I could tell that they

was both older men, maybe in their fifties, with silver hair, one sporting a goatee, the other a gold tooth. They stopped at the edge of the ridge.

"Can you trust them?" Geneviève asked.

I give her a look of contempt. I mean, I loved her, and she'd saved my hide, and she didn't have to be a nun—that was all well and good with me—but she had just asked one damned fool question.

"They just shot their cousin dead." I let it go at that.

"Señor!" Cousin Bowler called out.

I answered.

He said, "We cannot climb up to you with our hands like this."

With a grin, I told them, "We're a peaceable bunch. Just shuck off shell belts and revolvers. Leave them on the ground. Then climb on up. And welcome."

By grab, they actually shucked their hardware and started climbing.

Well, I considered shooting them both in their heads as they picked their path up the ridge. Probably would have done it had Geneviève and Rocío not been with me. They would have done the same to me. The two Hernandez cousins, I mean. Not Rocío and Geneviève. Instead of killing them, I helped Cousin Bowler up, even brushed off the bottoms of them fancy buckskin trousers he wore.

They removed their hats as they stood there, taking me in, stepping back from Rocío, and eyes practically bulging out of their skulls when they looked at Geneviève.

"Don't y'all want to know where that gold is?" I had to interrupt that love gathering. Made me all jealous.

"Where is it?" Bowler Cousin asked.

I give them one more look over. "Any of you birds know how to get to Crockett's Cave?"

They didn't look at me. Stared at each other. Then Black Hat Cousin repeated, "Crockett's Cave?"

"That's where the gold is. All of it."

That, I figured, was a lie worthy of ten Hail Marys to start off with.

"Señor," Cousin Black Hat finally said, "I live in San Miguel County, and my cousin here"—he gestured toward Cousin Bowler—"is from Chama, just below the border of Colorado. We are not familiar with this country at all."

Figured. But it was worth a shot.

Then Sister Rocío said, "I know where it is, Micah. I can feel it. It is this way."

Geneviève grabbed her arm before she stepped off and fell.

"It is this way," the blind woman said. "I feel it."

Chapter Thirty-four

We basically followed a blind woman like she was a divining rod.

I kept that Dean and Adams in my hand at all times and kept them eyes of mine on Cousin Bowler and Cousin Black Hat. Geneviève never let go of the Remington, never let them man-killing cousins get too close to her or Rocío. We went down, and the temperature dropped considerable as we'd climbed into the shadows out of the sun. 'Course, it wasn't freezing. Not in July. Not in the Valley of Fire.

Dark clouds kept approaching, and my nerves got tighter than a miser gripping a three-cent piece. Sister Rocío was humming. The two cousins wasn't saying nothing. We climbed over a sand-stone ridge, went back down in the lava, and kept walking south and west, then west and south. Geneviève held that big .44 in one hand, and the other gripped Rocío's arm, the blind nun acting like it was a Sunday stroll to church in the city of Rome.

Thunder rolled across the sky and lightning slashed to earth.

"Monsoon," one of the cousins said, pointing at the dark line beneath the cloud that told us it was pouring rain a few miles ahead.

"Micah," Geneviève called out. "Those clouds are moving fast."

"I know." I done a quick look behind me, then turned back to make sure the cousins weren't up to something no good. They wasn't. Then I realized what I had just seen, and slowly, almost forgetting about Cousin Black Hat and Cousin Bowler, I turned and stared again, and quickly faced front.

"There's no place to hide back there," I said, though that ain't what I'd been looking for. "Let's try to find the cave."

A hundred yards later, I smelled rain on the horizon, and it had turned downright chilly. Didn't want to catch my death in some thunderstorm, but I didn't think there was much I could do about it.

Off to the right, I saw Cousin Bowler waving his hat over his head frantically, and we all hurried over to that big old boy, who was pointing at an opening in the ground.

"Crockett's Cave?" Cousin Bowler asked.

"Absolutely," I said, though I didn't know for certain-sure. When I was hiding from them fellows from White Oaks, I must've come in through the other entrance, off to the west. Bowler went in first. Then Geneviève. Followed by me and Rocío, and I turned to make sure Cousin Black Hat followed, which he done. Moments later, we could hear the rain drenching the earth, but we was safe in Crockett's Cave.

A match flared. Cousin Bowler frowned. "Where's the gold?"

I pointed. They turned, saw something, and headed over.

The match went out, and darkness enveloped us again. The rain sounded odd, almost like it was echoing. Cousin Bowler spoke to Cousin Black Hat, and their voices bounced around the dark dungeon we'd come into.

A voice whispered right next to my ear, and I liked to have soiled my britches it scared me so much 'cause I wasn't expecting it. I calmed down because it was Geneviève.

"What are we doing here?" she said.

I could tell she was seething, but I answered her. "Well, it beats waiting out in the rain."

Another match flared. I heard Cousin Black Hat say, "What is that rabbit doing hanging upside down like that?"

The match moved, then got flicked rapidly out, or got dropped. All I know was that it was dark again.

In the darkness, Sister Rocío said, "It is not a rabbit, señor, but a Townsend's big-eared bat."

"Señor," Cousin Bowler called out, and his voice danced around the cave. "I see no gold."

"Of course not," I said, and started walking over to him. I reminded myself that I'd never done much planning, and most of the plans I'd come up with never had worked. This here time down in Crockett's Cave was pretty much a prime example of why Big Tim Pruett never trusted me to do more than saddle his horse or take his weighted dice and slip him a fair pair because I was good at sleight of hand and he didn't want to get run out of town on a rail.

Crockett's Cave, I read in *The Nation* while in the privy waiting to be hanged, ain't what one would call small. It was part gypsum, part limestone, with one big passage and a few shorter ones along the sides. The big room was about a hundred feet by three hundred. It smelled like dust.

About that time, I'd come up amongst Cousin Black Hat and Cousin Bowler, who struck his lucifer. The light made me back up, but then I seen the glint of something in Cousin Black Hat's hand, and I knowed it was a gun. Even if I hadn't noticed it right then, Cousin Bowler was telling me, "Do not speak loudly, señor, but talk in an easy voice. We do not wish to alarm the nun and the young—"

"She's a nun, too," I lied, and didn't feel no urge to say a Hail Mary or Our Father over that fib.

"Very well. My cousin has a Remington over-and-under .41-caliber derringer in his hand. I think he can see you long enough to put a bullet in your belly."

"Most likely," I said, but them boys didn't

know how fast I can move when somebody's about to shoot me in the stomach.

Nasty way to die. A bullet in the gut. I wonder if hanging's a better way to go.

"I see no treasure here, señor," Cousin Black Hat said. "Do you?"

"Of course you don't," I said, thinking to myself *because it ain't here, you damned fools,* but saying, "Because you don't leave a fortune in gold just sitting out in the open, even in a cave. You bury it."

Slowly but surely, I stepped between the cousins. The match went out, and I was in darkness, though I could still see light seeping through the opening to the cave. I was kneeling and saying, "You got to dig," when a new lucifer flared into life.

That give me a clear target, and I taken it. My hands scooped up all they could hold, and I flung guano into the eyes of Cousin Black Hat, you know, the one holding the derringer.

He used an English cuss word, which was good and accurate since that's exactly what I'd throwed into his nose and eyes and mouth. The match went out, and then there was this terrible scream, one of uncontrollable rage, and not close, but from the entrance to the cave.

It was complete darkness until I pulled the trigger on the Dean and Adams. The flash about blinded me, and the noise liked to have deafened me. Up ahead, near where I'd left Rocío and Geneviève, come cussing and a click that even where I was working the trigger on that .436 again I recognized as a Colt being cocked.

Then come more flashes, which sent pain through my eyeballs.

Something else I learned about Crockett's Cave. It's a big room, but when folks start shooting, it's hard on one's ears and eyes. Bullets ricocheted off the limestone, kicked up gypsum, and the roar of them guns proved terrible painful. A bullet burned my arm, right above the elbow. I had my finger on the trigger, but I couldn't see nothing to shoot at. But Geneviève was shooting, and somebody else had just entered the cave, and he was blasting away, too. Nobody could see nothing.

"During the gun battle in the depths of Hades, with thousands of bullets and arrows bouncing off the walls around him, The Bishop kept his nerves under absolute control. He knew to rush would rush him to death."

That's what that Colonel-fellow wrote about me and my adventures in *Valley of Fire, Shadow of Death; Or, The Bishop and the Ingots*, which I read three nights ago in one sitting. It ain't accurate, but the colonel never asked me for no information, though I did like him calling me "The Bishop."

Anyway, at that time, my nerves was cut open and sending panic through my body. I did have my finger on the trigger—that much, Colonel what's-his-name knowed what he was writing about—but there wasn't nothing to shoot at.

There was a scream off my left, but I was just seeing painful flashes of orange and red and white. Above the ringing in my ears and blood rushing to my brain, there was a voice. "You son of a bitch! I shall kill you, you son of a bitch. I shall give you exactly what you gave my favorite cousin."

Felipe Hernandez. I should have knowed. Never trust nobody.

He and his cousins had come up with a plan. The cousins said they'd killed Felipe, then that sidewinder had trailed us to the cave. The vindictive son of a bitch figured he could find a fortune in gold and avenge poor cousin Gomez.

I heard footsteps. Kept waiting for Cousin Bowler or Cousin Black Hat to finish me off, but they couldn't, on account that they was both lying dead, though I didn't know that fact till later. Well, my vision cleared at last, and I figured it was God letting me see myself die.

Hernandez had a torch in his left hand, a Colt in his right.

He squeezed the trigger. The Colt roared. Almost immediately, something burned across my neck. I heard that ping—well, I thought I did, but it had to be my imagination—and I cringed, because I never really want to get shot by a ricochet again. Before Hernandez could pull the trigger again, or just swing the barrel of that gun and crack my skull, he muttered, "My God. I am killed." And he was.

The torch dropped, and so did Felipe Hernandez, killed by a ricochet from his own gun.

The torch, still burning on the floor, give me enough light to know that the cousins wasn't worth my time no more. I didn't have much time left, because the rain had stopped, and the sun would soon sink. I wanted to get Geneviève and Rocío out of this cave, and find that gold, give them dead nuns a Christian burial, and get the hell out of the Valley of Fire.

"Come on!" I yelled, and headed for the opening, shining light, beautiful light, over me. "Let's go. Let's get out of here!" I was halfway out of the cave before I recollected that Sister Rocío couldn't see, so I come back down, helped them both up, telling them, "There's something I want y'all to see!"

Something glorious and wonderful and helpful.

Sister Rocío reminded me that she couldn't see. She went out first, while I had to wait for Geneviève, who eased back into the cave to fetch the bag of hardtack and jerky and Benigno's Remington .44.

"Let me have the gun," I told her.

She pulled it out, give it to me butt first. "It's empty."

I figured. So many shots had been bouncing around in the cave. I could feel the heat from the revolver, and shoved the Dean and Adams behind me. Thought I had two shots left in my .436.

"Did I . . . ?" Geneviève began. She swallowed. "Did I kill any of those men?"

"Ricochets got them all," I said. 'Course, I wasn't certain of nothing about Cousin Bowler and Cousin Black Hat. They might have shot each other. Might have been ricochets. Might have been their dead cousin Felipe. Maybe I'd lucked out and killed one. Might have been God.

From outside the cave, Sister Rocío said, "Micah!"

I grabbed Geneviève's hand, and led her into the dusk, smelling the fresh rain, feeling real good till I saw three other gents standing there. What I seen wasn't glorious and wonderful and helpful.

Chapter Thirty-five

Corbin give me a friendly nod and motioned at the long-barreled Colt in his right hand. The Pockmarked Man spit tobacco juice at one of them colorful frogs. He was holding a rifle.

"Hello, Bishop." Sean Fenn had Sister Rocío right in front of him, pressing a revolver's barrel against her temple.

"Pitch that gun you're holding back into the pit."

I done what he said. That Remington was empty anyhow, so it wasn't going to do me no good.

"Is the gold down there?" Fenn asked.

My head shook. "Just three dead men."

He grinned wider. "Well, I'm sure they'll have company." His eyes darted over to Geneviève. "Nice to see you, honey." He didn't mean it.

Back to me, he said, "Who's in the cave?"

"Felipe Hernandez and two cousins."

"Hernandez." It taken him a while to recollect. "From Las Vegas?"

I nodded.

He laughed. "Well, I'm sure glad he hadn't forgotten you. The boys and I were riding toward San Antonio when we heard the gunfire. Decided there was a good chance you would be involved in any shooting. Lucky us, eh?"

All I did was shrug.

"Where's the gold?"

When I didn't answer soon enough for his liking, which was immediate, he pressed the revolver tighter across the old nun's noggin, bending her head back, and causing her to groan.

"Sean . . ." Geneviève pleaded.

"Shut up!" Fenn roared.

"It's behind you," I said. "About two hundred, three hundred yards."

Fenn eased off with the Colt, but he didn't turn around. The Pockmarked Man did, though. Corbin just grinned.

"Talk," Fenn said.

So I talked. "Sister Rocío was jerked over the edge when all the mules—"

"Burros," the blind nun corrected.

"When all the . . . when most of the burros slipped on the ice—which means they had to be traveling on a trail." I nodded behind him. "That trail is as good as any I've seen going north-south."

"All right." That's all Fenn said.

So I recited him the poem.

> From the top of Ararat,
> We must climb down.
> Into the cañon
> Beside the King's crown,
> Where black meets the red.
> Into the second cañon,
> We walk with pain,
> Until we can touch
> The cross of Lorraine.
> Hallowed be the dead.

I had to explain the poem on the Cross of Lorraine that Geneviève had kept on her person all that time. It caused Fenn's face to crimson something considerable, but he ground his teeth, and kept that temper of his in check.

"So that's Mount Ararat behind me?" Fenn said with a snort.

"If you look at it from where I am, you can see the Ark," I said, studying it. "Coming over the trail, or looking at it from the north, you don't see it. But those burros toting the nuns and gold back in forty-eight had fallen off on this side. Rocío was looking up this way, looking north, not south."

The Pockmarked Man sprayed a lava rock with tobacco juice. "By golly, Fenn, I reckon you could say them boulders up on that hill resemble a ship of some kind."

Fenn chewed on his lip, and maybe his head tilted slightly like he was conceding my point. But all he said was, "So we've climbed down from Mount Ararat. Where's the gold then?"

"That ain't how I figure it, Sean," I said. "Sister Rocío was already in the canyon, so she'd already climbed off Ararat. She went into one of the side canyons."

Fenn give me that point, too. Then he made me repeat the poem, which I did, with some help from Rocío.

"Beside the King's crown?" he asked.

"My guess is it's a rock that looks like a crown. That's the canyon we need to enter."

"All right," Fenn said. "Let's find that canyon."

"Well, the problem there is that almost forty years have passed since she buried the nuns and the ingots," I said, feeling smart all of a sudden. "Flash floods. Lightning. Wind. Hail. That rock marking the canyon could be long gone by now."

"It's the first canyon," Rocío then told us. "Heading east. I couldn't carry gold and bodies very far, now could I?"

"Well, why in hell didn't you just write to take the first canyon?" The Pockmarked Man said, all haughty and inconsiderate.

"I do not question Lord Byron's choice of words," Rocío said. "Nor Longfellow's."

Corbin laughed. The Pockmarked Man picked his ear quickly, then brought that hand back down to the Winchester.

" 'Where black meets the red,' " Fenn repeated. "What's that about? Darkies and redskins?"

"Red and black lava," Corbin said, and I knowed right then that Corbin was getting tired of Sean Fenn. So was I.

"Well," Fenn said. "I guess we should try to find it before nightfall. Lead the way, Bishop."

Problem was, I couldn't lead the way. They'd see that Dean and Adams tucked in the back of my waistband, and that pistol was the only chance I had to get out of this pickle alive. 'Course, I didn't recollect how many shots I had left in that old gun. I thought only two. But Fenn had lowered his .44-40. Oh, he still held it, but the barrel was aiming at the sandstone dust, and Sister Rocío was standing in front of him. Corbin was staring at the country and the Ark. It really did look like a boat what with the sun sinking and the light fading and the sandstone rising above the black rocks and me standing in a puddle after that big rain shower.

"Micah," Geneviève whispered, "don't."

You see, she saw my hand reaching behind my back. It was a good feeling, I thought, her caring for me. I was about to die, and she didn't want me to, and I thought that if hers was the last voice I ever heard on this earth, that wouldn't be a bad way to go to my maker.

But it wouldn't be the last voice I heard, because I had to say something right then and there. "Sister Rocío. Ka-boom!"

Bless her heart, she remembered what I'd told her up on that ridge. Instantly, she went belly-first to the ground, and the Dean and Adams was in my hand. I saw Sean Fenn raising his Colt and thumbing back the hammer, but I didn't have no hammer to thumb back. All I had to do was pull the trigger, which I done. The bullet didn't pull right or left. I knowed because I saw blood spurt from Fenn's throat.

Scratch shot. I damned near missed him all together.

But the bullet must've broke his neck, because he went down without a word and the Colt he had been holding went disappearing down a crack in the black rocks.

I had a choice to make, and I figured I could only kill one of them, if I was lucky. It just struck me that Corbin might not hurt Rocío or Geneviève, but The Pockmarked Man would likely kill them both. So I aimed at The Pockmarked Man, who had already brought up his Winchester and was about to kill me.

Pulled the trigger, I did, and heard that percussion cap go snap, which ain't what I wanted to hear. A misfire meant I was dead since I wouldn't have time to pull the trigger again. Even if I had, it wouldn't have helped because the Dean and Adams was empty.

A gun roared, and I jerked, but didn't feel nothing, didn't see the puff of smoke from the Winchester. The rifle hadn't fired so I hadn't gotten shot, but The Pockmarked Man had. Blood and gore just sprayed out of his head, and he toppled over and landed like a ton of bricks is always landing.

When my ears stopped ringing and I quit shaking, I heard thunder way off in the distance where the clouds was dumping rain on some other part of the Tularosa Valley. And I heard Sister Rocío praying.

Geneviève stepped beside me, and she even put her arm around me, and we slowly turned to face Corbin together. I guess we figured he would shoot both of us dead, but that would be all right because we'd die together in each other's arms.

Corbin had holstered his Colt.

He pointed toward the spot that looked like it

might have been a crack in the black rocks, which must have been the first canyon Sister Rocío had said was there. "Let's find that gold."

So we followed him . . . into the canyon that might have once been beside something resembling a king's crown . . . and saw black and red lava, or maybe the red was pink sandstone. Didn't matter. It was another canyon, a box canyon, and we went there.

Certain-sure, we walked with pain—which come natural for Rocío, old as she was—and me and Geneviève, battered as we was. Even Corbin, whose high-heeled boots wasn't made for walking, especially over sandstone and cactus and lava rocks, walked with pain.

Until we could touch the Cross of Lorraine.

There it was. A two-barred cross made of rocks in the sand, undisturbed after almost forty years.

"Sister," I asked Rocío, "does the top of the cross point to the grave?"

"Yes." She sounded like a teenage girl. "Have you found it?"

Geneviève said, "I think so. I really think we have."

Chapter Thirty-six

So . . . we dug.

Well, not immediate, because it was dark by then. We slept on the wet ground in the duds we had on, didn't eat no supper, just drunk some water.

Night turned cool after all that rain, and Geneviève come up to me, like she'd done in the burning desert when we'd both come so close to dying and before we ever got the chance to send Sean Fenn to Hell.

She snuggled up real close to me, and I put my arm around her belly.

"I'm not sorry," she whispered.

"About what?" I asked.

"Sean Fenn."

I wasn't either. Fact was, if she hadn't been around, I probably would have done something fairly degrading to his body. Then again, we hadn't buried him or The Pockmarked Man. Hadn't even dumped him into the cave with Felipe Hernandez and his cousins—which was pretty degrading when you consider things.

That colonel fellow put none of that in his half-dime novel *Valley of Fire*. Instead, he had Corbin and the nuns and me fighting off about a thousand Modoc Indians, which I ain't never seen or knowed to even visit New Mexico Territory.

"Oh, Micah." She looped her fingers in mine and squeezed.

Since my lips was so close, and her hair smelled like fresh rain, and her neck was right there, I kissed it, and she giggled. I figured I'd tickled her, and decided against kissing her neck.

Till she told me, softly, "Do that again."

I obeyed.

"Let's run off to Mexico," I said.

"All right. I'll be Esther."

"I'll be your king."

"It'll be the Feast of Purim every day."

We laughed.

The colonel didn't put none of that in his book, neither. And that's all I'm saying about that night. Geneviève was a fine woman. She was a real lady. Bet she'll turn out to be a Mother Superior somewhere down the line.

Next morning, we didn't eat no breakfast. Corbin went back to fetch horses—his and The Pockmarked Man's and Sean Fenn's since they had come along the good trail, and ours, since we told him where ours was picketed—figuring we'd need all the animals we could find to pack that gold out of the valley.

We didn't get started on moving boulders and rocks and dirt till right before noon. By dusk, we'd gotten some of the stones moved away, but not many.

Corbin's hands was bloody, blistered, and dirty,

and mine wasn't no better. Geneviève had tore a gash in her right first finger, which she'd wrapped up with a strip from her already threadbare and ripped to shreds green and white checked shirt. We drunk hot coffee and ate fried salt pork and beans—Corbin and Fenn and The Pockmarked Man hadn't been skinflints when it come to their suppers and all—at the fire that night.

Corbin looked at Sister Rocío and said, like he couldn't believe it, "How did you get those boulders down by yourself?"

"With a machete," she said innocently.

"A machete?"

"Its blade was bent," she added, like that helped. Then she grinned. "But the Lord was with me."

Geneviève didn't come to me that night. Well, it had been a warm day and all.

Next morning, Corbin rode off for Carrizozo to bring back supplies. Honest, I thought he might have come back with some more fellows to kill me and take the gold for themselves, but Corbin wasn't that big of a fool. He wasn't gonna share with more than he had to. Besides, while he was gone, either getting the horses and mules, or bringing back tools and the likes, he was having an easy day while me and Geneviève was tearing our hands and fingers to pieces.

I couldn't be angry at Corbin, not yet. Not after he saved my life by killing The Pockmarked Man. He come back that afternoon with not only rope and picks and shovels, but he come back with a buckboard, too, pulled by two big draft horses that could certainly haul, we figured, $750,000 in gold ingots.

"Where'd you get the money to buy all this plunder?" I asked him.

"From Sean Fenn's billfold," he said like I was the dumbest fool this side of Texas. "Where else?"

After grabbing me a pickax, I followed Corbin and Geneviève over to our spot. Before I could swing, Corbin had unwrapped some brown paper and tossed something in my direction. It hit my chest, fell, and bounced off the ground. "You might want to put those on."

Good, comfortable deerskin gloves.

Things went better after that. Oh, it wasn't like a winning streak shooting craps, but hard work. We'd loosen a boulder, then it taken all the elbow grease Corbin and me and Geneviève could muster to roll the stone away. All the while, Sister Rocío sat in the shade, saying prayers, humming, and asking what she could do to help, God bless her soul.

Finally, there was a hole. I could reach in, but felt nothing. We dug with more purpose after that, then got to the point where Geneviève, tiny as she was, could squeeze through. She got in, turned herself around, stuck her hand out, and I handed her a candle while Corbin lighted the wick.

Smart fellow, Corbin. He'd bought candles and matches at the mercantile in Carrizozo, though me and Geneviève still had a box of matches, so we could've saved him two cents off his bill. We held our breath, and Geneviève, protecting the candle with the palm of her left hand, disappeared in the dark.

"Oh, my God!" was the first words out of her mouth.

The candle come out first. I taken it, tossed it aside, grabbed Geneviève's hand, and eased her out of the hole.

Sister Rocío stopped singing. She eased her way closer to us.

"You all right, ma'am?" Corbin asked.

"They're. . . ." Geneviève was shaken, like somebody had just stepped on her grave. "They're mummified." She crossed herself. "The nuns."

Made sense, of course, when you take into account how dry this country is and that the bodies had been sealed in that cave for close to four decades. Not many bugs would make it down there, so, sure, bodies would mummify a bit in country like we was in. Most certain. I figured it out and I ain't never set in on one of the Sisters of Charity's lectures.

"I have blankets in the buckboard," Corbin said. "We can lay the bodies of the nuns in one, wrap it up, load it in the wagon."

But that won't leave much room for the gold, I was thinking.

"That will be fine, Señor Corbin," Rocío said. "Thank you."

"*De nada,*" Corbin said, then poked me with the handle of his shovel. "Let's widen this some more."

We done that in no time, since we was all greedy.

"Please," Rocío said before we entered, "bring the bodies out. They have been denied consecrated soil for far too long."

It wasn't bad, I reckon. I mean, as long as we didn't look at the bodies too long and got them covered up with the blankets as soon as we laid their bodies on one. I didn't have no nightmares.

Corbin and me played pallbearers while Geneviève and Rocío sat in the shade and talked. They crossed themselves as each corpse was brung out, wrapped up, and taken to the buckboard.

When all the dead nuns was taken care of, Sister Rocío had us bow our heads. We taken off our hats, Corbin and me, and let Rocío pray.

"Thank you," Rocío told us. "Now, Sister Geneviève and I will be on our way."

"Ma'am?" Corbin said.

"To the mission at San Elizario. Near El Paso. That is where Lorraine and her comrades were going. That was to be their home. We shall bury those poor, young nuns. It is where they would

347

want to rest. That has been my dream for thirty-eight years. Then we will return to Santa Fe."

"But . . ." I wasn't thinking about the gold no more. I was thinking about me and Geneviève. "But Geneviève . . ."

"Micah," she said, and her eyes was just dancing, "it's not too late. Rocío says it's not too late. She says that I can still become a nun. Isn't it wonderful?"

"It is never too late for anyone," Rocío said. "Even you, Micah Bishop."

"Yeah." Corbin's dander was getting ruffled. "But what about the gold?"

Rocío's face got all sheepish, or as sheepish as a seventy-three-year old nun's face can get. "I am truly sorry, Señor Corbin, but there is no gold. The bandits stole it thirty-eight years ago . . . except for an ingot or two that they dropped after they left. They must have thought I was dead."

"You lied?" I said.

She shrugged. "I didn't really lie. At least, I tried not to. I just let you . . . interpret things. I said I never saw the bandits. Because I was unconscious. Things like that."

I sat down. Corbin dropped with me.

"You see," Rocío said. "It was the only way I could think of to save Micah from the gallows, and finally put Lorraine and our sweet, holy comrades in consecrated soil before I die. Sí, I guess one would say that I lied. A very bad falsehood. I am sure I will have a very stiff penance after my next confession."

Well, I reckon you know the rest of the story already.

We taken Geneviève and Rocío to Socorro after—you're damned right—me and Corbin went through that cave till we knowed for sure there wasn't no gold in there. We caught the train there for El Paso and seen the dead nuns planted in holy ground at San Elizario near that jail where, turned out, Corbin had once spent some time in, too. It was a beautiful ceremony. They didn't let me and Corbin take communion. After that, we brung Geneviève and Rocío back to the Sisters of Charity orphanage in Santa Fe, where both of them kissed me. Rocío on my cheek. Geneviève full on my lips.

Once they was back inside, Corbin suggested that we head to the nearest saloon to get roostered, but before we got there, he drawed his Colt and put the barrel against my spine. "You know, there is a fifty dollar reward for you in Las Vegas."

The double-crossing son of a bitch is why I'm writing this down in this dungeon. I knowed I should have killed him. Next time, I won't regret having to do it.

The law said that my first trial wasn't legal, but more of a miner's court, so they give me another one. A fair one. For the murder of Gomez since nobody actually knowed what had become of his cousin, Felipe Hernandez. I didn't think the second trial was fair, and I reckon, since Felipe Hernandez was dead in Crockett's Cave and couldn't drum up a big turnout to see his cousin's death avenged, nobody got word to the Sisters of Charity down in Santa Fe. It ain't like nuns read newspapers, or penny-dreadfuls that are published because that colonel what's-his-name had happened to be in Las Vegas when I was getting tried. The book come out about the time some judge said that my trial and sentence was legit, and I was to die.

Well, I reckon that's about all there is. I—

Just got time for some fast writing.

Moment ago, Evers come in and said, "There's a nun here to see you, Bishop."

"Is she young and beautiful?"

Evers said, "Not by a damned sight." He touched his head, which is still sporting a bandage. "I done learnt my lesson. This one is older than dirt, blind, and got only one arm." He snorted. "Calls herself . . . Esther."

"Esther?" I asked.

"Yep. Says she's here for the Feast of Purim, whatever the hell that is. I don't hold with none of that Catholic stuff. My ma was a hard-shell Baptist."

He mustn't have seen me grin, 'cause I knowed Geneviève was with Rocío, probably had a horse saddled for me out on the street. Guess word of my impending execution finally reached a Santa Fe orphanage and hospital run by nuns. Reckon I won't get my neck stretched after all.

God love the Sisters of Charity.

"Hell, Evers. Send her in."

Center Point Large Print
600 Brooks Road / PO Box 1
Thorndike ME 04986-0001 USA

(207) 568-3717

US & Canada:
1 800 929-9108
www.centerpointlargeprint.com